RALPH COMPTON:
NAVARRO

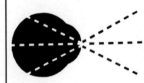 This Large Print Book carries the Seal of Approval of N.A.V.H.

A RALPH COMPTON NOVEL

RALPH COMPTON: NAVARRO

PETER BRANDVOLD

THORNDIKE PRESS
A part of Gale, Cengage Learning

GALE
CENGAGE Learning·

Farmington Hills, Mich • San Francisco • New York • Waterville, Maine
Meriden, Conn • Mason, Ohio • Chicago

GALE
CENGAGE Learning

LIBRARY OF CONGRESS CATALOGING-IN-PUBLICATION DATA

Names: Brandvold, Peter, author. | Compton, Ralph.
Title: Ralph Compton : Navarro : a Ralph Compton novel / by Peter Brandvold.
Other titles: Navarro
Description: Large print edition. | Waterville, Maine : Thorndike Press, 2016. | © 2005 | Series: Thorndike Press large print western
Identifiers: LCCN 2016006734| ISBN 9781410488305 (hardcover) | ISBN 1410488306 (hardcover)
Subjects: LCSH: Large type books. | GSAFD: Western stories.
Classification: LCC PS3552.R3236 R35 2016 | DDC 813/.54—dc23
LC record available at http://lccn.loc.gov/2016006734

Published in 2016 by arrangement with New American Library, an imprint of Penguin Publishing Group, a division of Penguin Random House LLC

Printed in Mexico
1 2 3 4 5 6 7 20 19 18 17 16

THE IMMORTAL COWBOY

This is respectfully dedicated to the "American Cowboy." His was the saga sparked by the turmoil that followed the Civil War, and the passing of more than a century has by no means diminished the flame.

True, the old days and the old ways are but treasured memories, and the old trails have grown dim with the ravages of time, but the spirit of the cowboy lives on.

In my travels — to Texas, Oklahoma, Kansas, Nebraska, Colorado, Wyoming, New Mexico, and Arizona — I always find something that reminds me of the Old West. While I am walking these plains and mountains for the first time, there is this feeling that a part of me is eternal, that I have known these old trails before. I believe it is the undying spirit of the frontier calling, allowing me, through the mind's eye, to step back into time. What is the appeal of the Old West of the American frontier?

It has been epitomized by some as the dark and bloody period in American history. Its heroes — Crockett, Bowie, Hickok, Earp — have been reviled and criticized. Yet the Old West lives on, larger than life.

It has become a symbol of freedom, where there was always another mountain to climb and another river to cross; when a dispute between two men was settled not with expensive lawyers, but with fists, knives or guns. Barbaric? Maybe. But some things never change. When the cowboy rode into the pages of American history, he left behind a legacy that lives within the hearts of us all.

— *Ralph Compton*

CHAPTER 1

Stuffing a blue receipt into his shirt pocket, Tom Navarro pushed through the Tucson Mercantile's main door and paused on the stone loading dock. The Murphy freight wagon was parked before the dock, and three Bar-V boys were loading the dry goods stacked at the dock's lip. The sunseared men in high-crowned, wide-brimmed hats and brightly colored bandanas sweated in the midday heat — above a hundred and five, if the rusty thermometer hanging on a porch post was right.

"Doggone, Tom," Lou Waters complained as he handed a twenty-pound sack of cracked corn to Ky Tryon, "why'd you have to pick the very middle of the day for this back-and-belly job?"

Navarro, the Bar-V segundo, glanced at the brassy sky, dug out his makings sack, and slowly shaped a cigarette. "I thought it'd be good to sweat some o' last night's tarantula juice out of your blood, before you headed back to the ranch. You looked a might deep in the pain barrel this mornin', and I know how a wagon ride over a bumpy desert trace can make you feel like that rat in your guts is pullin' your tongue down your throat sideways. Might cause you to lose that expensive lunch I bought you."

"Expensive?" Jorge Amado chuckled. The stocky Mexican standing in the wagon bed took a sack of cornmeal from Tryon and stowed it away with the flour, pinto beans, and coffee beans he'd already stacked neatly against the wagon's front wall. "It was free with the beer, Senor Tom."

"Was it? Well, hell. Next time, remind me to buy you boys a proper meal."

"Dang, Tom, cheap as you are —" The canteen's batwings squawked. Tryon, lifting another sack from the loading dock, glanced toward the cantina and froze.

The cantina was a flat-roofed adobe, painfully white in the unrelenting sun, with a brush roof and splintery batwings. The doors swung back and forth as a man stepped before them and stood beneath the brush arbor, staring at Navarro, thumbs hooked in his pistol belts.

He was a scrawny little hardcase with a long, horsey face, buck teeth, and a beard that hadn't seen a barber chair in months. A straw sombrero hung down his back, and his sweat-soaked white shirt was open clear to his belt buckle. Head tilted up, he regarded Navarro with slitted eyes, as though he were sizing up a bronc for riding. Several flies buzzed around his face, attracted to the smell of spilled beer and goat cheese, no doubt, but he paid them no mind. A short-barreled Colt with worn walnut grips rode in his low-slung holster.

Behind him, several faces appeared over the batwings. The grins shuttled between the little gunslinger and Navarro, who stood on the loading dock, casually smoking his cigarette while regarding the little man dully.

"So you're Tommy Navarro," the little man said. He had a high, screechy voice. " 'Taos Tommy' Navarro."

The three Bar-V drovers had stopped working. They stiffly slid their gazes between Navarro and the little hardcase. Navarro stared down at the man from under the brim of his flat-brimmed black Stetson with a snakeskin band, the brown paper quirley drooping out the right corner of his mouth.

His hard-angled face was wind-seamed and sunburned to the color of a dry-blistered cherry table. He might have passed for Mexican if not for the shell gray eyes set deep in spoked sockets and the prematurely silver hair and sideburns, trimmed weekly by the Bar-V's German cook.

"Kid," Navarro said, having sized the little man up for under twenty-five and the short-barreled Colt as a hand-me-down, "go back where you came from."

The kid swaggered out from under the awning. His bleary eyes said he'd been drinking most of the morning, and the swagger added that he didn't hold it well. "Taos Tommy Navarro," he said in his little-dog bark. "Well, well."

"Go home, kid."

"They say you're fast."

"I ain't gonna tell you again."

The kid stopped abruptly and held his hand above his holster. He glanced at the Colt Navy riding high in a soft brown holster on Navarro's right hip. "I bet you ain't no faster'n me."

Navarro scowled around the quirley at the other three drovers, frozen in their work positions, squinting in the brassy light. Navarro looked at the kid again, still holding his hand above his pistol, waiting, challenge in his glassy brown eyes.

He chuffed and turned, giving the kid his back and strolling over to another porch post to his right. He leaned his broad left

shoulder against the post and stared northward up Main at a string of freight wagons
pulled up before the livery barn.

"Get to work, boys," the ramrod told his
crew. "If we're gonna make it back to the
Bar-V before dark, we gotta start pushin'
soon."

"Hey, I was talkin' to you," the kid behind
him said.

Navarro did not respond. He was watching two Mexican boys running around the
freight wagons, loosing invisible arrows and
calling to each other in Spanish.

"Careful, Tom," Ky Tryon said as he stiffly
picked up a ten-pound keg of molasses.
Slowly, he turned to hand the keg to Waters,
who reached for it while eyeing the hardcase.

Navarro shrugged and continued staring
at the kids and the dog, puffing his cigarette.

"Don't turn your back on an open challenge, Taos Tommy," the hardcase warned.
"Folks gonna think you're chicken."

Navarro heard the *clomp* and *spur-ching*
of boots on the porch steps behind him. He
could smell the kid drawing close, and he'd
been right about the stale beer and goat
cheese, as well as chili peppers, sweat, and
horse piss.

The kid stopped. "I got a bet goin' over to

the cantina yonder. Ten silver dollars says I can blow two holes in your old chest before you even clear leather. Wanna try provin' I'm wrong?"

Navarro turned and faced the kid, his broad hat brim shading his dark face and searing gray eyes. "Kid, I got tired of drilling daylight through little punksticks like you a long time ago. Damn tired. I don't answer the challenge anymore. Never will again. Now go back over to the cantina, buy you and your friends a round on my silver" — he flipped the kid a cartwheel, which bounced off the kid's shoulder and hit the loading dock with a clang — "and leave me the hell alone."

The kid's nostrils flared. He glanced at the coin lying near his right boot. Behind him, laughter rose from the cantina.

He snapped his angry gaze to Navarro, took one step closer, narrowing the gap between them, and lifted his hand above his pistol grips. In a sneering voice, he said, "When I count to three, I'm grabbin' iron. You suit yourself."

The kid had just said, "Two," when Navarro's left hand leapt forward, grabbed the kid's gun from its holster, and almost casually tossed it into the street. The Colt Lightning landed in the dust with a plop.

The manuever had taken less than a second.

The kid gave a startled grunt as he clawed at his holster and stumbled back, his right hand coming up empty. "H-hey!" he complained, turning to the gun gleaming up from the gray dust.

Red-faced, cheeks bunching, he returned his gaze to the segundo towering over him. Navarro grinned, his teeth showing white against his tanned skin.

"You son of a bitch!" the kid snapped.

Turning, he walked to the lip of the loading dock. Navarro extended his right boot, tripping the kid, who gave an indignant wail as he stumbled forward and fell head-first off the dock's lip, into the finely churned dust of the street.

"Ooooh," Jorge Amado said from the wagon bed, wincing and beetling his bushy black brows.

The kid climbed to his knees, holding his right shoulder. "My arm, damn ye . . ."

Navarro lowered his tall frame from the loading dock. The kid's right right arm hung at an odd angle.

"Here, let me pop that back into place for you," Navarro said. He grabbed the kid's arm and brusquely jerked it back. With an audible crack, the ball of the arm snapped back into its socket.

"Awwww!" the kid screamed.

The kid screamed louder as Navarro grabbed both his arms and dragged him over to the stock trough on the other side of the wagon. The ramrod slammed the kid against the trough. The kid's screams died, his eyes fluttering, his head wobbling on his shoulders as the pain, heat, and alcohol combined to make him faint.

Navarro took a handful of the kid's hair and dunked his head in the trough, plunging it deep. He held him down for a good ten seconds, the kid thrashing his arms and legs against Navarro's iron grip. The ramrod bore down stiff-armed, still puffing the quirley clamped in his teeth.

He pulled the kid's head up from the stock trough. The kid took a deep, raking breath, water rolling off his face and pasting his hair against his forehead.

"How 'bout if I give you one more long drink so you can think more clearly about your future?" Navarro said.

The kid's protesting cry turned to bubbles as the ramrod muscled the head back down in the trough, causing water to spill over the sides, making mud around the kid's knees. Finally, Navarro jerked him out. The kid arched his back as he sucked air into his lungs, then fell forward vomiting water.

Navarro stood over him grimly, sucking the quirley down to little longer than a .44 shell. "I've just given you the benefit of the doubt, pip-squeak. I've decided you're just another shit-brained little hothead out lookin' to make a name for yourself by blowin' out my lamp. A minute ago, you didn't know better. Now you know better. You come around me again, I'm gonna trim your wick so low you'll never hold another spark." Navarro stepped forward and kicked the kid's side with the toe of his boot, throwing him onto his right shoulder with a whimpering groan. *"Comprende?"*

The kid coughed and finally nodded.

Navarro turned to the cantina, where three wide-eyed faces peered over the batwings. "Davis, Potter, Jurgens — get your asses out here and haul your friend back inside the saloon," he snarled.

The three Circle-6 riders filed through the batwings, all looking sheepish, brush-scarred chaps flapping around their legs.

"Sorry, Mr. Navarro," said the tall, long-haired blond named Potter, a flush rising beneath his tan. "We were just funnin' the kid."

Arnie Jurgens, whose father Navarro had scouted with out of Fort Bowie some years

15

ago, said, "He was braggin' all mornin' about how fast he was. Then we seen you pull up in the wagon" — he shrugged — "and we bet him he wasn't as fast as you."

"Thanks for tellin' him who I was, Arnie. 'Preciate that."

"Sorry, Tom."

"Take him inside and keep him there till I'm gone. Then you boys best haul your sorry tails back to the Circle-6." He looked at the stocky young Jurgens, whose plump face was a pale oval below his gray felt sombrero. "I have a feelin' your pa had other things for you to do in town besides goading tinhorn gunslicks into lead swaps and putting burrs in my bonnet."

When the three had hauled the young hardcase back inside the cantina, Navarro retrieved the kid's gun from the street and tossed it onto the porch roof. He turned to his own three men, who were regarding him grinning.

"What the hell are you boys lookin' at?" Navarro whipped his dead quirley into the street. "You're burnin' daylight!"

CHAPTER 2

In a high hanging valley of the Santa Catalinas, Karla Vannorsdell was helping her grandfather's Mexican maid, Pilar, clean the old patriarch's high-ceilinged study, and thinking about the tall Mexican boy who'd become her beau. She ran a feather duster over the rearing bronze Morgan horse on her grandfather's map table.

The feather duster paused on the horse's cocked tail. Eyes suddenly bright, the color rising in her cheeks, Karla turned to the older woman and said quickly, because she had to share the news with someone and the maid was the only other woman on the ranch, "Pilar, Juan and I are going to be married."

The words, so long considered, shocked Karla almost as much as they did Pilar.

The plump maid had been dusting the broad, hide-covered desk fronting a vast, oak-framed map of Arizona Territory. She

17

whirled, round brown eyes snapping wide. "Karla!" she exclaimed, then, fearing someone had heard, peered self-consciously at the room's open doors.

The girl was relieved to have told someone. She'd been harboring the secret for weeks, since Juan had proposed to her by the spring-fed waterfall under Antelope Peak. Pilar stared at her, her eyes dark and fretful.

"Aren't you happy for me, Pilar?"

The older woman blinked, then let out a long, silent breath. "Senorita, has Juan discussed this with your grandfather?" She dropped her arms to her broad, round sides. "Have *you* discussed this with your grandfather?"

"Why should I?" Karla said, unable to keep the defensiveness out of her voice. "It's our decision. We will make our own plans!"

When Pilar said nothing, Karla turned to her, her smooth-cheeked, heart-shaped face flushed with beseeching. "Surely if we love each other, there will be no trouble. Isn't that right, Pilar?"

The older woman dropped her eyes demurely and let her gaze stray across the official papers and clothbound account books littering the huge desk before her. She said gently, "It is a different world here than the one you are used to back east, *mi amor.* In the East, I think things must be *libre como un pajaro.*" She looked around the room searchingly. "How do you say? *Looser.* Here, the old traditions . . . they are still followed. Especially by men such as your *abuelo,* Don Vannorsdell."

"But —"

"Karla!" The burly voice rose beyond the office, on the heels of a door slam.

She turned to the door as boots clacked on the flagstones in another part of the house.

"Karla, are you here?" her grandfather's voice boomed in the cavernous dwelling.

Karla glanced at Pilar once more, reluctant to end the conversation, then lifted her chin to the broad, open entrance to the hall. "In your office, Grandpa!"

The pounding had grown quieter as the man bent his old legs for the kitchen. It grew louder now as he approached the office. Paul Vannorsdell's stocky figure appeared in the dim doorway, a craggy, florid face under a flat-brimmed leather hat, the brim of which looked mouse-chewed.

He peered into the room. "What on earth are you two doing in here?"

"We are cleaning your office, senor," Pilar hurried to explain, raising her feather duster as if for evidence.

"We are cleaning and discussing the womanly aspects of love," Karla said, good-naturedly jibing the old man.

When she'd first come to the Arizona Territory from Philadelphia, after her parents had been killed in a train collision, she'd found her grandfather, whom she'd never met, to be every bit the irascible old hermit her mother had once told her he was. In the two years since, however, Karla had probed the chinks in his armor, and had even gotten him to laugh a time or two.

At the moment, however, that armor was solid. The gray-brown eyes did not smile. The carefully trimmed gray-brown mustache capping his thin upper lip did not so much as twitch. Vannorsdell's shoulders seemed to pull together for a moment, tensing. His craggy face flushed slightly, and then, visibly suppressing an angry impulse, he crouched and forced a cunning smile into his eyes as he beckoned to Karla. "Come on, daughter. I have something to show you outside."

Reluctant to snap away from the passion of the previous conversation, Karla frowned. "Outside?"

"Hurry!"

A moment later they were descending the

20

broad fieldstone porch steps — the stocky old Dutchman in baggy trousers and a doeskin vest, the young brunette in green jeans and plaid flannel shirt, her hair pulled back in a pony tail and secured with a turquoise-studded barrette. Her jeans stretched taut across her rounded hips and thighs. She wore a horsehair belt, which she'd braided herself, and high-heeled brown boots with red stars tanned into the pointed toes.

They crossed the hard-packed ranch yard surrounded by adobe-brick outbuildings, to one of several peeled-log corrals east of the L-shaped bunkhouse. The west-angling sun softened the light and the pulsing heat, tinging the adobes with pink and conjuring brown shadows.

Several of Vannorsdell's sweaty, dusty drovers stood near the corral, smoking and talking. Hearing the screen door slap shut, they turned to Karla and her grandfather, shaping whiskery grins around their brown paper cigarettes.

Inside the corral stood the rancher's number two man, Dallas Tixier, holding the head stall of a fine white Arabian. The horse shook its small, elegant head and lowered its broad snout, peering at the group with wary curiosity. Its high-set tail swished once, and its copper eyes reflected the pink hues of the adobes. Beside the animal, Tixier grinned, squinting his blue eyes and flashing a gold eyetooth under his black sombrero.

Placing her hands on the corral's top rail, Karla whistled. "Who belongs to that fine animal?"

The old man quirked a grin. "You do."

Karla's mouth fell open but she didn't say anything.

Vannorsdell announced proudly, "Born in Arabia, that fine animal was. A prince from one o' them fine desert castles raised him from the best bloodstock anywhere in the world. I bought him from a rancher near Soledad."

Karla studied the old man, skeptically. The drovers flanked him. They said nothing as they smiled at Karla. "He's . . . for me?"

"Sure he is." Vannorsdell glanced conspiratorially at the men behind him, winked, and turned back to his granddaughter.

Karla looked at the fine Arab, which shook its head impatiently and snorted. It wasn't her birthday or either of her dead parents' birthdays or any other special day that she could remember. Finding no discernible reason for the present from a man who rarely gave presents of any kind, much less

Arabian horses, she turned back to her grandfather, frowning. "But why?"

"Don't look a gift horse in the mouth." The old man laughed. The men behind him chuckled. Vannorsdell jerked his head at the Arabian. "Go get acquainted, girl!"

Karla studied the horse again. She couldn't help feeling she was being led into a trap of some kind. She felt guilty for such a notion. In the two years she'd known him, she'd gradually grown to, if not love, at least respect her grandfather. But it had been a hard-won respect, a regard that the old frontierman's ill temper and narrow-mindedness frequently poked and prodded and sometimes even strained to the breaking point.

"What're you waitin' for?" the old man urged, his voice climbing high.

Karla glanced at him, shrugged, hitched up her jeans with both hands, and crouched through the fence. She crossed the corral and held out her hand to the horse. The Arabian's round eyes appeared as wary as hers.

Keeping its cream tail high, it backed a step, and Tixier, holding the halter rope taut in his gloved right hand, said, "Ho now." The horse lifted its snout, glared down at Karla, and twitched its nose.

"Easy, boy," Karla said gently, lifting her

hand to its snout. "Easy, now. There . . ."

She turned to her grandfather, who was staring over the corral at her, with the dusty drovers lined out to his left. Still half expecting the ground to open beneath her feet, Karla raised brows bleached by the desert sun. "I don't know what to say."

"Senorita," said Dallas Tixier, shaping a grin as he peered at her from under the horse's cocked head, "I think your eyes say it all."

Karla looked the horse over, ran an appreciative hand over its shivering withers. "How old is he?"

"Three," Tixier said. "A fine, fine animal."

"He's saddle-broke," Vannorsdell called to her. "A good rider. Calm, too, for an Arab. I told Tixier to find me a good, calm horse that won't turn twister at rattlesnakes or prairie dogs . . . since you ride all over creation," he added with a disapproving tone.

Karla's frequent riding of the greenest broncs in her grandfather's remuda had been a bone of contention between them. Vannorsdell didn't think a young woman should ride anything but old mares with a sidesaddle, much less wear men's denims, boots, and a pistol on her hip. And she shouldn't ride *every day*. As headstrong as the old man, Karla had won that battle, but she helped Pilar cook and clean, as well.

Tixier offered the halter rope to Karla. "There is some light left, senorita. Why don't you take him for a ride around the buildings? Shall I get a saddle . . . ?"

"Why not?" Karla said, running a hand down the gelding's smooth, arched neck, across the well-defined withers. Her shoulders loosened. So the horse really was hers. It wasn't a joke or a trick of some kind. And what a magnificent beast he was, too.

She turned a genuine smile to her grandfather. "Thank you, Grandpa," she said. "He must have been awfully expensive."

Vannorsdell flicked a dismissive hand.

Cantering hooves sounded on the trail east of the ranch yard. Karla turned her gaze that way, where the low sun cast long, sharp-edged shadows along the ground. A rider on a sleek pinto moved up the hill toward the ranch headquarters, his low-crowned sombrero bobbing above the dense chaparral sheathing the wagon trail. As the rider approached, Karla saw the red bandanna flopping around the man's neck, the gray flannel shirt, brown vest, blue charros with gold stitching down the outside of the legs, the red sash around his waist.

"Juan," she said, her full lips spreading a smile.

She released the halter rope and crawled through the fence. As she made her way across the yard, toward the entrance portal into which the Vannorsdell name and the Bar-V brand had been burned, her grandfather barked, "Better wash for supper, boys."

As the men dispersed, spurs softly chinging as they headed for the bunkhouse, Karla stood by the portal, smiling as she watched the approaching rider appear around a bend in the trail, and pass through the headquarters' open gate. Silhouetted against the painted western sky, the rider halted the pinto before her, his face shaded by his broad-brimmed hat.

"Well, well, well," she greeted, jamming her hands into the back pockets of her jeans, shifting her weight coquettishly, "what brings you here in the middle of the week, Senor Juan? Don Renaldo give you your walking papers?"

"Hello, Karla," the young man said, looking down at her but lifting his eyes to regard someone behind her.

She glanced over her right shoulder. Her grandfather stood before the corral, chest out, shoulders back, looking toward her.

Vannorsdell cleared his throat, turned, and bent his old legs for the ranch house.

She turned again to Juan, who sat his saddle with a tense set to his shoulders. His handsomely chiseled, clean-shaven face was framed by his hat thong and by the long dark curls spilling down from his hat.

When he said nothing, just looked at her with troubled eyes, she said, "Would you like to come inside?"

"I cannot stay long."

Karla studied him, rocked back on her heels, and swept a strand of hair from her face. "Is something wrong?"

Again, the young vaquero looked behind her. She turned another look over her shoulder. Her grandfather stood on the house's wide veranda, looking toward her and smoking a long, thin cigar.

She turned back to Juan, her eyes wide with confusion. She opened her mouth to speak, but Juan cut her off. "Karla, I came here to tell you good-bye."

"Good-bye!" she repeated. It was as if he'd slapped her across the face.

"I am leaving the Territory. Going back to *Mejico*."

Only two days ago, they'd picnicked along Antelope Creek, flirting and joking . . . and planning their future together.

Haltingly, trying to absorb his words, she said, "Juan, I thought . . ."

"I see now that it would not work, *mi amore.* I am a *Mejicano.* A *bean* eater." He glanced at the house again. "You are a *Norteamericano.* You must marry a fair-haired gringo." He cuffed his hat off his head, revealing a full head of sweaty dark brown hair.

Her heart thudding, Karla stepped up to his horse, placed a hand on his knee. "Juan, it *will* work — if we love each other."

He shook his head and looked off. When he turned back to her, his lower lip trembled. He bit down on it. "You're new to this country. This is the way it works here. I wanted to stop and tell you good-bye so you wouldn't wonder what happened when you didn't see me again."

Karla felt as though a large bone were lodged in her throat, and her eyes burned. Her voice trembled as she spoke. "It's my grandfather, isn't it? He told you not to see me anymore."

"Don't be mad at him, Karla. He's right. If we got married, what would we do? Where would we live?"

"Here!" Karla cried. "You'll work here — for my grandfather."

The vaquero laughed without mirth and,

squeezing her hand in his, leaned down and gazed lovingly, apologetically into her eyes. "I love you, Karla. But vaqueros don't marry gringas." He reined the horse around and galloped out through the gate, his gold-brown dust powdering the mesquite and creosote behind him.

Karla stood for a long time, listening to the fading thuds. Anger burned within her, and she wasn't sure who she was angrier at: Juan or her grandfather. Tears rolling down her cheeks, she wheeled and strode stiffly toward the house.

She found her grandfather in his study, smoking in his chair behind his desk. His hat was off; his silver hair had taken its shape.

Karla stopped just within the door, took a deep breath. Her voice was even and hard. "You ran him off. You told him not to see me again."

Vannorsdell regarded her sympathetically, the cigar smoldering between the index and middle fingers of his right hand. "Karla," he said with a reasonable hunch of his shoulders, "he's a Mex."

Karla stared at him, felt the pressure building, feeling more hatred for her grandfather than she'd ever felt for another living thing. "Bastard!" she screamed.

She turned and — her smooth suntanned cheeks mottled red — ran from the room.

CHAPTER 3

Tom Navarro's spry paint followed the meandering desert trace through a notch in the hills, around a long bend hugging a dry wash on the left, and into a shallow canyon. Scrub pines and mesquite stippled the boulder-strewn slopes on both sides. Behind Navarro, the wagon rattled and drummed, the beer and wine casks sloshing near the tailgate.

Amado, Waters, and Tryon rode behind the lumbering Conestoga, slouched in their saddles, faces dimming beneath their hat brims as the sun sank low.

The supply trip to town was normally a much-coveted assignment — especially when the fun-loving Tixier led the crew. It wasn't as much fun when Navarro led. The silver-haired frontiersman and ex-gunslinger ran a tight ship, allowing the men to stay in town only two nights and never past midnight either night. And they could cavort only with the doves Navarro deemed acceptable — namely, those who would not put a man on his back with a burning case of the pony drip. Men with the drip couldn't ride or do much of anything but lay abed and howl.

And howling, as Navarro said, "ain't what the boss is payin' us for."

Navarro halted the paint and dismounted to remove a windblown branch from the trail. As he grabbed the horn to mount again, he froze and lifted his head to the slope rising on the right side of the trace. Holding his breath, he pricked his ears.

He'd turned fifty that March but he still had the ears of a coyote, and he'd heard something just now. Wasn't sure what but it didn't sound natural. There wasn't a lick of wind. The birds were oddly silent for this time of the day. It had cooled some, and the birds usually fed and fought and called reminders of their boundary lines from early dusk to good dark.

Hearing nothing else, Navarro swung up into the saddle. The wagon hammered along behind, slowing as it approached Tom. Tryon must have seen the cautious set to Navarro's shoulders.

"What is it, boss?"

"I don't know." Navarro glanced around.

It was getting late for an Apache attack. The desert Indians wouldn't normally fight at night, for they worried that, if they were killed after dark, their souls would get lost on their way to the next world. "Stay alert. I'm gonna ride up the southern slope and take a look around. Keep moving. I'll catch up to you in a bit."

Tom swung his horse forward and gigged it down the twisting canyon trail. After fifty yards, he turned the horse left off the main trail and followed a narrow game trail, spotted with deer and rabbit scat, high onto a pine-clad mountain shoulder. He rode up and over the shoulder and into another canyon.

Soft thuds rose from below. He glanced into the canyon. Several blacktail deer, led by a spike buck, clattered up the opposite slope, their white rears and knobby black tails bobbing as they scattered into the mesquite and pinions and disappeared over a rocky knob.

Navarro gazed after the deer and fingered the horn handle of his .44. Could be Apaches that spooked them. Possibly a bear. Navarro had killed a grizzly out here late last fall, after the grizzly had butchered several head of Bar-V beef. Or maybe they'd heard Tom's own hoof falls. It was damn

quiet out here tonight, with no birds singing, no coyotes howling the sun down.

Navarro was rounding a thumb of cracked
andesite when, up the slope on his right,
beyond a boulder snag, a horse blew. Navarro reined his paint to an abrupt halt and
shucked the Winchester repeater from the
saddle boot beneath his right thigh. Holding his reins in his gloved left hand, he
cocked the rifle with his right and snugged
the brass butt plate against his hip.

He sensed more than heard the bullet slicing the air to his left. Throwing his chest
flat against the paint's neck, he heard the
bullet buzz over his right shoulder a split
second after the rifle's crack rose from
downslope.

He reined the horse left and, staying low,
swung his rifle toward the downslope side
of the hill, where two men crouched in the
rocks and shrubs. Navarro fired the Winchester. One-handed, he jacked another
shell and fired another round.

His first round barked off a rock. His
second took one bushwacker — a short
hombre in a dirty plaid shirt and a straw
sombrero — through the high right side of
his chest. He only saw the man begin to fly
backward down the slope when the second
man fired. The bullet smashed into the

paint's chest with a cracking thump. As Navarro shook loose of the stirrups, the horse reared, twisting and falling as it screamed.

Navarro hit the ground on his right shoulder, dug his boots into the gravel, and flung himself forward and out of the falling horse's path. The second bushwacker fired again, the flames stabbing from the end of the barrel, the bullet smacking a slender nub of rock two feet before Navarro's face.

The rock finger disintegrated, but it had been enough of an obstruction to knock the bullet wide with an echoing spang, stinging Navarro's face with only shards of rock and lead.

Cursing, hearing the horse's final anguished throes to his left, Navarro rose to his left hip, aimed at the second bushwacker just as the tall slender gent in a floppy hat and buckskins levered another shell into the chamber of his Henry rifle.

Navarro shot the man low in the belly. As the man groaned and dropped to his knees, firing the Henry into the rocks at his feet, the Bar-V segundo remembered the sound he'd heard upslope.

Jacking another shell into his Winchester's chamber, he pushed himself to his feet, ran across the trail, and crouched at the upslope's base, behind rocks and twisted cedars.

He was edging a look up the steep, rocky grade when a bullet slammed into the rock a foot above his head, kicking up dust and stone slivers, which peppered the trail and dead horse behind Navarro like hail.

"Think you're tough now, you son of a bitch!" The screechy, indignant voice of the kid from the cantina echoed around the canyon several times before it faded.

Pressing his back to the slope and clutching his rifle in both hands, Navarro swallowed the dry knot in his throat and fingered the Winchester's trigger. The kid. The son of a bitchin' stupid-ass kid!

The wiry little firebrand had found some amigos in Tucson, probably sleeping off drunks in the livery barn or the town's lone boardinghouse. Intending to set up an ambush in the canyon, they'd taken a shortcut from town. Navarro had heard them on the ridge and busted their little fandango wide open.

Only they'd killed a good horse, one that Navarro had raised from a Colt and gentled in his own little paddock behind his cabin.

And the kid had the high ground. . . .

"Come on out here, you old duffer!" the kid called. "Think you can make sport o' me now! Ha!"

The rifle popped. The bullet smacked the same rock the previous one had smacked, making Navarro's ears ring.

Tom looked to either side. Straight above, the hill bulged, forming troughs on either side. From the angle of the kid's shooting, he must be snugged up in the left trough. The hill's bulge would prevent him from seeing what was going on in the right trough.

Navarro wheeled right and, crouching to keep his head below the bulge, began climbing the trough. The kid fired another round at his old position, the rifle's report echoing. Navarro climbed between boulders, occasionally losing his footing in the chalky shale. Once he dropped to a knee, but pushed up and on, grabbing at boulders and shrubs for purchase.

"Come on outta there, ye old bastard!" the kid cried, his voice muffled. "Show yourself now, ye damn coward." Another echoing shot.

Navarro climbed between two cracked boulders leaning away from each other, grabbed a pinion, and hoisted himself to the ridge top. Lots of gravel up here and spots of bobcat sign.

In the west, the sun was falling fast beneath fleecy golden clouds, bleeding deep into the jagged purple ridges.

On one knee and looking around, Navarro caught his breath, admonished himself to go easy on the rum-soaked Cubans Vannorsdell blessed him with on occasion, and scuttled around the rocky bulge, following the goat path down the other side.

The kid's rifle had popped three more times before Navarro, heading downslope one slow step at a time and leveling the rifle out from his right hip, crept around a boulder and stopped.

The kid was hunkered behind a rocky shelf, his Spencer repeater propped in a notch of a flat rock. The kid yelled another jeering demand from behind his cover and jacked another shell in the Spencer's breech.

Ten yards behind him, Navarro said, "Kid, you're wild as a corncrib rat and dumb as a dog barkin' at a knothole."

The kid froze.

"I tried to educate you," the Bar-V segundo said. "But it looks like I'm gonna have to put you down."

The kid stayed where he was, facing the downslope, his Spencer cocked and aimed at Navarro's old position. His right shoulder twitched. He didn't seem to be breathing. Between the sweaty curls pasted to his shirt collar, his neck was growing crimson.

Finally, he whipped around, bringing the Spencer to bear, stretching his lips back from his teeth in an outraged snarl.

Navarro's rifle spoke five times as Tom stood, gray eyes narrowed, feet spread, shooting and cocking, shooting and cocking.

The kid got off only one shot as Tom's shots ripped through his chest, drawing a small circle over his heart. The kid's head snapped back against the rock, eyes blinking rapidly, each shot holding him there for the next. After the last shot had blown through his spine, he sighed and slowly slumped to his right, relaxing, the Spencer slipping from his hands.

Behind him, the rocks dripped red.

At the bottom of the slope, a rifle barked. A horse whinnied. The rifle barked again. A man yelled.

Navarro climbed over the shelf the young firebrand had used for cover, and hurried down the steep, rocky slope, breaking his descent by grabbing pinion and mesquite branches.

Several more shots rose to his ears.

"Whatcha think you're doin', ye greaser bastard?" he heard Ky Tryon complain.

At the bottom of the slope, Navarro

turned left onto the game path he'd been following when he'd been bushwacked. He stepped around his dead paint, traced a bend around the mountain's shoulder, and stopped.

Ky Tryon lay upon the trail, clutching his extended left leg with one hand, his six-shooter in the other. Blood oozed between the fingers of the hand clutching his thigh. Tryon's face was pinched with pain.

Right of the trail, downslope, the stocky Mex in the dirty plaid shirt was moving slowly up the slope toward Tryon. His sombrero hung down his back, and his long silver-streaked black hair fell over his shoulders. He moved awkwardly, obviously in pain from his wounded shoulder, his Winchester in his right hand.

"Stop there, amigo," Navarro called.

The Mex wheeled toward him too quickly, then lost his balance and dropping. As his right knee hit the ground, the rifle went off, sending the slug several yards off Tryon's right shoulder.

The man cursed loudly in Spanish as, on both knees now, he took the rifle in both hands and began fumbling another shell into the chamber. He didn't look at Navarro but kept his pain-twisted, sweating face on the rifle as he cried and cursed and fought

the lever, caught against a half-ejected cartridge.

Navarro brought his own Winchester to
his shoulder, quickly aimed, and fired.

The round plowed through the Mexican's
head, just above the hairline. The man flew
back onto a half-dead juniper, arms pin-
wheeling, the rifle clattering onto the rocks
and gravel to his left.

Navarro lowered the Winchester and ran
to Tryon. The drover looked at him through
pain-sharp eyes.

"Came up to help you out," he rasped.
"Damn Mex smoked me."

"I told you to wait below."

"Well, I didn't — okay, Tom?" Tryon
barked and sucked air through his gritted
teeth.

Navarro turned. "You see the other one?"

"What other one?"

"Wait here."

Navarro moved quickly but cautiously
down the slope, peering around boulders
for the tall man in buckskins. The light was
dying quickly, the shadows thickening, making him look twice behind prospective cover
before moving on.

After he found the thick blood pool where
he'd shot the man, it didn't take him long
to track him to where he'd crawled, smear-

ing blood thick as oil, fifty yards down the slope and west of his previous position. The man sat with his back to a deadfall pine.

He literally cupped his guts in both his ham-sized hands. The wound smelled like fresh blood and excrement.

When Navarro's shadow fell across him, he sighed and lifted his chin from his right shoulder. His big face with a mallet nose and tiny eyes was sweat-soaked, the beads turning crimson as a fleeting shaft of dying sun broke through a notch in a western ridge.

"Please, mister," the man groaned, tongue cracking dryly, "just a drink of water . . ."

Navarro glanced up the slope at Tryon and at the dead paint — nearly as good a horse as he'd ever owned — stretched across the path as though dropped from the sky.

"How 'bout some lead instead?"

Navarro raised the rifle and fired.

CHAPTER 4

Navarro driving, Amado following on his buckskin and leading Ky Tryon's horse, the Bar-V wagon raced through the descending night, following the deep-scored wagon trail into the high country where the saguaros thinned and cottonwoods began appearing in swales, with cedars, sedge, and broomgrass growing thick along the benches.

The Bar-V sat in a high valley that, from the granite crests looming over it, resembled two giant hands cupped together at the heart of a long, bulky mountain. The sky was lit up like a Mexican Christmas tree when the wagon thundered through the yard's wooden portal, whipped past the corrals and blacksmith shop, and squawked up to the bunkhouse, Navarro sawing back on the reins and bellowing, "Hoah now . . . *hoooo-ahhhh!*"

The bunkhouse door had opened as the

wagon passed under the portal, and several silhouetted figures stood on the porch, hatless, cigarette smoke billowing around their heads in the still night air.

"Why you boys so late?" asked Dallas Tixier, stepping off the porch with several others. "I was beginning to think the senoritas had talked you into staying another night."

Navarro wrapped the reins around the brake handle. "A coupla you men help Ky inside. He's got a bullet in his left thigh. Someone tell Joe to break out his medical kit and put water to boil."

In Apache country, bullet and arrow wounds were as commonplace as horse throwings or saddle galls. Without any to-do, three men helped Tryon out of the wagon and inside, one of the men saying, "Ah, Christ, Ky, I seen whores' hickies worse than that."

When the kid was inside and the stove had been fired up for water, the wagon driven up to the back of the main house for unloading, Tixier turned to Navarro. "What happened, Tommy?"

Navarro curled his lip. "Bushwacked in Arrowhead Canyon."

"Apaches?"

Navarro shook his head. "Some younker

44

fancied himself the next William Bonnie."

"You put him down?"

"Like a chicken-thievin' hound."

Tixier returned his long black cigar to his teeth and lowered his gaze to Navarro's left arm. "Looks like you need some attention there, your ownself."

Navarro glanced at the torn sleeve and dried blood. He hadn't realized he'd been grazed until after he'd killed the man in buckskins and was helping Tryon onto his horse.

"Just a scratch." Navarro turned away, looked westward toward the open range capped in stars.

Tixier blew a long stream of smoke. "What're you thinkin'?"

"I'm thinkin' I'm feelin' restless. Might need to move on again soon. Maybe a horse ranch up in Montana." Tom turned to Tixier, the half-Mexican, half-Pima he'd scouted with out of Fort Bowie, fighting Apaches before they had tired of army ways and had taken up the ranching life. "Would you come with me?"

"It's cold up there, ain't it?" Tixier said around the cigar in his teeth.

"I'll get you a fat Indian woman."

Tixier shifted the cigar and grinned. "Then, hell, I'd think about it."

Navarro retrieved his saddle, which he'd wrestled off the dead paint, and hefted it onto his left shoulder. "I'm goin' to bed."

He'd started away from the bunkhouse, heading for his own cabin near the creek, but Tixier's voice stopped him. "Trouble up to the house tonight." He inclined his head to indicate the sprawling adobe fronted with shrubbery and a wide front veranda, several windows sprouting lantern light.

"What kinda trouble?"

"The senorita and Don Vannorsdell," Tixier said conspiratorially. Light from the window flanking him glistened off his gold eye tooth. "Her vaquero came to say *hasta luego.*"

Navarro looked toward the house, sighed deeply, shifted the saddle on his shoulder, and walked eastward across the yard. He crossed a narrow arroyo and tramped through the chaparral to the shack that had been here long before Vannorsdell had moved to the valley — a squat, boxlike adobe with a sagging brush arbor silver limned by starlight.

He mounted the porch and reached for the door latch. The motion was stillborn.

Wheeling left, he dropped his saddle, saddlebags, and rifle boot and snapped his horn-handled .44 from his holster. Thumbing back the hammer, he extended the gun to the hammock hanging beneath the arbor and in which a shadowy figure lay.

He stood tensely, gun extended, staring.

"Go ahead and shoot," Karla said, her voice small and brittle.

Navarro tipped the Navy's barrel up and depressed the hammer with a ratcheting click. "Know how close I just came to perforating your fool hide?"

"I don't want to live anymore, Tommy."

Navarro sighed and holstered the weapon. He stooped to pick up his saddle, straightened, and threw open the door. "You'll get over it . . . him."

He walked into the dark cabin that smelled of mesquite smoke, tanning grease, and dry adobe. He dropped the saddle on the floor behind the door, lighted the hurricane lamp on the table, walked back out to the porch, and gathered up his rifle boot and saddlebags. He carried the tack into the dimly lit, rough-hewn cabin, dropped it on the single cot against the left wall, beneath a small crucifix that had hung there when he had moved in, and removed his cartridge belt.

Bootheels thudded softly. He looked up to see Karla moving through the door, an Indian blanket wrapped loosely about her shoulders, her light brown hair hanging free.

Her tan heart-shaped face was drawn, sun-bleached brows furled.

"You heard?"

Navarro nodded, dropped the gun belt on the cot, and threw his hat on top of it.

"The old bastard drove him off," Karla said.

Navarro grabbed the red-rimmed washbasin off the table and left the cabin through the back door. He filled the basin at the well pump, having to work the squeaky handle several times before the water came up, then stooped to let the chill stream douse his head. Blowing water from his lips and rubbing it out of his close-cropped hair, he straightened, returned to the cabin, kicked the door closed, and set the basin on the table.

He sat heavily down in one of the two spool-back, cane-bottom chairs, which creaked under his weight. The water felt good, running down his head and under his shirt, soothing his sweaty sunburned neck. The girl stood by the door, her back to the wall, watching him as though waiting for him to say something.

"You didn't really think he was going to let it go anywhere, did you?" Navarro asked, jerking his shirt out of his dusty denims and beginning to unbutton his left cuff.

"It's not up to him. It's up to me and Juan."

Working on the buttons, Navarro glanced at her from beneath his gunmetal brows. "Karla, you've been out here nearly three years now. You know better."

She pursed her lips and spoked her eyes, making her voice hard. "I love Juan. If my grandfather loved me, that would mean something to him."

Navarro unbuttoned his shirtfront, removed the shirt, and tossed it over his hat and tack on the cot. He took a knife from a scabbard lying under a yellowed illustrated newspaper on the table, and began cutting away the bloody sleeve of his long underwear shirt.

"What happened?" Karla asked.

"Some younker reminded me why I like to stay to home."

When he'd cut through the sleeve above the elbow, he winced as he pulled the blood-soaked cotton away from the graze. He set the sleeve aside and inspected the burn — a half-inch gash along the outside of the arm, about halfway between the elbow and shoulder. The blood had gelled, nearly dried.

Karla moved away from the wall and slumped into the chair across from Navarro. "Did any of our men get hurt besides you?"

"Tryon took a bullet in the leg. Went all the way through. Didn't hit the bone." He winced as he dabbed at the cut with a damp cloth. "Damn lucky."

"Did you kill them?"

"Yep." Navarro glanced at her. "Bring me that roll of bandages from my war bag, will you?"

Karla got up, retrieved the torn cloth wrapped around a stout cottonwood stick, and set it on the table. Then she turned to the cupboards against the back wall, and produced a bottle. She set the bottle on the table beside Navarro, then turned back to the cupboards.

"All my bellyachin'," she said guiltily. "And you and Ky were shot."

Hearing her rummage through his airtights stacked neatly in the cupboard above his larder box, Navarro popped the cork from the bottle, held his arm over the bloody water in the basin, and doused the cut with whiskey. He winced and sucked air through his teeth as he lifted the bottle to his mouth, took a long pull, then set it on the table and began wrapping a bandage around his arm, closing it firmly around the cut.

He cut the bandage from the roll, took one end in his teeth, set the knife on the table, and tied the knot one-handed.

"Does your grandfather know where you are?"

She was opening a can of tomatoes with a rusty bowie knife. "He thinks I'm in my room."

"He wouldn't like you bein' here."

"Why wouldn't he? You don't have any bean-eater blood, do you, Tommy?"

"Don't get sassy. Your place isn't here, with me and my kangaroo rats. It's up at the big house with your grandfather."

She set a tin plate on the table beside the whiskey bottle. It was filled with canned tomatoes, crackers, and chunks of roasted venison from the buck he'd brought down from the high country last week. "I'd make you something proper at the house, but I'd just as soon not go near the place again."

"You don't have to cook for me, girl. I work for you, remember?"

Karla took the basin off the table and dumped it in the backyard. Navarro was eating the food she'd prepared while hearing the pump squawk as she ran water over the basin. When she came back in, she returned the basin to the table and took two water glasses from the cupboard. She set them on the table, slumped back down across from him, and poured two fingers of whiskey into each.

"You're drinkin'?" he said, raising his eyebrows as he picked up one of the glasses.

"I learned it from you, remember?" She smiled, knocked her glass against his, and took a sip. She smacked her lips and sighed. "Just like you taught me how to ride, how to track, and how to shoot — you taught me how to drink."

"That was beer."

"Grandfather doesn't have any beer around the house. Just rye whiskey, and cognac and port for visitors."

"Christ." Navarro threw back half his whiskey, set the glass on the table, and cut off a chunk of venison with his fork. "You're gonna get me fired."

She sipped her whiskey, leaned forward on her elbows, and propped her drawn face in her right hand. "We've talked a lot about horses and shooting and such, but you've never told me if you've ever been in love before."

Navarro chewed, swallowed, and indicated her glass with his fork. "That's the whiskey talkin'."

"Have you?"

He paused, a fork of tomato and meat halfway to his mouth. He stared at the food for two seconds, then shoveled it into his mouth. Chewing, he nodded. "Christ, I'm fifty years old. Of course I've been in love, a time or two."

"What happened?"

"First woman died durin' the War, while I was off fightin' it. The second . . ." He paused again, wiped a hand on his jeans, took a sip of the whiskey, and set the glass down. He forked the last bit of meat, frowning, his heavy brow ridged. "The second . . . well, I should've known better." He jabbed the meat into his mouth and chewed.

"Uh-oh."

"What?"

"I sense drama. A little Shakespearean tragedy in the life of Taos Tommy Navarro?"

Avoiding her eyes, Tom ate a cracker soaked in tomato juice and shook his head. "Just the common old tragedy visited on every one of us, we live long enough."

She splashed more whiskey into his glass, then into hers. Her voice thickened a little, and she pooched her lips out. "Come on, Tommy, tell me. I'm heartbroke."

Navarro tossed the fork onto his empty plate, leaned back in his chair, cleared his throat, and probed his teeth with his tongue. "She was the widow of the second man I killed — outside of the War, that was."

53

"Gosh," Karla said. "Go on."

"The man was town marshal of Pueblo, in the Colorado Territory. He was planning to kill a friend of mine in cold blood. I shot him in a fair fight. In his pockets, I found a picture of a pretty, innocent-eyed girl. I paid her a visit, to explain my side of it."

"And you fell in love?"

Navarro nodded.

"What happened?"

"We were together for a couple months when her dead husband's brother, the marshal's deputy, got wind of who I was. He pulled a gun on me, in a Denver eatery. Cordelia got between us, took a bullet in the neck. She died in my arms."

Karla ran a slender index finger around the rim of her glass as she studied it. "What a romantic tragedy."

Navarro lowered his head and ran a rough hand over his damp hair. "Not so romantic. Just a tragedy."

"And the deputy?"

"Killed him on the spot. It was self-defense, but that doesn't matter when you kill a lawman. So I ran out. Left her there. Never been back to Colorado."

"There wasn't anything you could have done."

He sat stiffly, hands on his thighs, staring

at the table. Finally, he grabbed his glass, threw the whiskey back, and stood. "I've had a hard day, and I'm goin' to bed."

"Oh, please, Tommy. Don't kick me out. I don't want to go back to the house tonight. I don't want to be alone!"

"You can't stay here." He picked up his plate and tossed it into the wreck pan on the range.

"I'll sleep on the floor."

Navarro turned to her, drawing his mouth wide to speak. She gazed up at him with such heartbreak and beseeching that he let the objection die in his throat.

He sighed. "All right. You can have the cot. I'll sleep in the hammock." He pointed an authoritative finger at her. "But you're out of here at sunrise. This ain't proper, and if the old man finds out, he'll likely have me tarred and feathered and run out of the country!"

Tarred and feathered, hell. Men were strung up for lesser offenses than sharing sleeping quarters with young women. He'd get her up at first cock crow, send her back to the house. She'd have calmed down by then.

Later, after he'd been lying in the hammock for an hour, unable to sleep and thinking about Cordelia, he heard a click.

He reached for the gun beneath his pillow, but stopped. The click came from the door, which opened slowly. Karla stepped out.

"What's the matter?" he said.

"Can't sleep." Before he knew what she was doing, she'd rolled over him and, distributing her weight evenly, snuggled up against his shoulder.

"Hey, what in the hell are you doing?"

"I'm lonely and I want to sleep on your shoulder."

Navarro didn't say anything. He lay there awkwardly, wrapping one arm around her shoulders because he didn't know what else to do with it. His muscles tensed. She didn't say anything, either, but her chest rose and fell as she breathed. Her shoulders quivered, and he felt a wetness on his chest, where her face lay against it. She sniffed back tears.

"I'm sorry, Karla."

"I'm going to ride out and find him tomorrow. I'm going to bring him back and I'm going to tell my grandfather that if he doesn't let us marry, I'm leaving."

"Where would you go?"

"Anywhere Juan wants to go."

"Juan's a vaquero. He rides from job to job, just like the rest of us saddle tramps."

"He's not just a saddle tramp. He writes poetry."

Navarro sighed.

They lay there for a long time. Finally, she quit crying and rested her head against his cheek. He felt the brush of her eyelashes against his face as she blinked. Her breath was a faint rasp through her parted lips. Her breasts pushed against his side. Smelling the lilac water she'd washed with, the faint pumpkin aroma of her hair, he ran his hand down her back, feeling the womanly curve of her.

A discomfiting warmth rose within him.

"I can't sleep all shut in like this," he grumbled, dropping his right foot to the floor.

As he slid out from beneath her, she said, "Where you going?"

"Inside. And you're going home."

"Tommy . . ."

"You heard me." His voice was stern. "Git!"

She sat up and looked at him defiantly. "I won't ever go back there."

"You don't have anywhere else to go. Now *git!*"

She struggled to her feet, wrapped her blanket around her shoulders, and stalked off the porch in a huff. "You're a bastard, Tommy!"

"Yes, I am." With that, he went into the

cabin and slammed the door behind him.

It took him another hour to fall asleep. He didn't know how much time had passed before boots thumped on the porch. Someone pounded on the door.

"Tommy!" Dallas Tixier called.

Navarro lifted his head from the pillow, groggily glanced around the shack. Golden light poured through the sashed windows, winking off the bottle and empty glasses on the table. For the first time in years, he'd slept past dawn.

"What is it?" Navarro growled.

"It's the senorita," Tixier said. He threw open the door and peered in, his bushy black brows knit beneath the brim of his high-peaked sombrero. "She's flown the coop."

CHAPTER 5

Navarro and five other riders were mounted and waiting before the big house. The sun hadn't yet climbed above the horizon, and the clear sky above the ranch was lighter than the land. The smell of mesquite smoke still peppered the fresh air.

After Pilar had discovered Karla's empty bed, she'd awakened the old man. Still in his pajamas and slippers, he'd ordered the hands, just rising in the bunkhouse, to scour the grounds. When they'd found no sign of the girl, and had discovered the Arabian gone, Tixier had fetched Navarro.

The house's stout oak door opened and Vannorsdell walked out, tucking his shirt into his baggy riding denims. "I can't believe she'd pull such a stupid stunt," the old rancher said, as Jorge Amado handed him the reins of a black quarterhorse gelding, saddled and waiting. The rancher grunted and wheezed as he climbed into the saddle. He turned to Navarro, who wore a white cotton shirt with blue pinstripes, suspenders, and bull-hide chaps over blue denims. "Doesn't look like she slept in her bed at all last night. What in the hell do you think she's up to?"

"Looks to me like she went after her Don Juan."

"Do you think she's really that goddamn crazy in love with that bean eater?"

Navarro shrugged. "You know Karla."

"If that crazy girl started out when she told Pilar she was going to bed, she's a good seven, eight hours ahead of us."

"I tracked her from the corral to where she left the main ranch trail, heading south. With any luck we'll ride out a few miles and run into her, heading back."

"And when we do, I'm gonna tan her hide," Vannorsdell said, gigging the black across the yard and riding abreast of Tom. The other hands fell in behind. The old man grumbled, "Worrying me like this, pulling me away from my work . . . I have a meeting up at the Circle M later this morning."

When they'd trotted through the main gate, Navarro, the best tracker of the bunch, galloped out ahead of the pack, Vannorsdell staying about twenty yards behind. The stocky old man was an awkward rider.

60

Although he prided himself on his abilities, he rode like he was riding a pinwheeler, as though he were always about to chin the moon, his bolo tie whipping over a shoulder, one arm flopping back like a broken wing. He never had fallen, however — at least, not when Navarro was around. Together they'd ridden every swale and ridge line on the old Dutchman's sixteen-thousand acres.

The girl's trail wasn't hard to trace, following, as it did, the old horse trail leading straight south through a notch in the Alder Bluffs, then angling west along Copper Creek. Navarro rode with his jaws set. Just like a girl to do something this impulsive and downright dangerous.

Karla had ridden with Navarro out this way several times, and she knew the country, but this was a godforsaken place, where danger lurked under every rock and cactus. Even seasoned drovers wouldn't drift out here alone. If the heat, falling rock, mountain lions, and diamondbacks didn't get you, the Apaches would. And horses, even Arabians, were known to tumble down ravines.

And then there were the diabolical sun and lack of water. . . .

Damn fool girl.

What made Navarro even angrier was the

guilt he felt at turning her out last night. If he'd let her stay at his place until she'd settled down, she might not have pulled such a plug-headed stunt in the first place. . . .

Also, he was afraid. At the moment, he wanted to tan her hide as badly as her grandfather did, but Navarro and Karla had developed a special bond over the past three years. He'd never fully realized it before, but getting close to her, hunting and riding together, he'd sort of gotten an inkling of what it must have been like to have a daughter.

This riding after her lost love gave him another inkling, and soured the first one more than a tad.

"Damn," he said, after they'd ridden an hour. He was at the top of a rocky knoll, looking around.

The other men had halted below to loosen their saddle cinches and give their mounts a blow. Vannorsdell was squinting up at Navarro. "What is it, Tom?"

Navarro reined his piebald down the other side of the knoll. Ten minutes later, he appeared again at the top of the knoll. "I found the trail. Mount up."

They'd ridden for another hour and forty-five minutes through a rocky draw, with saguaros and barrel cactus on both steep slopes, when Navarro leaned out from his saddle and frowned down at the trail. "I'll be a . . ." he muttered.

Vannorsdell was riding behind him, beside beefy Rob Miller, who had only one ear, the Apaches having taken the other two months after he'd begun riding for the Bar-V. "Tom, what is it?" the rancher asked.

Navarro rose up in his saddle and looked around. A flush rose in his face, darkening the already dark cherry skin. "I'm not sure we're on Karla's trail."

Vannorsdell rode up to his left. "What are you talking about?"

"She's been givin' me one hell of a time trackin' her — I'll tell you that."

"Karla? How can she be hard to track?"

"She's been obscuring her trail."

Vannorsdell scowled at him. "How?"

"She's been riding over the hardest ground she can find. Taking shortcuts between canyons. In some places, she's been rubbing out her trail or obscuring it with sand and rocks."

"Where in the hell did she learn how to do that?"

Navarro sent his gaze up the wall to his left, then up the one to his right. His horse blew and stomped its right front hoof. Navarro frowned down at the animal.

"What is it?" Vannorsdell asked.

"Ole Crowfoot here — he's actin' a mite wily. Like we might be on Apache sign instead of Karla's." Navarro dismounted and, holding the reins in his right hand, hunkered down on his haunches. He traced the outline of a hoofprint in the clay-colored sand and gravel in the sparse shade of a spindly pinion. "This print here ain't shod."

"You mean to tell me we might be following Apaches instead of Karla?"

Navarro felt the flush of embarrassment. "I think she lost me back in Manzanita Gulch."

"Tom, how in the hell does my granddaughter know this country so well? And where in the hell did she learn to obscure her sign like that?"

Navarro toed a stirrup and swung into the saddle. "I reckon I taught her, Mr. Vannorsdell." Without looking at the rancher's reaction, he turned to the men behind him. "Keep your carbines to hand and your eyes skinned. I might have just rode us up the asses of about a half dozen Apaches."

The men muttered as Navarro started out, shucking his own Winchester from the saddle scabbard under his right thigh. He jacked a shell into the breech and set the rifle across his saddle bows.

Karla was probably heading for the San Pedro River. That was the best corridor for a ride toward Mexico. Navarro would probably cut her sign there, in the San Pedro Valley, but the four Apaches, who looked to be no more than an hour or so ahead, could make getting there a little rough.

The longer he rode under the hammering sun, the more certain he became that Karla had not come this way. He didn't see the print of a single shod hoof. Somewhere, she'd made a clean break from her previous trail.

Navarro had taught her well.

Behind him, Vannorsdell and the hands rode Indian file, not talking much, their saddle leather squeaking, their horses' shod hooves ringing off stones.

Around them, cicadas whined. The heat was a heavy pall. There was no wind. At three in the afternoon, Navarro heard a deep, distant rumble. He hipped around in his saddle and peered over a cone-shaped mountain of rock. Behind the mountain, the sky was the color of a ripe plum. A hair-like line of lightning sparked. Five seconds later, thunder growled.

Vannorsdell followed Navarro's gaze, then turned back to Tom. "Movin' slow. Looks to be headin' south. Maybe it'll skirt around and miss us."

"Maybe," Navarro said, turning forward and riding on. If that storm carried as much rain as it appeared, these gullies would be rivers soon, and Karla's tracks would be obliterated.

A half hour later they were climbing toward a pass, along an ancient Spanish trail skirting a wash to their left. Pines, mesquite, and cholla grew around them, and mountain goat scat littered the flat, black rock mushrooming along the wash. In natural rock bowls they found water dotted with grass seeds and dead and hatching insects, and stopped to let the horses draw, then mounted and continued climbing the steepening, winding trail.

They'd stopped at another tank to let the lathered horses drink, when Jorge Amado blew air through his teeth. "Look at that, Tom."

Navarro followed the stocky Mexican's pointing finger, to a column of smoke billowing out from a rocky knoll about a hundred yards ahead and slightly south. Navarro poked his hat brim off his forehead and bit down on the brown paper quirley in his teeth.

His shell gray eyes, spoking at the corner,

stared hard at the smoke. He slid them left across the wash. Another column rose about two hundred yards ahead, from a jumble of black rock shaped like a sleeping bear. The column rose straight up, in a series of staggered charcoal puffs.

"Ain't it just a wonder how they do that?" Tom said, a tenseness beneath the mock-jovial tone.

"You know, Mr. Navarro," said Rob Miller, "every time I see smoke talk like that, my other ear starts to ache somethin' crazy."

"Apaches are men, same as us," Hector Potts said, squatting to fill his hide-covered canteen with the tepid water.

Vannorsdell stepped up beside Navarro. He was smoking a stout cigar. "I reckon I forgot to tell you, Tommy — while you and the other boys were in Tucson, a cavalry detail from Fort Apache stopped at the ranch. Nan-dash is off the reservation again. They said he killed an itinerant trader. Slow-cooked him in a clay pot over his own burning wagon."

Navarro grinned sardonically and blew smoke through his nostrils. "That's nice to know."

"Sorry, Tommy. I was going to tell you today."

"Today would've been a good time."

"You think they're layin' for us?"

"Could be. We cut Karla's sign again, about twenty minutes ago. She came this way. The Apaches came later."

Vannorsdell studied him, his tobacco-stained teeth showing through his dry, parted lips. "You think they have her?"

"There's only one way to find out." Navarro turned. "Hector. Charlie. Let's mount and see what all the smoke's about."

Hector Potts was an old Indian trader who'd married one of Cochise's daughters several years back, before she'd died of a stomach complaint. Charlie Musselwhite had been a drover since he was tit-high to a mustang dam. He'd fought Indians from Dakota to the Mexican border and still had his hair, because he'd learned to fight by their rules. Because of their knowledge of Indian ways, Navarro had hired both men himself.

Musselwhite, with his spiky corn yellow hair and perpetually amused brown eyes, had already kicked out of his boots and was on the ground pulling a pair of well-worn mocassins onto his feet, grimacing with the effort. Hector Potts had his Colt Bisley out. Tonguing the right corner of his mouth with concentration, he slowly turned the cylinder, making sure all six chambers showed brass.

The hair on the back of his neck prickling and his stomach feeling light, Navarro dropped his quirley, stubbed it out in the gravel, and grabbed his Winchester. He jacked a shell into the chamber, off-cocked the hammer, and mounted his horse. Glancing at Vannorsdell, he said, "The rest of you wait here."

"What if you don't come back?" Rob Miller said. He turned away to urinate on a shrub.

"You can send my fortune to Aunt Bess in Paducah," Navarro said.

"Robbie, do you think Arliss will still love me if I come back without my hair?" Musselwhite asked Miller, doffing his hat and grinning over his shoulder as he gigged his horse after Potts and Navarro. The drover had been sparking the working girl of a neighboring rancher for the past three months.

"Hell, no," Miller called after him.

CHAPTER 6

Navarro reined his piebald to a halt in a round cup in the sloping desert floor shaded by several large mesquite trees and stunt cedars. The manzanita grass grew thick.

Keeping his voice low, the Bar-V segundo said, "Let's leave the horses here."

"You know how I feel about walkin', Tommy," Hector grumbled.

"How do you feel about tryin' to level a shot at a running Apache from the back of a crow-hopping mount?"

"Oh, I'm just jawin'," Hector said, dismounting. "Sure wish I had me a pair of mocassins like Charlie. Those look right soft on the feet, they do. . . ."

When they tied off their horses to the mesquite trees, still speaking barely above a whisper, Navarro said, "Let's split up. I'll head toward the smoke column on the left. You boys head for the one on the right. If you see the girl and can get her out without

70

getting her and yourselves killed, do it. If the Apaches are too close, leave her. We'll meet down with the old man and the others in two hours and palaver up another plan."

"Why don't you take Hec, Tommy?" Charlie said, holding his Colt's revolving rifle in both hands. "He moves too slow for me."

"I move too fast for both of you. Go!"

Navarro turned and, holding the Winchester in his right hand, walked north through the cracked, sun-blasted boulders, descending the slope to the bottom of the dry wash. He climbed up the far side of the wash and wended his way through the boulders, some as large as Murphy freight wagons.

Halfway to his destination, he ducked low between a cedar shrub and the fallen skeleton of a barrel cactus, and shot a look up the hill. The smoke was gone. He looked right. The smoke was gone over there, as well — only loose rock piles spiked with dry brown grass under an arching sky.

Cool air moved against his back, drying the sweat beneath his collar. A raindrop struck his right ear. He swung a look behind him.

The plum clouds had moved closer, shepherding gray rain curtains. The sky over Navarro was still bright, but it wouldn't be in about ten, fifteen minutes. Lightning forked across the purple front, and thunder rolled.

He turned forward just in time to see a shadow flit between two rocks about forty yards ahead and left. Another flitted over a rise before dropping into a shallow swale nearly straight ahead. Navarro had only glimpsed the second shadow, but he'd seen the shoulder-length hair flying around a head band, outlined by the brassy sky behind.

Navarro crawled straight back down the rise for thirty yards. He moved left around a huge chunk of pitted black lava. Behind him, thunder rumbled, growing in volume. The light grew wan, and the cool wind picked up, lightly swirling dust.

Tom hunkered down behind a rough-edged black rock, doffed his hat, and peered around the left side.

One of the Apaches slipped around a boulder, slick as a snake, moving toward Navarro's last position behind the dead cactus. He was a lean kid with the traditional red bandanna, bare-chested and wearing only a loincloth and knee-high leggings. A deerhide quiver was strapped to his back, five or six arrows protruding from the top. Winding around rocks and cholla, he moved up behind where Tom had been only two minutes before, and slowly raised his bow and arrow.

Navarro heard a rock click and turned left. The other Indian was moving in from the other direction — a chubby kid with pitted cheeks, dressed similarly to the first but with a big bowie sheathed on his hip. His right eye had been sewn closed over the empty socket.

Navarro shuttled his gaze to the first brave. The young Chiricahua had just discovered that Navarro had left his previous position. He wheeled to the other brave and muttered something Navarro, who knew a smidgin of the guttural language, couldn't hear above the rising wind and rumbling thunder.

Navarro stepped out from behind the rock. Seeing him in the periphery of their vision, both bucks wheeled toward him, startled.

Navarro raised the Winchester and fired, blowing the first kid straight back into the cactus. The other buck, sensing Tom had the drop on him, had wheeled away as Navarro shot his friend. Not seeing the boulder two feet to his right, he tripped over it, falling face-first in the gravel, losing his bow and arrow and giving an indignant groan.

Navarro's second shot, squeezed off as the

kid had fallen, blew shards from the rock.

Tom ran toward the rock. The kid climbed to his feet, wheeled toward Navarro, and cut loose with a high-pitched shriek as he clawed the bowie from his hip and ran toward Tom. He was twenty feet away and closing fast when, facing the buck, straight-backed, feet spread, Tom casually raised his cocked Winchester, squinted businesslike down the rifle's barrel, and blew a neat, round hole through the Indian's head.

The kid stopped, head snapping back, arms flying straight out from his shoulders. The bowie flew from his hand and clattered in the rocks. He stood like a broken ship's mast for several seconds, then fell straight back like a drunk gandy dancer falling into a bed.

Navarro ejected the spent shell, jacked another into the breech, and lifted the rifle to his shoulder, looking around. He'd have bet a fresh venison shank and a pint of mescal that these two younkers weren't the only two Chiricahuas up here.

Keeping the rifle raised, he moved ahead toward the jumble of rocks at the ridge line, where the smoke had originated. The wind blew him from behind, chilling the sweat under his shirt. Rain pelted him, splotching the rocks and bringing up the smell of sage and creosote. The moisture beads glistened on his rifle stock.

Keeping the rifle raised, he moved slowly up the hill.

He was near the crown, where a steep wall of red sandstone rose from powdery sand, when he spied movement on his left periphery. He whipped around and dropped to a knee as a copper-faced Indian crouched over a flat-topped boulder, aiming a strap-iron arrow at him.

Navarro had just snugged the Winchester to his shoulder when the arrow snapped away from the cedar bow and wheezed about three inches off the nub of his left shoulder. Navarro fired twice, quickly, not hearing his own casings fall from the breech.

The Indian gave a cry and disappeared in a blood spray.

Spying more movement on his right, Navarro turned again. As lightning flashed and thunder cracked wickedly, filling the air with the smell of brimstone, two more Indians appeared, bolting toward him through a doorlike cleft in the sandstone ridge. The rain had started in earnest, great white buffeting sheets, and the Indian's mocassins splashed through the puddles as they bolted toward Navarro.

Tom shot one as he paused to nock his

arrow. An arrow careened toward Tom from his far right, but the wind caught it, sent it clattering onto the rocks over his left shoulder. As his breath was sucked out of his lungs by the chill wind, rain sluicing over his hat and washing down his face, Navarro cocked a fresh shell into his Winchester's breech.

A lightning bolt sliced out of the murky gray rain and slammed into the stone ridge with a cannonlike boom, showering the entire area with blue-white sparks and the fetid odor of burning hair. Tom raised his gaze in time to see the other Indian, who had just loosed an arrow, leaping toward him, only three feet away and screeching like the devil's own hound.

The Apache dove into him, driving the rifle down and out of his hands. Navarro heard the rifle clatter against a rock. Tom hit the ground on his back, the Indian screeching and driving against him, digging his knees into Tom's thighs as he rose up and lunged toward Tom's face.

Instinctively, Navarro reached for the Indian's right wrist, caught it three feet from his face and raised his eyes to it. A razor-edged pig sticker with an upturned tip and hide-wrapped handle was aimed at his throat. Navarro had stopped it just before that savage blade had cored his Adam's apple.

Thunder cracked, for a second drowning the Indian's maniacal, unwavering screech.

Lightning flashed again, glinting off the knife blade and off the savage black eyes staring down into Navarro's own, filled with barbarous glee. The Indian had placed both hands on the knife's handle, pushing with all his weight against Navarro's right hand.

The blade tip slid down to prick Navarro's neckerchief. An eye wink later, the blade poked through the neckerchief and into Tom's neck, sharp as rattlesnake teeth.

The Indian's lips stretched back from long, thin teeth crooked and brown as old fence posts as the brave sucked a breath. His quivering chest expanded against Navarro's right, weakening forearm.

Tom pivoted slightly right. Grunting and grimacing as he held the knife back with his right hand, he brought up a rock in his left, and smacked it hard against the Indian's head.

The buck's renewed screech died stillborn as he fell onto his left shoulder. The Indian, sluggish from the blow, climbed to his knees and began crawling away from Navarro. Navarro jerked onto his own knees, grabbed the Indian's right foot, and pulled him back down.

The Indian jerked his foot from Navarro's grasp. Crawling forward, he scrambled to his feet. Navarro did likewise, reaching for his Colt, his hand coming up empty. He must have lost the revolver in the scuffle. The Indian flew toward him in the driving rain.

Navarro pivoted left, stuck his foot out, grabbed a fistful of the Indian's hair, and pulled. The brave tumbled over Tom's outstretched foot, dropping to his knees.

He was coming up again as Navarro leapt toward him. Spying movement on his right, sensing another Indian heading his way, Navarro rammed his right fist into the face of the brave before him. He rammed the face again, another pistoning blow, feeling the nose give beneath his fist and turn flat to the face, feeling the thick, wet blood on his knuckles.

A rifle popped to Navarro's right, nearly coinciding with another thunderclap.

Navarro leapt at the dazed Indian staggering bloody-faced before him. He got behind the buck, wrapped his right arm around his neck, cupping his chin, and jerked the head to the right and back, hearing the crunch and branchlike snap. He'd intended to use the dead buck as a shield, but the rain had made the Indian's skin slick, and he lost his grip.

As the body dropped before him, he cast his gaze straight ahead.

A stocky savage with a prunelike face stood on a rock about fifteen feet up the grade, his soaked calico shirt buffeting in the wind, sopping silver-streaked hair drawn back.

He had a Henry rifle raised to his shoulder and was siting down the barrel at Tom's forehead. Navarro felt like a deer trapped in a locomotive's rushing light.

Thunder clapped, rattling his ear drums. At the same time, a witch's finger of a shimmering lightning bolt jutted out of thin air twenty feet above and to the Apache's right. The bolt was gone in an instant, leaving the Indian limned in flickering sparks, like those from a blacksmith's forge. The electricity jerked down from his arms and out over his rifle, etching it precisely in the gray air before Navarro.

The Indian bellowed as the light faded.

He dropped the rifle, fell straight down from the boulder, and lay flat on his face, limbs akimbo. Flames traced a black circle in his shirt, just below his left shoulder blade. The flames were quickly snuffed by the rain. The man's hair and mocassins continued to smoke and sizzle as Navarro turned away, retrieved his Winchester, and dropping to one knee, brought the rifle up to his waist and looked around through the driving rain.

He knelt there for a long time, letting the rain pound him, watching the lightning flash off the rocks. Somewhere behind him, a tree was struck with a thundering crack followed by the rustling and cracking of falling branches and then the dull *whump* as the trunk hit the ground.

The storm had settled on this rocky knoll, cloaking Tom in a murky, dusky gauze.

Finally, when nothing else moved ahead or around him, Navarro retrieved his revolver and holstered it. Taking the Winchester in both hands, he crept up to the rocky ridge, slipped through the doorlike notch, and dropped to a knee, swinging the Winchester's barrel back and forth before him.

No movement here, either.

Looking around the buckling boulders, he found only the gray remnants of a fire and a pile of green cottonwood limbs. In a hollow about thirty yards from the crest, he found the mud-smeared tracks of five Indian ponies in the soft sand near a spring. Broken tree limbs littered the sand. Apparently, when the storm had hit, the horses had jerked their reins free and run.

Navarro took cover in the V between two boulders, and when the lightning had drifted east, he made his way back over the ridge top, found and reshaped his hat, and continued down the other side.

"Tommy!" a voice called above the wind.

Navarro turned. The rain had let up but the clouds still hovered low. Twenty feet downslope and left stood the short, bulky, water-logged shape of Paul Vannorsdell. The rancher's black stood white-eyed nearby, the rancher clutching his reins.

"We heard the gunfire and were comin' up, but the damn lightning held us back!"

Navarro moved toward him. "Where's Charlie and Hector?"

"Back down where you left the group. Potts took an arrow in his hip."

Navarro looked at him.

A grim expression swept the old man's face. He shook his head and said fatefully, "No sign of my granddaughter."

"Goddamn it!" Navarro brushed past the rancher, heading down the slope to find his horse. Like the Chiricahua ponies, the piebald had probably torn loose and galloped ten miles away by now.

"Where you goin'?" the rancher called after him.

"Home!"

CHAPTER 7

In the small cave where she'd taken refuge from the storm, Karla woke with a start.

She turned left, fumbling with the Winchester carbine with which she'd slept across her breast. She quickly jacked a round into the magazine and got her right index finger through the trigger guard. At the same time, she peered through the cave's arched opening, only three feet high, through which milky dawn light washed.

Heart thudding, Karla held her breath, straining her ears to listen.

Outside the cave rose sibilant sniffing and panting sounds. A rock rattled, and a scratching, tapping sounded, punctuated by the clinks of shale being knocked together.

A shadow appeared in the opening's far right edge — a coyote or a fox, head low, ears pricked. It sniffed busily, a musky, urinelike smell wafting from its coat.

"Shoo!" Karla whispered.

The beast squealed softly, a clipped howl. It withdrew its head and vanished, its hurried footsteps quickly fading with distance.

Karla's heart skipped a beat. She exhaled and lowered the Winchester. She sat with her wool blanket over her legs, her saddle and saddlebags behind her, for nearly a minute. When her heart had regained its normal rhythm, she set the rifle down, tossed aside the blanket, felt around for her low-heeled, high-topped riding boots, and pulled them on.

She retrieved the Winchester, climbed to her knees, and ducked through the opening, straightening and holding the rifle across her thighs. She wore tight denims and a cream flannel shirt, the tails untucked. Her brown hair fell straight across her shoulders, mussed from sleep. As she stood staring silently across the narrow, dark canyon opening before her, and at the patch of gray sky streaking the serrated rim, the cool morning air shoved against her, fresh from last night's rain.

There was barely a breath of breeze.

She hardened her jaw, tensed her back against the doubt, the apprehension and loneliness squeezing her lungs.

"Taos" Tommy Navarro had taught her how to survive in the desert. He'd taught her where to look for water and game. How to shoot and ride. How to track and cover her trail.

She would not return to her arrogant, meddling grandfather. That was what he was expecting her to do, with her tail between her legs, begging for his forgiveness. She meant to find Juan, and that was what she'd do.

Juan's uncle owned a rancho fifty miles south of the Mexican border, in a small canyon feeding the San Pedro. Hopefully, Karla would catch up to him later today or early tomorrow. What she and Juan would do then, she hadn't thought through entirely. All she knew was that she loved him, that he loved her — she'd seen it in his eyes even when he was telling her good-bye — and that her grandfather would have no say in their future.

Sitting against the cave wall, the rifle between her raised knees, she waited until the murky dawn light spilled over the ridges and down into the canyon, showing the crannies and hollows, the rocks and the spiky shrubs. She pinned her hair under her man's range hat, gathered her gear from the cave, and stole down the narrow trail winding through boulders to the grassy hollow where the Arabian stood, double-tied to a mesquite and hobbled so it couldn't bolt during last night's storm.

Before she'd left the ranch, Karla had filled one side of her saddlebags with grain. Now she placed a feedbag over the Arabian's head. As she saddled the horse, the grinding of its teeth filled the quiet air — a reassuring sound amid the eerie quiet after the storm.

Her imagination kept conjuring Apaches stealing down the slopes around her, but she resisted them, forcing instead the more pleasant memories of listening to her flint-haired vaquero beau read his love sonnets to her in Spanish while nearby their tethered horses cropped the meadow grass or a spring murmured through rocks.

A half hour later, she rode west along the spongy canyon floor, the Arabian's hooves making sucking sounds in the freshly eroded silt and sand. Around noon, she picked up the stage road cleaving a valley between two bald mountain ranges. She was about to rein the horse off the trail, toward a distant cottonwood copse, where she'd probably find a spring keeping the trees so green, when the smell of something burning touched her nostrils.

She peered around. A mile or more ahead, a thin column of black smoke rose above a rocky knoll. She stared at the smoke warily. Tom had told her that, if she ever found herself alone in the desert, to regard smoke with caution. Smoke often meant an Indian attack, and the Indians might still be around.

Finally, Karla batted her heels to the Arabian's sides, moving slowly ahead. She shucked the carbine from the saddle boot, jacked a shell into the magazine, lowered the hammer to half cock, and rode with the rifle across her thighs.

She'd ridden three-quarters of a mile and was rounding a wide bend when the Arabian stopped abruptly and, sniffing the air, pricked its ears and whinnied.

"Easy, boy, easy," Karla said, running a hand down the animal's fine neck and urging it forward.

She moved around the bend and stared across a low jumble of rock and cactus. Urging the reluctant horse closer, she studied the mound of fire-blackened wood as small flames licked here and there from the wreckage, black smoke swirling and rising.

On a flat panel tilted against a high wagon wheel half buried in ash and sand were the words, in gold-leaf lettering, BUTTERFIELD OVERLAND EXPRESS. Strewn about the rubble were the oblong remains of charred bodies, marked by half-burned hats and boots. A silver-plated revolver, untouched by the flames, shone between the still burning spokes of a wheel.

The wagon tongue was still burning, the horses gone, probably led off by the Apaches.

The Arabian whinnied and sidestepped, fighting the bit. Karla leaned over the horse's neck, cooing gently, as she studied the deep ruts the stage had carved in the sand when it had left the main trail, bulling over cactus and scattering rocks. All around were the relatively fresh prints of unshod hooves.

A chill engulfing her, Karla peered back along the powder white trail obscured by shimmering heat waves and the glaring sun. What looked like a body lay sprawled on the trail fifty yards away.

Karla was about to ride on and investigate when a high-pitched bark rose on her right. With a start, she turned that way, swinging the rifle out before her.

Two enormous black turkey buzzards, with faces like ancient bald men, stared at her furiously from fifteen feet away. Near them a small man with short gray whiskers and thin brown hair lay on his back among small stones and a barrel cactus. He wore faded blue denims, suspenders, and a cartridge belt and holster, the revolver missing.

Five arrows protruded from the man's chest, each centered over his heart. Two more jutted from his thighs. His ankles were crossed as though he were only napping; one arm was flung wide while the other gloved hand lay upon his bloody chest, loosely wrapped around the base of an arrow.

His blue eyes stared unflinching at the sky. His lips formed a perfect "O" of frozen shock and horror.

One of the buzzards, standing near the man's empty holster, gave another angry squawk and leapt in the air, beating its dusty wings. The other skitter-hopped several feet away, its skinny throat swelling as it breathed. Shadows glanced across the sand, and Karla looked up to see three more of the big carrion eaters swirling amid the smoke from the burning stage.

Feeling sick and making a conscious effort to keep in her stomach the jerky she'd eaten for breakfast, Karla gigged her horse back toward the trail. She looked cautiously around as the Arabian walked tensely, its tail swishing anxiously. Karla held the carbine's butt against her hip socket. She felt as though a crouching Apache were centering an arrow on her back.

Ten yards from the trail, she reined back abruptly. She'd heard something. Her gloved hand fingering the Winchester's trigger, she raked her gaze across the desert scuffed by the stage and a dozen horses.

"Kar-la." It was a wheezy rasp, like her name spoken by two yucca blades scraping together.

Her eyes whipped this way and that, finally settling on the stone her gaze had traveled across several times before. There was something odd about the rock. It seemed to move.

She stared at it tensely, her stomach squeezing. The rock appeared to turn slightly. The bottom third moved up and down, a slit widening and closing as her name was muttered again in the same anguished chords barely discernible above the cicadas' whine and the snapping of the flames.

Karla's heart raced as she gigged the horse across the trail and up a sandy rise. The rock capped the rise. Only it wasn't a rock. It was a man's head, the skin of the face drawn up and back over a thick mane of black hair. The blood-filled brown eyes stared luridly out at her, unblinking. The lids had been hacked off.

Again the mouth moved. "Kar-la . . ."

Her heart turned a somersault, and the desert tipped violently to one side, then to the other. She nearly fell from the saddle. Grabbing the horn, she dropped the carbine, vaguely heard it smack the sand beneath the horse. The Arabian lifted its head high and left, trying to turn away from the grisly spectacle.

"Juan," Karla sobbed.

As she shook her right boot from the stirrup, the Arabian reared and twisted backward, throwing her off its back. She fell sideways in the sand, landing on her hip and shoulder. If there was any pain from the fall, it didn't register. As the horse bolted away, Karla turned to the head staring at her glassily from the sand pile overrun, she saw now, with large red ants.

Sobbing uncontrollably, tears blurring her eyes, Karla climbed weakly to her knees, began climbing the mound toward Juan.

"Karla," rose the rasp again, barely heard above Karla's own cries, "come no closer."

"Oh, Juan," she said, phlegm thickening in her throat, tears washing down her cheeks. As she gained the top of the mound, feeling occasional ant nips, like cuts from glass shards, on the undersides of her arms and legs, she dropped down to her elbows and spread her open palms on either side of his head.

Juan's mouth opened, the bloodred tongue flicking between bloody lips. "Shoot me, Karla."

"I can help you," she cried, digging feebly into the sand beneath his chin.

"No! I don't want you to see what they did." Juan's voice cracked with a grating sob. *"Sangre de Christo!* Shoot me, Karla. I *beg you!"*

Karla ceased her digging, lowered her head to the sand between her outstretched arms, before Juan's bloody head.

"Bring the gun," Juan whispered. "Karla, please!"

Karla raised her head, regarding his pain-glazed eyes. Drunk with horror and sorrow, she climbed feebly to her knees. She stood, turned, and walked heavily back down the hill. She dropped to her knees, picked up the Winchester, and placed her right index finger through the trigger guard. She drew the hammer back. It clicked as it caught.

"Hurry!" Juan called, his mouth stretching wide.

Karla stood and walked slowly up the hill, the carbine hanging slack in both hands. She regarded Juan again through sun-gilded tears — her romantic vaquero lover who'd written and recited poems to her in Spanish.

"Do it!"

She dropped to a knee, raised the carbine's butt to her swollen cheek, centered the bead on his forehead. "I love you, Juan."

She didn't wait for an answer. She closed her eyes as she squeezed the trigger. The rifle cracked, the butt jerking solidly against her face, the sulfur peppering her nose.

Without looking, she turned away, walking slowly down the hill, and dropped to her knees. She did not open her eyes for a long time, until she heard the thud of hooves racing toward her.

As if waking slowly from a deep, troubled sleep, she slowly turned her head left. Men on horseback galloped toward her — a half dozen copper-skinned men on short-legged mustangs, their long black hair flying in the wind, red or blue bandannas gleaming in the sun.

The hooves thundered, growing quickly in volume, until Karla could feel the earth vibrating beneath her knees.

She watched them almost impassively. An instinctive fear grew within her, but it was surmounted by fury burning up from deep within her loins, quelling her tears and drying her cheeks.

Watching the men gallop to within thirty yards, she picked up the carbine, ejected the spent shell and jacked a fresh round into the breech. Standing, she spread her feet and brought the rifle to her shoulder. With an eerie calm, she snugged the butt against her shoulder, cheeked up to the stock, and centered a bead on one of the half dozen riders bouncing above the sage and threading through the chaparral.

She squeezed the trigger, and the rifle popped, spitting smoke and flames. The rider had anticipated the shot, and ducked, expertly swerving his horse to the left. The slug smacked off a boulder behind him with an angry echoing crack. The warrior whooped and jerked his bull-chested paint back toward Karla, savagely beating the horse's flanks with his heels.

Karla tried another shot, again missed. She ejected the spent shell, rammed another into the chamber, and fired at a brave only ten yards away. Screaming and howling like a devil loosed from hell, the brave dropped over the right side of his horse as the slug sliced the air where his chest had been. He bounded upright, jerked his rawhide reins sharply left, and slammed his blaze-faced dun directly into Karla.

She was out before she'd hit the ground.

Five minutes later, she lay belly down over the back of a Chiricahua war horse as the Apache braves lit southward across the hills, whooping.

Behind them, the piled white ashes of the stage smoked.

The buzzards lit upon the dead driver and commenced to feed.

Juan's raw, ant-streaked face, the bullet hole in his forehead streaming bright red blood, glared skyward.

CHAPTER 8

Navarro and the other Bar-V men had a long night's ride through intermittent rain. They stopped at a line shack to tend to Hector Potts' left hip and to feed and rest the horses before resuming their trek through the mud. Well after midnight, the sky clearing to show several stars and a gauzy moon, they passed beneath the portal of the Bar-V headquarters, the yard a rumpled, wet quilt before them.

"Tommy," Vannorsdell said, riding beside Navarro, "you're the best tracker I've ever known. . . ."

"Don't worry — Dallas, Charlie, and I'll ride out first thing in the morning on fresh horses. We'll get her back."

"You better take more men than that."

"With less dust and fewer sun reflections, we have a better chance of slipping through Apache country with our oysters."

"That damn girl. I'll tan her hide."

"She's in love."

"She has her father's blood. He was a wild one, that boy. It was pure luck he got rich readin' for the law back east."

They reined up before the barn. As the other men dismounted, Vannorsdell turned again to Navarro. "You think I was wrong to run off her Don Juan, don't you?"

"It ain't my say."

"What if it was your say?"

Navarro dismounted and reached for the latigo cinch. "Then I'd say you were wrong."

Vannorsdell stared down at him, then dismounted, tossed his reins to one of the other men, and stalked off toward the house, where Pilar stood on the porch with a dully glowing lantern.

Silent, the men tended to and stabled their mounts, then stalked off to bed. At dawn the next morning, after only four hours' sleep, Navarro, Dallas Tixier, and Charlie Musselwhite saddled fresh mounts and, with a mule outfitted with three weeks' trail supplies, mounted up and gigged their horses through the main gate.

Behind them, Vannorsdell watched grimly from the house's front porch.

"I don't know, Tom," Tixier said when they'd ridden an hour through the same country they'd ridden yesterday. "The sign's gonna be hard to pick up after the storm."

"You're right, Dallas," Navarro said, leading the procession through a rocky draw made slick by the fresh mud. "But I think I know where she's heading."

"Where?" Musselwhite asked behind him.

"Mexico."

"Ah, hell," Tixier said.

They rode through the midday heat blasting off the rocks, resting their mounts for ten minutes every hour. Navarro skirted the canyon in which they'd run into the Apaches, swerving south and then east along a maze of interconnected creeks and washes. He was off Karla's original trail but hoped to pick it back up along the San Pedro.

If she'd gotten through the Apaches, that was.

They were following a wash the Army called Weeping Squaw Creek, a scout having come upon a squaw mourning over the body of her dead husband there in '68, when Tixier reined his grulla mustang to a halt near a lightning-blasted cedar. He looked up the rocky ridge on the other side of the narrow, deep wash.

"Not agin."

Navarro followed the mestizo's gaze. Smoke puffed from a notch in the brush and saffron rocks, about halfway up the ridge.

All at once, the three riders reined their mounts off the trail and into the wash, their horses leaping the six feet to the damp, sandy bottom pocked with coyote and bobcat prints. Navarro shucked his saddle gun and dismounted, dropped his reins, and ran crouching to the opposite cutbank. He jacked a round into the Winchester's magazine and turned to Tixier shouldering up to the bank on his right.

"Not much smoke for Apache talk."

"Maybe they don't have much to say."

"Or maybe they've already said it," Musselwhite added, his white teeth flashing between sunburned lips as he thumbed back the hammer of his Yellowboy repeater.

Tixier turned to Navarro. "Could be the senorita."

Navarro stared at the smoke, then off-cocked his Winchester and handed it to Tixier. "Cover me." He hoisted himself up the ledge, took the rifle back from the mestizo, and dashed through the brush. When he made the mountain's base, he hunkered down behind a boulder and stole a look up the slope.

The smoke was still rising, webbing on a breeze. It was a steady column, not like the

intermittent puffs of an Apache signal fire.
More like a cook fire.

Navarro scurried up the slope, weaving a
slanting course up the mountainside, following a game path pocked with deer and
racoon scat. He stayed low, dashing between
shrubs and boulders, keeping an eye skinned
for sunlight reflected off gun barrels or the
flatiron of an Apache arrow.

Halfway to the smoke, he paused for
breath, then continued parallel to the ridge,
leaping from rock to rock, nearly tripping
when his boot slipped into a crack. When
he started smelling the smoke and charred
meat, he slowed to a walk, breathing
through his mouth and bringing his feet
down carefully.

He climbed the slope above the encamp-
ment. When he figured he was directly
above the fire, he paused behind a boulder,
listening. Hearing nothing, he leapt onto
the boulder and raised the Winchester, siting down the barrel at the figure squatting
by the small blaze in a rock ring, roasting a
rabbit over the flames.

Sensing someone behind him, the man
dropped the meat in the fire and whipped
around, falling back on the ground and
slapping the covered black holster on his
right hip. The man was young, well under

thirty, and clad in blue cavalry garb, captain's bars on his shoulders. He wasn't wearing a hat, and his straight brown hair was dusty and damp. Dried blood lay over a nasty gash on his right temple. His eyes widened fearfully as he fought the Army-issue Colt from his holster.

"At ease, soldier," Navarro said, lowering the Winchester.

The captain jerked his head up at the man looming over him. He froze with his hand on the grips of the Colt half out of its holster.

"I'm friendly," Navarro said, turning, leaping onto a lower rock right of the boulder, then down into the camp.

The soldier sat by the fire, his rheumy blue eyes acquiring a wary cast. He looked addle-pated. "Who're you?" he asked thickly, keeping his hand on the Colt's grips but leaving the gun in the holster.

"Tom Navarro, segundo of the Bar-V ranch."

The soldier looked at him, as if he were hearing the words from far away. He snugged his Colt back down in the holster.

"What's your handle?"

Again, the young soldier squinted up at him, fisheyed, as if sifting through a brain fog for words. "Me . . . I'm, uh . . . Jonah Ward."

Navarro glanced at the gold bars. "*Captain* Jonah Ward."

The young man nodded dully.

Navarro hunkered down on his haunches and laid the rifle across his thighs. "What happened to you, Captain? Why are you alone out here?"

Ward glanced away and ran his palm slowly down his tunic, stained with dry brick red blood that had run down from his temple. "I lost my command. The whole patrol wiped out. Twelve men. Apaches."

"When?"

"Two days ago."

Navarro fingered the Winchester. "You the only survivor?"

"Sergeant Tanner and a scout were with me for a while, but they both died from their wounds . . . yesterday, I think." Ward's breath caught as, pondering, he suddenly remembered. "The sergeant died yesterday morning. Tingsla died a few hours later. They were hit bad." Ward's eyes filled with tears and he dropped his gaze.

"Where did this happen?"

Ward blinked his eyes clear, and he shook his head. "Can't recollect. A lot of confusion. I remember we entered a canyon.

102

Turned out to be a *box* canyon. The Apaches were laying for us. I was hit with a tomahawk, and the sergeant threw me over my horse and led me out."

"Sounds like you might have run into Nan-dash's reservation jumpers. We ran into a few last night ourselves."

Ward nodded. "Nan-ta-do-ka-dash. We'd been on his trail for three days, out of Fort Apache." He seemed to think about that, then balled his sun-blistered cheeks and squinted up at the Bar-V segundo. "What are you doing out here, Navarro?"

"Trailin' a girl. My boss's daughter."

"Good Lord."

"Ran away from home to be with her vaquero beau."

"Heaven help her." Ward looked at the rabbit he'd dropped in the fire. The flames had turned it black.

"Hungry?" Navarro asked.

"I snared that rabbit, didn't want to risk a pistol shot. I haven't eaten since the morning before the attack. No canteen, but last night's rain filled the rock tanks." Ward snapped his teeth and looked chagrined. "I reckon I've been a little disoriented, Mr. Navarro."

"No horse?"

Captain Ward shook his head. "The sergeant's horse ran off last night, during the storm. I need to get back to Fort Apache. Can you help me?"

"Fort Apache's north. We're heading south. We can drop you off at Fort Dragoon."

"That'll do."

Navarro took the young man's arm. "Come along, Captain. My two partners and our horses are down below. If you think you can ride, I'd like to get a couple more miles in before nightfall."

Ward nodded as he climbed to his feet and straightened his dusty tunic. "I can ride."

Ward was a little wobbly on his feet — Navarro figured that the tomahawk had rattled his brains around plenty — and they took their time descending the slope, Tom leading the way but turning often to help the younger man over the larger rocks and through brush clumps.

When they gained the creek bottom, Navarro introduced the captain to Tixier and Musselwhite, who were smoking black cheroots while their horses drew water from a spring they'd found several yards east. Navarro gave the captain several twists of fresh jerky from his saddlebags, mounted his buckskin, pulled Ward up behind him, and gigged the horse out of the draw and onto the trail they'd been following before they'd spied the smoke.

Navarro heard the captain eating hungrily behind him as they rode. When the captain had finished the jerky, his head fell forward against Navarro's shoulder, and soft snores rose up from the young soldier's chest.

"They get younger every year," Tixier said just behind Navarro's grulla.

Tom shook his head and reined the horse around a sharp trail bend, flushing a skinny coyote from a clump of mesquite and Mormon tea on his right. The dun-and-cream coyote ran up a knoll, tail down, glancing sheepishly back over its left shoulder before disappearing down the other side.

The riders had just brought the canyon of the San Pedro into view ahead when the sun sank behind them, flooding the canyons and valleys with deep, cool shadows. Night was the best time for traveling in Apache country, because the Indians wouldn't fight after dark, but Navarro didn't want to continue and risk overlooking sign of Karla.

She was heading south, but they were leaving country foreign to her, and she might've gotten turned around anywhere. Navarro didn't want to think about the possibility that Apaches might have nabbed her even before she'd reached the San Pedro.

He, Tixier, and Musselwhite might be chasing a wild goose, but until they found Karla, either dead or alive, they had to continue scouring all the ground they could.

They made camp in a deep hollow at the base of a pinion-covered ridge, staking the horses and the pack mule out on long ropes so they could graze and draw water from a run-out spring. Navarro and Musselwhite gathered wood while Tixier, the best cook of the three, hauled out the utensils, sliced beef and potatoes into a skillet, and boiled coffee. They ate silently, the sky a bejeweled, black velvet blanket arcing over them, coyotes yapping from ridges, nighthawks swooping.

Captain Ward said little, just stared into the fire with the troubled expression of someone who'd endured more than he'd been ready for. In deference to the young man's condition, the others didn't say much, either.

When Navarro had finished his supper and scrubbed his plate with sand, he fished a tequila bottle and cloth bandages from his saddlebags, and hunkered down beside Ward.

"Tip your head toward the fire, Captain."

Ward turned to him, frowning curiously.

"That's a deep cut those 'Paches opened

on your noggin. Looks like you got a couple pounds of sand in it. It needs cleaning."

"I'll be all right."

"You'll probably live, but I see no reason to go around with your head full of sand when you don't need to."

"Could pus up on you, Captain," Musselwhite said as he poured himself another cup of coffee. "If it turns green, one o' those Army surgeons might decide to amputate."

Musselwhite chuckled at his own joke. Tixier shook his head. Ward said nothing, just tipped his head toward the fire with an expression of strained tolerance.

"You'll have to forgive Charlie's sense of humor," Navarro said, splashing tequila on a bandage. "The rest of us do."

"Don't listen to him, Cap," Musselwhite said. "I keep everyone in stitches around the Bar-V, I do." Leaning toward Navarro, he picked up the tequila bottle and splashed a dollop into his coffee, then reached around the fire to splash a finger into that of Tixier, who was enjoying a dessert of sour dough biscuit and prickly pear jam. Pilar, who was sweet on the old mestizo, or half-breed, had given him a jar of jam for his birthday.

Navarro splashed more tequila on the bandage and scrubbed the captain's temple with vigor. Ward frowned into the fire, his head moving with Tom's tending.

"Apaches," Ward said, as though talking to himself. "They don't fight like soldiers . . . like men."

Navarro tossed the cloth into the fire, picked up another from his lap, draped it over the lip of the bottle, and shook more tequila onto it. "How's that, Captain?"

Ward's nose wrinkled angrily. "They fight like children . . . like cowardly schoolyard bullies."

"You got that right, Captain," Tixier said. "That's why the Army needs to change the way it fights them."

"I attended West Point," Ward said, lifting a defiant glance at Tixier. "I trained under the best fighting men in the world."

"No, you didn't," Navarro said, again rubbing around the edges of the captain's wound. "The best fighting men in the world, second only to the Cheyenne, are the very Apaches that butchered your patrol. Your West Point commanders are fine when it comes to fighting other white men, but when it comes to fighting Apaches, the best teachers are the Apaches themselves."

Ward turned his skeptical eyes to Navarro. "What would you propose?"

Navarro tossed the second bandage into

the fire, took a long pull from the tequila bottle, and reclined against his saddle, crooking an arm behind his head. "I'd propose what I *did* propose and got laughed at for. That the Calvary of the Southwest abandon the blue woolen uniforms with the shiny brass buttons for buckskins, that they ride unshod horses in very loose formations, *and* at the first sign of conflict, dismount and take to the hills and the rocks, the way the Apaches do."

"Hear, hear, Tommy." Musselwhite saluted with his cup and drank. "If we hadn't fought so damn *civilized*, I'd have a lot fewer friends on the other side of the sod."

"You men served?" Ward asked, glancing around.

"*Sí*," Tixier nodded. He was sharpening his bowie knife on a whetstone — slow, even strokes — occasionally testing the edge on the black hair curling on his corded brown forearm. *"Contracto exploradors."*

Across the hollow rose the thuds of a rock rolling down a hill, the sounds sharp in the quiet air.

"Away from the fire!" Navarro rasped, reaching for his rifle and rolling into the shadows.

CHAPTER 9

His rifle cocked, the barrel resting on the rock before him, Navarro stared at the scrub pinions and low boulders on the other side of the fire. Beyond lay the arroyo from where the sound of the falling stone had come.

Low voices sounded — men talking to one another in hushed tones. There was the thud of a shod hoof.

Navarro glanced around the camp. Captain Ward lay to his right, behind a low, flat-topped rock, his cocked pistol in his right hand and resting in the weeds beside the rock. Ahead and left was Tixier, leaning back against a low shelf extending out from the base of the slope behind them. Charlie Musselwhite lay several yards before the fire, stretched prone, extending his own rifle into the shrubs brushed with amber fire-light, and into the arroyo beyond.

"Helloooo the camp," a voice called from

somewhere out in the darkness.

"Name yourselves!" Navarro returned.

A short, tense silence. The fire before Navarro snapped, and the coffeepot chugged. Ward thumbed back his Colt's hammer, making a soft *tch-tch-click*.

"Well, our mama's done already named us," the stranger said, his voice slow and buoyed with humor. He sounded young, maybe a teenager. "But if you mean, *tell* you our names, it's Trav Cheatam and Tall "Sawed-off" Gomez. We're friendly if you are."

Musselwhite gained his feet and ran forward into the shrubs, peering into the arroyo with his rifle snugged to his shoulder. "What's your business?" he called.

"Business? We ain't got no business. We was just wonderin' if we could share your fire. We been ridin' all day, and our horses are spent."

Navarro stood and moved warily across the camp, sidling up to a scraggly pinion growing out of a sandy hump and peering into the arroyo. He didn't have to speak very loud for his voice to carry in the hushed night. "Come on in."

He waited, rifle extended from his hip. He saw Musselwhite's silhouette in the trees to his left. Tixier had moved up to the arroyo,

111

on the other side of Charlie. They all had a good shot of anyone coming in shooting, and out here, you never knew who you were going to run into.

The *clip-clop* of slow-moving horses rose to the left, coming from east along the arroyo. Two figures appeared, moving side by side — an average-sized gent in a tall hat and a short, squat man wearing a sombrero, with silver flashing along his saddle. They stopped within a few feet of Tixier and the taller man wearing the high hat said, "There any grass?"

"Down there," Tixier said.

He, Musselwhite, and Navarro watched the men move westward along the arroyo, dismount, and stake their horses out with the Bar-V mounts and the pack mule. It took them fifteen minutes to unsaddle their horses and rub them down before they appeared out of the western shadows, approaching the camp with their saddles on their shoulders. Navarro and the others had waited, rifles at half-mast but hammers at half-cock.

"Sorry to trouble you, gents," the taller man said as he and the shorter man wearing the sombrero approached Navarro.

"No trouble," Navarro said mildly. He stepped to one side, so the two strangers could pass before him. "There's coffee on the fire, and extra grub. What's ours is yours."

"Thank you, mighty kindly," the taller one said as he and his friend stepped through the brush and headed for the fire tucked back in the hollow. He wasn't that tall — well under six feet, but he was a good three or four inches taller than his partner wearing the sombrero, who still hadn't said anything. Both wore six-shooters on their thighs, and walnut rifle stocks protruded from the scabbards they carried with their saddles.

"Cozy camp ye have here," the taller one said conversationally as he tossed down his saddle and blanket roll. "We couldn't even see your fire but from one little point on the ridge over this cut."

"That was the idea," Navarro said, moving back around the fire but keeping his eyes on the two newcomers. Both had stooped to arrange their gear, but they kept an eye skinned on Navarro and the others, who were drifting back to the fire.

By the guttering firelight, the Bar-V segundo studied each newcomer in turn. The taller man was just a kid, eighteen or nineteen, dressed in sloppy trail garb except for the expensive-looking top hat. He had a long face with dumb eyes and buck teeth making his clean upper lip bulge. His body was soft and fleshy, and he had the rounded hips and thick thighs of a heavy girl.

The shorter man was slightly older, a moon-faced Mex who grinned continuously and shyly while keeping his eyes lowered, occasionally glancing up from beneath a single black eyebrow.

He wasn't much over five feet five, his large head sitting without benefit of neck on abnormally wide shoulders. His short arms were as thick as most thighs, his thighs as thick as most rain barrels. He didn't look cunning enough to be a gunman, but he wore two silver-plated Smith & Wessons down low, in buscadero holsters. Both pearl-gripped revolvers shone through the sparely built holsters, glistening with oil.

"Yessiree, ye can't be too careful out here," the kid said, rummaging around in his saddlebags. "Say, you boys ain't run into any Apache trouble, have you?" Producing two tin cups from the saddlebags, he turned to Navarro sitting on a rock across the fire.

"A little." Tom leaned forward, picked up a scrap of thick cowhide, and used it to lift the speckled-black coffeepot from the flat rock in the fire. He extended the pot to the kid. "Joe?"

"Don't mind if I do," the kid said, extending a cup in either hand. When Navarro had filled both cups, the kid gave one to his Mexican friend sitting on his knees to the kid's right. The Mexican knelt on his stubby thighs, eyes lowered, as though offering confession.

"Careful," Navarro said. "It's been on the fire awhile. If your friend there was to drop one of those fancy six-guns in it, why, I'd say it'd probably float." He cut a quick glance at Tixier sitting on a deadfall to Navarro's right. Returning his strained amiable smile to the kid and his silent companion, Navarro raised his own cup in a salute, and drank.

"Strong — that's how we like it," the kid said, lifting the cup to his lips. He blew ripples on the coffee and sipped. Making a face, he swallowed and shook his head, showing his buck teeth. "And whooo-eee, it sure is strong! Thanks for the warning. Appreciate it."

Navarro glanced at Ward. The captain assumed his previous position to Navarro's right, leaning back against his saddle, holding his cup in both hands as he watched the fire. He appeared to have gone back to his previous thoughts, as well, staring into the flames but no doubt seeing the Apaches who had ambushed him and his detail. He seemed no longer aware there were strangers in their midst.

The kid had followed Tom's gaze to the soldier. "Hidy there, Cap. You is a cap, ain't ye? I ain't never served, but my old man, he was in the Army till I was ten, so I savvy the stripes and bars and such."

Ward had turned to the kid slowly and only nodded, then lifted his cup to his lips and sipped. While Ward leaned toward the pot to refill his cup, Charlie Musselwhite said, "Your old man was in the service till you were ten? He musta got out — what? — five years ago?"

"Ah, I'm older'n that," the kid said shyly. He blew on his coffee, sipped, and made another face. "Coffee like that, who needs firewater?"

Navarro decided to go ahead and fire off his question. It wasn't polite, but there was something fishy about these two, and he didn't care if he offended them. "Where you two headed — Cheatam and Gomez?"

Tixier flashed him a look over the blade he was again sharpening on the whetstone.

The kid regarded Navarro levelly, his eyes cool. He didn't say anything for nearly a minute. Then he set his cup down and removed his opera hat from his sandy blond head. He played with the hat's narrow brim. "We're headed down *Mejico* way." He let a little grin pull at the corners of his mouth.

"What's down *Mejico* way?"

"Our employers." The kid glanced at his buddy, the froggy, servile Gomez, then glanced around at the others. "We hunt Apache scalps and sell 'em down there, and then we go visit Tall's sisters and cousins in Escorpion. It's a town, in case you didn't know — in a canyon a hundred miles into *Mejico.* They say there's all kinds of spiders in there, and that's where it got the name, but me, I been down there three, four times now, but I ain't never seen a single one. But I seen plenty of Tall's sisters and cousins. *Muy bonita!*" He chuckled and twirled his hat in the air, caught it one-handed.

Tixier said, "A lucrative business, hunting Apache scalps?"

"When they're in season!" the kid piped, glancing again at his buddy, pleased with himself. Gomez knelt there, his coffee in his dark hands held low against his round belly, smiling at the ground before his knees. His teeth made a craggy white line below his black mustache, which drooped down around both sides of his mouth.

"Sounds dangerous," Navarro said.

"No more than sport huntin' wildcats,"

Cheatam said. "Of course, we don't work alone. We're ridin' to meet our bunch at Contention. Me and Gomez here — I call him Tall on account of his name is Tulare-cito and he's so short — we got waylaid by the senoritas over in Wakely. They just wouldn't let us leave — would they, Tall?" He didn't wait for Gomez to respond. "We're ridin' hard to catch up. We'd still be ridin', but our horses were ready to plum give out."

The kid stuck his hand inside his hat, held it shoulder high, and gave it a twirl. Watching the spinning hat, he said, "Where you boys headed?"

"After a girl," Navarro said. "You haven't seen one out here — a white girl — have you?"

"We ain't seen no girls since Wakely," the kid said. "What's a gringa filly doin' out here? Don't she know Nan-dash's off his reserve and madder than an old wet hen?"

"No, I reckon she doesn't," Navarro said, dropping his grim gaze to the rocks around the fire.

"Well, too bad for her, but good for Tall and me and the rest of our bunch. We thought we weren't gonna get any huntin' in before headin' back down to Mexico, but now that Nan-dash is runnin' off his leash

118

again, we might get a little scalpin' in, after all." He flipped his hat in the air and caught it with both hands, then ran his finger against the high black crown.

"Kid," Navarro said, leaning out over the rifle laid across his knees, "you either set that hat on your head or set it aside. I'm not going to tell you twice."

The hat froze in the kid's hands. He looked at Navarro, dumbstruck. The others looked at Tom, as well, the captain's wide eyes sliding around in their sockets. His right index finger stopped tracing his cup's rim.

Navarro's stare didn't waiver from the kid. Gomez looked up demurely, the fire's two main flames flickering in his dark eyes.

"Mister," the kid said haughtily, "I don't know what's got into you, but —"

He flipped the crown of the hat toward Navarro and jammed his right hand inside. Navarro bolted to his feet and raised his rifle to his shoulder, the rifle booming twice, the explosions like cannon shots within the hollow. Both shots took the kid in the face, one above his left brow, the other an inch below his left eye. He jerked once with each shot. Jaw slackening, eyes snapping disbelief, he twisted slightly right and fell slowly back to the ground.

A small-caliber gun snapped inside the kid's hat, blowing a hole through the crown and plunking a wild slug into the fire, throwing up sparks.

The pocket pistol had no sooner popped than Gomez had bolted off his stubby thighs, his small hands a blur as they clawed up his pearl-gripped Smithies. He'd nearly raised both guns before Tixier and Musselwhite, leaping off their heels and grabbing iron, extended their pistols at him and fired, Tixier shooting three quick rounds into the right side of his head, Musselwhite triggering one shot into his chin, another through his heart.

Gomez was punched up and back, screaming and firing both pistols into the air. He hit the mountain wall, bounced off, and fell in a heap at the base, both blood-splattered pistols still clutched in his small hands. He lay on his back, staring up at the sky, working his eyes and mouth and rubbing the hammer of the right Smithy with his thumb, feebly trying to cock it.

Smoke curling from the barrel of his long-barreled Colt, Tixier walked over to Gomez, planted his right boot on the gun he was trying to cock, extended the Colt, and drilled another round through the Mexican's head, killing him.

Captain Ward had bolted to his feet and stumbled back, his pistol hanging low in his right hand. Mouth agape, he turned to Navarro. "How'd you know that kid had a gun in his hat?"

Tixier and Musselwhite turned to Tom, their eyes puzzled.

"Saw reward dodgers on both of them in Tucson the other day. They and one other son of a bitch are wanted for murder and horse theft up around Prescott." Tom shook his head. "He was just too damn in love with that hat."

"Horse theft, eh?" Musselwhite said.

As if on cue, one of the horses whinnied.

"Let's go meet the third son of a bitch." Rifle raised, Navarro bolted through the brush.

CHAPTER 10

Several yards out from the hollow, Navarro quartered left along the ridge base and stopped, allowing his eyes to adjust to the darkness. Farther left along the arroyo, the horses were tethered in a patch of high grass surrounded by mesquite trees. Their shadows moved among the denser shadows of the brush and the arroyo's western bank.

A shadow wearing a hat moved among the horses and the lone braying pack mule.

Navarro had taken two steps forward when red-yellow light blossomed from between two mesquite shrubs. The gun's report reached Navarro's ears at the same time the slug slammed into the rock wall over his right shoulder. He threw himself forward, hitting the ground as another shot rang out.

The horses whinnied and clomped around, snapping brush. Hooves pounded as a couple galloped off.

Gaining his feet, Navarro moved west along the arroyo, remaining near the base of the rock wall and keeping the grass and shrubs between him and the shooter. In his vision's periphery, several more shadows moved — his own men spreading out across the arroyo.

"He's near the horses," Navarro called. "Hold your fire."

Tom dropped behind the boulder as, keying on his voice, the shooter squeezed off another shot. The slug spanged off the rock wall where Tom had just stood. Navarro extended his Winchester over the boulder, made sure the horses were clear, then fired into the powder smoke webbing around a mesquite tree.

As his slug ricocheted off the ground, Navarro bolted out from the boulder and ran to the trees. Shots exploded to his left. Dropping to a knee, he turned to see the fire blossoms of two pistols — three quick shots, then two more as if in afterthought.

To his right, a horse screamed and hooves thudded in the arroyo's soft sand. Navarro whipped around as a shadow flitted across the arroyo, faintly limned by blue starlight and heading into a southern cleft.

"Sumbitch's lightin' a shuck, Tommy!" Tixier called, his boots thudding as he ran.

Navarro ran after the shadow, his cocked rifle held high in both hands. When he'd run forty yards, he saw the cleft the rider had taken — a narrow, rocky feeder cut meandering south. He walked into the cut, hugging the cactus and shrubs growing along the western edge, then paused, holding his breath.

Hooves thudded into the southern distance.

"Where is he, Tom?" Musselwhite said behind him.

Navarro shook his head and stole along the cut, hearing the footsteps of Charlie, Dallas, and Captain Ward approaching from behind, Tixier's breath rasping loudly. Someone kicked a rock, stumbled, and cursed.

"Looks like the bastard got away," Musselwhite said when they'd all walked about thirty yards and were rounding a western dogleg in the narrow defile. "Don't think he got any of our horses, though."

Navarro stopped, dropped to one knee, and touched a black smear in the rocks. He rubbed the fresh blood between his fingers.

He stood and walked another twenty more yards, again stopped. A man lay sprawled across a spindly shrub in the lee of a large boulder. One arm had caught on the boulder, the other on the shrub, and his head sagged between, so that it looked like he was half lying, half kneeling. Navarro walked slowly up to the body and saw that half his head had been blown away. The blood glistened faintly in the long black hair curving down the back of his buffalo-hide tunic decorated with large red flowers.

Navarro turned and brushed angrily past the other three men who'd walked up behind him and were staring at the dead man. Tom cussed loudly, the oath echoing, and headed back down the cut.

"What's he so mad about?" Captain Ward asked Tixier. "At least they didn't get the horses."

Musselwhite answered, "No, but we'll have to move camp now. Every Apache within twenty miles probably heard those shots."

When they'd chased down the two loose horses, Navarro and the others broke camp, saddled up, and rode off down the arroyo.

Two hours later, they made a second, hasty camp along a shallow sandy wash in the open desert, surrounded by creosote and catclaw. They picketed the horses and mule close and kept their coffee fire small and smokeless.

Hunkered down beside the low flames and clutching his coffee cup in his right hand, Navarro glanced at Tixier and Musselwhite, then stared into the star-shrouded desert. The young captain was already curled up in his blankets, snoring.

"At first light, you boys turn back," Navarro said tonelessly.

Charlie and Dallas glanced at each other, the firelight shunting shadows across their sun-seared faces. "What're you talking about?" Musselwhite asked.

"The farther south we get, the deeper into Apache and Yaqui country we get, and the more border bandits we're gonna run into." Navarro sipped the coffee. "No point in you boys risking your hides for that fool gringa. I'll track her alone."

Dallas lay back against his saddle, drew one half of his blanket over his body, and tipped his hat over his eyes. "You'll track her alone. That's a good one, amigo."

From across the fire, Charlie looked at Navarro. "You moonblind, Tommy?"

At first light, the four men saddled up and rode east, meeting up with the deep canyon of the San Pedro as the bottommost point of the sun bled up from the eastern mountains. At ten o'clock they intersected the old Butterfield express route leading south to the mining camps in the Dragoon Mountains. Not long after that, they came upon a ruined stage filled with charred bodies, an arrow-pierced body lying nearby, the man's eyes eaten out by buzzards.

"Tom!"

Hunkered over the dead man, Navarro looked up. Dallas stood at the bottom of a sandy knoll, staring at a black rock at the knoll's crest.

The mestizo spoke without turning around. "Come over here!"

Navarro, Musselwhite, and Captain Ward tramped over to Tixier. Tom glanced up at the black rock the mestizo seemed so taken with. He glanced again. The object was no rock but a human head, skinned and sun-raisined, the eyes eaten out, a single bullet round in the forehead.

"Those people are savages," Ward muttered.

Tixier looked at Navarro. "He look familiar, Tommy?"

Navarro stared at the head. He'd met Karla's Don Juan one time, when he'd run into them riding out on the prairie, then seen him again from a distance. The square jaw and the hair under the peeled skin were Juan's.

"Christ," Navarro said, rubbing his jaw

and looking around at the unshod tracks in the sand.

"What's that out there?"

Navarro turned to Ward, followed the captain's pointing finger across the chaparral, to a horse grazing about a hundred yards off, at the bottom of a low sandy ridge.

Navarro wheeled, walked over to his buckskin tied to a greasewood clump, and mounted up. He spurred the horse into a lunging gallop across the chaparral. When he was thirty yards from Karla's horse, it bolted. Navarro kept the buckskin on its trail, overtook it, grabbed the reins, then turned the buckskin back to the others waiting at the bottom of the sandy knoll capped with Juan's bloody head. The nervous Arabian ringed its eyes with white and fought Navarro's grip on the reins but seemed pleased by the presence of other horses.

"Well, she made it this far," Charlie said.

Navarro dismounted, tied the Arabian to a mesquite tree, and climbed back aboard the buckskin, reining the horse to the backside of the sandy knoll. "Let's have us a close look around, gents."

The others mounted their horses and joined Navarro's search for Karla's body, riding slowly across the flat, peering under every rock and cactus within a two-hundred-yard circle of the stage. Navarro felt sick to his stomach. The stage had obviously been run down by Apaches.

And Karla and Juan had been involved.

Like Juan, she was probably dead. He half hoped she *was* dead. The Apaches were not known for coddling their prisoners.

When Navarro had ridden around to the south side of a large clay-colored boulder a hundred yards north of the stage, he reined in the buckskin suddenly. A bloody corpse shone in the sun — what was left of one, anyway. Navarro raked his graze across the grisly leavings.

It wasn't Karla. The coyotes had left only a torso, but it was a man's torso.

As much as Tom didn't want the Apaches to have Karla, he was relieved it wasn't her.

"Well, it looks like they have her," Navarro said when, after an hour of searching, they all returned to the trail just south of the burned-out stage. "Or at least they did when they left here."

"We'll be trackin' 'em, then," Musselwhite said, removing his canteen from his saddle horn. His buoyant tone belied what they all knew — if she wasn't dead, she probably wished she were. And tracking her down would probably get them all killed.

Navarro looked at Ward sitting the Arabian. "Captain, you have a horse now. Fort Bowie's that way. See that crease between those two ranges cropping up yonder? You'll want —"

"I'll stay with you men."

"Where we're goin' ain't exactly conducive to good health." Navarro canted his head, indicating Dallas and Charlie. "I'd be shed of these two reprobates, if they didn't tend to stick like ticks on a coonhound."

"You men saved my life," Ward said. "I'd like to do whatever I can to help. Besides" — the soldier lifted one shoulder — "it's a scouting mission."

Navarro glanced at Tixier and Musselwhite. Both men shrugged. Tixier shucked his bowie from the scabbard on his cartridge belt, flipped it around, and extended it handle-first to Ward.

Musselwhite said, "Cap, those buttons on your coat sure are shiny."

Ward looked at the knife before him, then lifted his puzzled gaze to Navarro. Wiping sweat from the inside band of his black Stetson, Navarro said, "No brass buttons on this scout, Captain. A Yaqui could spot the reflections from the Sea of Cortez."

Ward's blistered forehead crinkled. "This is a uniform of the U.S. Army. I can't just

130

—" He stopped, regarded the granitelike faces surrounding him. With a sigh, he took the knife, cut the buttons and bars off his tunic, and returned the knife to Tixier.

"Let's find your girl," he said.

The Apaches weren't hard to track, for they'd done nothing to cover their trail. Navarro counted eight sets of unshod prints moving in no great hurry. They were a confident bunch, which meant they were extremely dangerous.

They were no doubt Nan-dash's crew from the San Carlos Reservation, holing up deep in the Dragoons and planning more raids on the White Eyes. Segments of the group were no doubt wreaking havoc somewhere in the region even as Navarro and his cohorts chased the bunch who'd attacked the stage.

Navarro kept expecting to find Karla's body, used up and butchered, along the trail. Funny, his feelings toward her. He'd never had a daughter, but a daughter was what she'd become to him. She was too young to be anything else. If Vannorsdell hadn't ordered him to go after her, he'd have gone, anyway, the old man be damned. He'd not return to the Bar-V until he'd retrieved her, dead or alive.

If she were dead, the richest part of his recent life would be gone. Thinking about it returned him to the loneliness he'd known before she'd arrived, a shy, mousy little waif in a straw boater and braids.

Navarro and the others were crossing a narrow valley between two rocky, nameless ridges when they came upon a dead horse and a rider in grubby trail garb. At least, what was left of him had been clad in trail garb. The man's horse had been partially butchered and cooked over a chaparral fire.

Navarro probed the ashes with his right hand.

"How old, Tommy?"

"Two, three hours."

Musselwhite looked southeast along the Apache's trail twisting through the brush and dipping into a swale where five cotton-woods flashed in the late-afternoon sun. "We're gettin' close."

Tixier was chewing jerky in his saddle and casting his brown eyes at his horse sniffing the breeze. "My mare — she smells 'em."

Navarro snorted, mounting his buckskin, then reaching across and snagging a stick of jerky from Dallas' open shirt pocket. "It's you she smells, you dirty half-breed!"

"No," Tixier said, waiting, studying his horse as the others pulled out. "It's 'Paches, all right."

They found the body of the dead man's partner among the cottonwoods, stripped and hacked apart, two young coyotes circling the carcass. Leaving the coyotes to their carrion, they continued across the valley, crossed the ridge beyond, and found the headquarters of a small ranch operation still burning, the sooty smoke a dark column against the sky's fading light.

Three dead men and three dead horses were strewn about the yard, and farther along they came upon six dead cows and a dead vaquero, the young cowboy's entrails strewn for nearly a hundred yards across the rocks and sage.

"Savages," Captain Ward said as they rode past the carnage.

"You ain't seen nothin'," Musselwhite replied.

On the other side of the valley, they followed a dry creekbed up among high, craggy peaks spotted with mesquite and pinion. The sunlight was weakening, and the pines and cliffs shaded the trail.

When they'd been riding along the wash for an hour, Navarro halted his horse and lifted his head to listen. Faintly, the sound of Indian chanting and a slowly beating drum came to his ears.

He couldn't see much, as the wash was on his left and a high wall of granite on his right. He dismounted and retrieved his field glasses from his saddlebags. He tossed his reins to Musselwhite, walked up the saddle they'd been climbing, and disappeared around a bend.

Behind him, Tixier dismounted and sniffed the air. "Smell that?" he said to Musselwhite and Ward. "Roasting mule."

A quarter hour later, Navarro came back. The others had dismounted and loosened their saddle cinches, giving their horses a rest.

Navarro said, "Far as I can tell, they've bivouacked atop Gray Rock. They probably posted guards, so we'll leave the horses here and walk the rest of the way."

"Ah, Apacheria," Musselwhite said ironically as he mashed out his cigarette with his boot toe. "I have so many fond memories."

Chapter 11

Navarro grabbed his reins, led his buckskin a hundred feet back along the trail, then followed a game path into the wash. When he and the others had tethered the horses and the mule to roots and shrubs, they grabbed their canteens and shucked their rifles from their saddle boots. Musselwhite sat down to lace his mocassins.

"Think ole Nan-dash is gonna remember us, Tommy?" Tixier asked, his grin showing the gold tooth in his dark, angular face. His short, scruffy beard was dust-glazed, his weathered sombrero pulled low on his forehead.

"Well, I would hope so," Navarro said with a wry smile, "after all we meant to each other."

He climbed out of the wash and tramped along the trail. Behind him, Ward turned to Tixier. "What'd he mean by that?"

"A few years ago, we spent a whole winter

prospecting right under his nose," Tixier said. "He got onto us eventually, though, and we had one hell of a time gettin' out of there. A year later, we ran him down for the Army, and the bluecoats corralled him on the reservation."

They climbed several ridges and crawled through a ravine. The sun fell and the night gathered rapidly, offering a refreshing chill. There was no moon yet, but several stars kindled in the east. Coyotes yammered on the higher peaks, and a blue jay shrieked down the ridge to their right.

Occasionally as they walked, coming out of trees or topping a rise, they saw their destination — the boulder-strewn granite scarp the whites called Gray Rock, standing several hundred feet above the low apron slopes around it. The natives, who saw the peak as sacred, had been holding religious ceremonies on its crest for centuries.

As the men tramped toward the mountain's base, the drums, rattles, and chants drifting down from the peak pricked the hair on the back of their necks.

They waited until good dark, when the guards posted on the jagged rock formations along the mountain's crest couldn't so easily see them, then climbed the trail twisting along its base. The trail was sheathed in boulders, cedars and pines, but in places the trail was exposed to men looking down from the mountain's rim.

The last quarter mile was a hard climb over boulders, then up over the lava mushrooms and steep granite walls. Twice they had to avoid the roving, rifle-wielding pickets smoking their pungent Mexican tobacco.

The drums and chants were louder now, as though coming from only a few yards away. The musk of roasting mule and the tang of pine smoke hung heavy in the chill air. A crimson glow flickered across the distant pines stippling the mountain's saucer-shaped, rock-ringed crest.

Ten feet ahead of Tixier, Navarro stole along a lava bed, then stopped suddenly. A rasp sounded to his right. Throwing up a hand for the others to freeze, he turned toward the sound.

An Indian sat not twelve feet away, perched on a flat boulder, a rifle draped across his thighs. The brave faced the canyon, away from Navarro, long hair wafting in the breeze. He was smoking a cigarette. The breeze blew the smoke away from Tom, but he caught a faint whiff of the pungent tobacco now. He smelled the man, too — the rancid sweat and bear grease and the musky odor of horse and mule.

Navarro stared at the man's back, pondering. He glanced back at Tixier, a silhouette standing motionless ten feet behind him, on a low rise of rock. Musselwhite and Ward stood several feet behind him, rifles raised. Dallas shrugged.

Navarro laid his rifle flat on the ground, pulled his dagger from his belt sheath, and crept slowly up the rocks. When he was three feet from the guard, the man coughed suddenly, blowing smoke, bending forward over his rifle, and turning his head to his right.

Spying the man behind him, the guard's head jerked toward Navarro and up. Tom leapt forward and buried the dagger deep in the man's lower back, severing the spine. Navarro wrapped his left arm around the man's mouth, pulling him off the boulder and holding him until his death spasms ceased.

Tom wiped his knife blade on the man's leggings and looked around. Fifty yards beyond, the fire's glow flicked across the rocky escarpments and pines, licking at the black sky.

Navarro sheathed the knife, picked up his rifle, and waved the others on. He stole along the lava flow, across a dip, then climbed a boulder-strewn ridge and crawled out over a lip of pocked boulders and wind-gnarled cedars, the fire flaming high in a low, saucer-shaped hollow a hundred feet below.

The large, pyramidal blaze was ringed by twenty-five or thirty Apaches, all facing away from Navarro. Chanting to the drums and rattles that rose like God's angry heartbeat, they marched in place, arms raised above their heads, some wielding spears.

Before the group, a middle-aged man knelt before a smaller fire, sprinkling a dust-like substance over the flames. This was Nan-dash, a little grayer and more lined than Navarro remembered, but still square-shouldered and lean-waisted, hawk-nosed, pinched-lipped, his tiny zealot's eyes set close.

He wore a beaded deerskin vest and an umber headband. A medicine pouch hung from a leather thong around his neck. His silver-streaked hair hung loose, his forehead and cheekbones slashed with war paint.

On either side of him, feathered lances poked up from the earth, their tips shrouded in flames.

Navarro dropped his gaze to the main fire. His insides shrunk, tightening. On either side of the fire, two women had been staked out, spread-eagle, like hides for stretching. They were naked, sweat-soaked skin glistening in the fire's hot glow.

The one on the left side of the fire was Karla. Navarro didn't recognize the captive on the right — probably taken, like Karla, on the dash from the reservation. Both young women cried and struggled against the leather thongs holding their hands and ankles fast to the stakes.

Navarro lunged forward with his rifle. Tixier grabbed his arm and smiled. "There's twenty-six of them. Only four of us."

Navarro stayed where he was, every muscle drawn taut. To his right were Musselwhite and Ward, the firelight sliding shadows across their faces.

Navarro dropped his gaze to Karla struggling futilely against the leather ties, bending her knees as she tried to work her ankles free. His heart hammered. He resisted the urge to leap into the hollow, shooting.

At the head of the chanting, dancing warriors, old Nan-dash gained his feet. He turned to one of the braves before him on his right, and nodded. He turned to one on his left and nodded again. Both braves whooped with joy, dropped their loincloths, and pushed through the group to the girls.

The young lady whom Navarro didn't know gave a scream as one of the braves fell between her spread legs. As the other brave threw himself atop Karla, she turned her face away, gritting her teeth with anger and revulsion.

Navarro snapped his rifle to his shoulder, quickly sighted, and fired. The bullet drilled the brave atop Karla through both ears. As the brave slumped onto Karla's shoulder, Navarro gained his feet, levered another shell, and fired into the Apaches, who were now jerking their heads around, dumbfounded. One clutched his belly and stumbled backward, knees bending.

"Idioto!" Tixier yelled as Navarro leapt down the ridge, levering the Winchester.

Two more Apaches dropped before the others figured out what was happening. While three-quarters of the group turned and ran, several threw knives or tomahawks. Most sailed wide. Navarro deflected a tomahawk with his Winchester, then shot the brave who'd thrown it as the man turned to run with the others for the wickiups and probably to fetch a rifle or a bow and arrow.

Navarro fired another shot and ran toward Karla. Tixier, Musselwhite, and Ward were laying down good cover fire behind him, the gunfire echoing around the canyon, wounded Indians screaming as they dropped. Navarro kicked the dead brave off Karla's shoulder and knelt down.

"Tommy!" she cried.

Navarro set the rifle aside and shucked his bowie. A bullet sizzled between them, and he lifted his head to see that several Indians had fetched their rifles. One knelt twenty yards away, levering another shell into his smoking Henry. Navarro dropped his knife, grabbed his rifle, and was about to shoot the brave when a bullet from behind him took the man through the brisket.

Grabbing the bowie, Tom cut the thongs binding Karla's wrists to the stakes, then those binding her ankles. He snatched a horse blanket from beside the fire, and threw it over her.

"Can you stand?"

Clutching the blanket to her breasts, she nodded. He helped her up and shoved her toward Tixier, who was shooting and running toward them, flanked by Musselwhite and Ward. As Dallas, extending his Winchester in his left hand, grabbed Karla with his right, Musselwhite dashed around the fire to the other girl.

She stared up at him, unseeing, her chest

still, mouth drawn, face frozen in terror. She'd literally been scared to death.

A bullet burned a furrow atop Navarro's right shoulder. A brave dashed from the other side of the fire, leaping toward him with a long knife in his hand. Navarro kicked the brave in the groin and smashed his rifle butt against his lowered head, cracking his skull with an audible crunch.

Rifles snapped a staccato din as Navarro ran back toward the rocky scarp, at the base of which Ward and Musselwhite shot from kneeling positions, Ward triggering his revolver, Charlie levering his Yellowboy, spraying the entire hollow and causing sparks to fly up from the fire. The Indians whooped and returned fire, their slugs chipping shards from the rocks around Charlie and the captain.

Navarro was nearly to the scarp's base when he felt the beelike sting of a bullet slicing into his calf. It tripped him up momentarily, and he turned to squeeze off a shot. The Winchester clicked empty.

He swung a glance up the scarp. Tixier was helping Karla over the broken boulders. They were moving slowly, as the girl was barefoot and weak. His rifle apparently empty, Dallas paused frequently to trigger his pistol into the hollow. His right arm was bloody, and blood trickled from a bullet burn on the left side of his neck.

Throwing down his rifle and turning to Musselwhite and Ward, Navarro yelled, "Pull out!"

Charlie squeezed off another round and straightened. He was turning to follow Ward up the scarp when a bullet punched into his side. He fell back against a boulder with a grunt. Navarro fired at two braves running around the fire, dropping one and halting the other, then turned back to Charlie.

The carrot-topped tracker gained his feet, holding a gloved hand to his bloody side. "I'll make it!"

Navarro was on one knee, shooting into the Indians dashing at him, sometimes four at a time. He held them off for a few more seconds. When his pistol was empty, he turned and climbed the rocks behind him, noting the blood Charlie had left on the boulders.

Bullets spanged off the rocks around him. His calf burned. He felt the wetness atop his shoulder, the blood dribbling down his collarbone.

He zigzagged through the boulders and, pausing behind a jagged monolith to reload his Colt, turned his gaze down the slope. Old Nan-dash himself was leading a handful of whooping braves up the scarp, leaping from rock to rock, pausing only to loose arrows or trigger their Henrys and Civil War–model Springfields.

Thumbing the last slug through the Colt's loading gate by feel, Navarro cast another glance up the slope. Tixier and Karla were out of sight. Ward had just made the ridge and turned now, peering back down and yelling something at Musselwhite several yards behind him. Charlie had paused, quartering toward Navarro. In the flickering firelight, Tom saw his drawn features, the sharp rise and fall of his chest.

"Keep going!" Navarro shouted, then swung toward the charging Indians and cut loose with his Colt. They were moving too quickly, spread out across the rocks, and he only killed one, clipping another's thigh.

Old Nan-dash's deep voice rose with savage glee. "Nav-ar-oooo!"

Tom turned and lunged over the rocks, making the ridge a minute later, finding Charlie stumbling along the crest, heading back the way they'd come.

Navarro caught up to him, pulled the scout's pistol from his cross-draw holster, turned, and fired two shots back along the ridge, hitting little but rocks and air but holding the Apaches at bay. Shots rose farther back along the hollow, and several Apaches seemed to be turning back. Navarro grabbed Musselwhite's arm and led him after the others, whose shadows moved along the black eastern ridge, their shadows dancing ahead.

He found Tixier, Ward, and the girl crouched by a low, steep wall of boulders, breathing hard. Karla was on her knees.

"It's a steep drop over the lip," Dallas said, his right arm bloody, his revolver in his right hand. "Can't see much."

"Don't see as we have much choice!" Navarro said, swatting the scout's good arm.

When Tixier and Ward had both negotiated the rocks rimming the mountaintop and disappeared over the lip, Navarro helped Musselwhite. "Ah, Christ, Tommy," the scout grumbled. "Apacheria . . ."

"I'll buy you a steak in Tucson."

"I prefer one of Pilar's rump roasts . . . buried in onions. . . ."

"Picky bastard."

When Musselwhite had gone over the ridge, Navarro turned to the loud whoops rising behind him. Shadows bounced among the rocks and shrubs, moving toward him fast.

He grabbed Karla's shoulders, lifted her to her feet. "I'm gonna climb up, and you give me your hand."

Using his hands and wincing against the pain in his wounded calf, he climbed the sharp rocks. When he'd gained the ridge, he lay down and reached back over the other side, extending his hand to the girl.

"Reach for it!"

Clutching the blanket with her left hand, Karla rose up on her toes and extended her right. He glanced behind her. A shadow with whipping hair was ten yards away and closing. Navarro extended Musselwhite's revolver and triggered two shots as an arrow smacked the rock a foot beneath his chin. The Indian grunted and staggered back.

"Tommy!" Karla cried.

Navarro leaned farther out over the ridge and grabbed her hand. He'd lifted her two feet off the ground when something hard struck his forehead. The blunt end of a tomahawk, he knew, as the night dimmed and sounds grew faint.

The girl's wrist slipped from his sweat-slick hand.

Her brittle voice came from a great distance. *"Tommy, don't leave me!"*

Eyes fluttering and dimming, Navarro slid down the slope behind him. Gravity and unconsciousness enveloped him at the same time, and he went rolling down the ridge, into the darkness of the canyon yawning below.

CHAPTER 12

Karla watched Navarro's eyes flutter and his head slip back over the ridge. "Tommy!" she screamed.

The exclamation had barely died on her tongue before sharp breaths and running footfalls sounded behind her. She whipped around. An Indian loosed a savage whoop and slapped her once with the back of his hand, once with his open palm. The blows staggered her.

As she fell to her knees, the brave grabbed her wrist. He'd jerked her halfway to her feet and was turning back toward the hollow when a shot sounded behind him. The bullet whomped through his chest and exited his lower back, spraying blood onto the rock wall to Karla's right.

The brave fell, knocking Karla to one knee.

"Hey!" A man's voice rose from the rocky slope dropping toward the hollow.

Heart thudding, both cheekbones still numb from the Indian's blows, Karla cast her gaze down the incline. A white man stood with his feet spread on two separate boulders, a rifle in his hands. It was too dark for Karla to make out his features, but she saw he wore a white man's shirt, duster, and Stetson.

White men had come. Thank God.

Hope lightened her heart and she wanted to run to the man, but embarrassed by her nakedness, she remained on her knees, crouching low and holding her arms across her breasts.

"My friend fell down the mountain!" she cried, lifting her head to indicate the rocky lip above. "Please help him!"

The man kept his eyes on her and made his way up the rocks, crouching over his extended rifle. As he came closer, she saw the leering grin on his hard, craggy face. Her hope died, replaced by the old, needling fear. The man was white, but the lascivious expression told Karla he was no better than the savages from whom she'd just escaped.

"Well, what do we have here?" he said, lips stretching back from his teeth.

Karla knelt with her arms across her naked breasts, and watched the man approach, his hard features taking shape in the darkness.

In the hollow behind him, rifles flashed and popped. Bullets screeched off rocks. White men whooped and hollered.

"Look at you, little missy," said the man approaching Karla, the lewd grin frozen on his bearded cheeks. "You ain't got a stitch on!"

Karla jerked her glance toward the dead Indian. The brave's rifle lay only a few feet away. She glanced at the white man again. He was only ten yards away, closing slowly, as though approaching a wild animal.

Karla lunged for the rifle, scooping it off the ground, and automatically jacking a shell into the chamber.

"Hold on!" the man ordered. "Just hold on, little miss. You don't wanna shoot me. Why, I'm your friend! I done saved you from the savages, didn't I?" He glanced at the dead Indian sprawled near Karla's feet.

He spread his arms in supplication, the rifle in one hand, aimed toward the sky. His shaggy brows furrowed, but the lewd, confident grin remained as he continued walking toward her, one step at a time.

Karla stood and extended the rifle. She'd fired a Henry before, but this one felt like lead in her hands, which were weak from being tightly bound with rawhide.

151

"Don't come near me," Karla said, fear and fatigue trilling her voice.

The man took one more step and stopped. "Okay," he said reasonably. "Okay, we'll do it your way."

"My friend is Tom Navarro, segundo of the Bar-V ranch," she said nervously, loosening and tightening her grip on the Henry. "He's fallen down the mountain behind me. He's hurt. My grandfather will reward you generously for helping us."

"Sure, honey, I'll help," the man said woodenly, running his flat eyes across her chest. "Just put the gun down, and I'll help you . . . and your friend. . . ."

He took another step. Karla's jaw tightened, her muscles tensing. "Get away!" A sob slipped through her gritted teeth. Her mind kept returning to Tommy, lying broken somewhere on the other side of the slope behind her. She had to get to him.

The man, grinning, had lowered his arms. Suddenly, he lunged toward her, whipping his rifle toward Karla's. Before his Winchester connected with her Henry, Karla squeezed the trigger. The man grunted as the bullet tore through his belly. His momentum carried him another stumbling step forward. Dropping his rifle and slapping both hands to his middle, he fell to his knees.

Face bunched with pain, he looked up at her, eyes wide with shock. His voice was tight, barely audible. "Why, you little . . ." One hand on his belly, he reached with the other for the rifle angling across his right knee.

Panting, hearing panicked grunts squirting up from her throat as though from someone standing beside her, Karla backed away from the man and quickly levered another shell into the Henry's chamber. She centered the rifle on the man's chest, steeled herself, and squeezed the trigger.

The rifle clicked empty.

Karla's thudding heart fell hard. The man was bringing up his own rifle, grunting and cursing, his hand shaking. Karla took her own rifle by the barrel and lunged toward him, swinging the butt in a broad arc. It smacked his head so hard that Karla's wrists cracked painfully.

The men fell on his right shoulder and lay quivering.

"Otis? Where the hell are ye, boy?" The man's burly voice rose from downslope and several yards right of where the first man had come up.

Looking that way, Karla saw two shadows

darting amid the tall pines and jumbled rocks and boulders. Victorious whoops and laughter rose from the hollow.

"Come on, son," the man on the slope called again, his voice filled with laughter. "We done got 'em all, every blasted one. I got ole Nan-dash's hair right here!"

Giving a startled cry, Karla dropped to her knees. She set the rifle down and jerked her head around. Before her, rocks clattered under the boots of the men climbing the slope. She peered up the ridge from which Tommy had fallen. If she tried to climb it, the approaching men would see her.

"Otis, let 'em go! It's time to dance!"

Karla heaved herself to her feet, stepped over the dead Indian, and bolted behind three boulders wedged atop one another and shielding her from the hollow and the men climbing the slope. Looking around for an escape route, hearing the footsteps growing in volume behind her, she stole out from behind the boulders, edged over a little lip and into a hollow. A dark crevice shone in the rocks at the base of the lip on her left.

Moving to it, the sharp stones cutting her bare feet, she squeezed between the rocks and into the hollow, gritting her teeth against the jagged edges slicing her back, belly, and thighs. When she was wedged in the cramped hollow, she peered out from between the rocks.

She saw little but a pine looming ahead and left, more rocks and shrubs dropping along the slope to the hollow. Flickering light from the Indians' fire, now taken over by the scalp hunters, edged up from below, giving the night an eerie luminescence. Victorious whoops still rose, punctuating the muttered conversation.

By the voices, there must have been twenty white men down there.

Scalp hunters.

Karla knew the breed. They'd visited the ranch on occasion, seeking water and grain for their horses — hard, soulless, blood-stained men with crusted Indian scalps hanging from their saddles. Enshrouded in flies and reeking of death.

"Look what I found!" a man shouted, laughing. *"Tiswin!"*

Back toward the dead scalp hunter, a man yelled, "Bing, I found him!"

Running boots clattered on rocks. Silence. The two men spoke, their voices too low for Karla to hear clearly. She drew her limbs together as much as she could in the shallow, irregular niche, and ducked low behind a rock, squeezing her eyes closed.

After a minute, the rocks clattered again. One of the men grunted deeply, as though shouldering a great weight. "Otis, you stupid bastard," one of the men said through a strained sigh. "You let that wet-behind-the-ears 'Pache take ye down! Vern, don't forget his scalp."

The footfalls faded as the two men headed back down the slope toward the hollow.

The tension in Karla's body relaxed slightly. Listening intently, she heard no other nearby sounds, only those of the revelry below the hill. Smoke wafted to her nostrils, smelling of mesquite and a meat other than mule. Beef. Her mouth watered. She hadn't eaten in two days. The Apaches had allowed her only a half sip of water from a bladder flask.

Tommy. How could she get to him?

Peering around the rock before her, she saw that the glow of the fire had increased. With that much light, she wouldn't be able to climb the ridge without being seen from below.

Suppressing her thirst and hunger, she thought through the dilemma. As she did, a horse whinnied somewhere on the other side of the mountain. If she could get to the horses, she might be able to mount one and ride through the narrow crevice the Apaches had used to attain the ridge.

Once down, she could skirt the mountain's base and, hopefully, locate Tommy and the other Bar-V men.

She'd wait here until the scalp hunters, drunk on the Apache's *tiswin,* had gone to sleep. . . .

As she waited, the cool of the desert night settled around her naked flesh, raising pimples along her back and arms. It got so cold that her muscles ached and her teeth clattered.

So gradually as to be almost imperceptible, the firelight faded and the celebration waned. When all but three or four of the voices had died, Karla waited another hour, transporting herself mentally to a summer hay meadow not far from the Bar-V headquarters, where the hot sun enshrouded her.

But then she thought of Juan, saw him as she'd seen him last, his skinned, blood-drenched face protruding from the ant-covered sand. She heard her own rifle shot, and though she hadn't looked at Juan after she'd pulled the trigger, she now saw the hole the bullet had drilled through his forehead.

Her heart contracted. Sobs racked her, tears flowing from her eyes and coursing down her dusty cheeks.

"Juan," she cried softly.

Suddenly realizing all the sounds from the hollow had died, she lifted her head and peered around the rock. The night was still, the stars vivid. A light breeze blew, and a single wolf howled.

Wiping the tears from her cheeks with the heels of her hands, Karla crawled out of the niche and looked around. Nothing moved. Except for the wolf, all was silent.

The breeze biting her, and the rocks chewing at her feet, she followed a path of sorts through the rocks and pines around the edge of the hollow. She moved slowly, swinging her gaze in all directions.

Several times she found the scalped bodies of dead Apaches, blood on their hairless skulls. By now she'd seen so much horror, and was so chilled and terrified, that the grisly sightings barely registered. Navarro, Tixier, and the others foremost on her mind, she stepped over or around the bodies and, avoiding the very center of the hollow, where the dying fire glowed wanly and where intermittent snores resounded, made her way to the other side of the mountaintop. The Apaches, and probably the scalp hunters, had picketed their horses there, in the willows and curl leaf growing along a spring.

Amid the scarps and pine snags, it took her a long time to find the horses. When she did, she also found a bridle hanging from a branch.

Holding the bridle low at her side, she moved slowly toward the herd grazing on long picket ropes or reclining in the grass along the spring. She singled out the shortest one standing off by itself, and moved to it slowly, wincing at the thorny brush beneath her feet.

Seeing her, the little paint shied, sidled away, giving its tail a single angry swish. Karla cooed to the mount, holding her soiled hands out placatingly.

"Shhh . . . it's all right," Karla said, her voice shaking with the rest of her. "Oh, what a handsome horse you are. . . . That's all right. . . . Don't be afraid."

As much as she felt the need to hurry, she took her time with the paint, speaking to it softly and letting it get used to her smell, before slipping the bridle over its ears. Because of her stiff legs and sore feet, she needed three tries to leap up onto its back, and when she finally got settled there, she reined the horse westward across the brushy bench. Two horses whinnied behind her. Before her and to the right, another jerked with a start, leaping off its rear hooves and running out to the end of its rope.

She set her teeth against the noise and heeled the horse into the cleft in the rock wall. The trail dropped steeply, throwing her forward over the horse's neck. Twisting and turning between the jutting stone walls, the little paint picked its way, its hooves clipping stones, the jolting ride causing Karla's sore muscles to scream and her bare rump to burn against the horse's coarse hide.

It took a good quarter hour to get to the bottom of the mountain. When the paint finally leveled out at the base of an apron slope buried in mesquite, Karla reined back and heaved a long sigh of relief.

She was just about to bat her heels against the horse's ribs and begin making her way south along the mountain's base, when the sound of crunching gravel rose on her left. Acrid cigarette smoke peppered her nostrils. She whipped her head toward the sound and the smell. A man in a battered bowler hat stood wielding a rifle and an enraged scowl, a crooked quirley protruding from his thin lips.

Before Karla knew what was happening, the man had grabbed her left arm and pulled. He was short but powerful, and the tug jerked Karla instantly off the paint's back. She hit the ground hard, her head glancing off a stone.

"Goddamn girl!" the short man snapped, dropping to his knees beside her and brusquely grabbing her chin in his callused right hand. He gave her head a violent shake, rattling her brains around. "Where the hell you think you're goin'? Huh? Where on earth you think you're *goin'*?"

CHAPTER 13

"Come on, Tommy. Get your ass up now."

The deep, gravelly voice came from a long ways away. Someone was shaking him.

"Tommy?"

Behind the voice and high above, rifles snapped. Navarro blinked hard. Sharp nails probed his brain. A blurred figure was hunkered down beside him. Navarro smelled sweat and blood. He wasn't sure if it was his own or someone else's or a mixture of both.

Tixier's emaciated, bristled face took form. The mestizo knelt beside Navarro, his slumped shoulders rising and falling sharply with his strained, wheezing breath. "We gotta get outta here, Tommy. All hell's broke loose. Can you walk?"

Navarro winced against the nearly overpowering ache in his skull, rolled onto a shoulder, and looked around. He and Tixier were on a sand- and scree-strewn slope.

Fifty feet above was the lip of the ridge they'd fallen down.

"Where's Charlie . . . Ward?"

"Ain't seen 'em. I was climbin' down when you fell past me."

Karla's voice echoed behind the ringing in Navarro's ears. "Tommy, don't leave me!"

He grabbed Tixier's sleeve. "Where's the girl?"

"She's still up there, Tom. Come on. We gotta get outta here . . ."

Navarro gained his feet with effort and stared up at the ridge. "You go, Dallas. I'm not leaving without her."

"We ain't in any shape to fight 'Paches no more tonight." Tixier leaned forward, planted his hands on his knees. He heaved a heavy, wheezing sigh. Blood glistened on his arm, and his knees were shaking as badly as Navarro's.

Tom studied him, the two images of the man moving in and out of painful focus. Tixier was right. Neither he nor Navarro was in any shape to climb back up the mountain. Even if they could, they'd be of no use to Karla.

Hearing the sporadic shooting on the mountaintop, which evoked in his damaged skull more anxiety than curiosity about who the Indians were still shooting at, Navarro

163

gently pulled Tixier's good arm. "Come on. Let's find our horses. . . ."

He tramped heavily down the slope, looking back to see Tixier moving slowly after him, reaching for rocks as though drunk. Crawling over boulders and cat-stepping over sand slides, they made their way down the mountain's aproning slopes. Twice the banging in Navarro's head brought him to his knees and Tixier had to prod him with a boot toe and several jerks on his arms to get him moving again.

He'd just stumbled over a cactus skeleton when something to his right, on the other side of a low, square boulder, caught his eye. A human form. Navarro glanced at Tixier mincing sideways down the slope ahead of him, then stepped around the boulder to his right, and looked down.

It was Musselwhite, lying facedown, arms and legs spread, head turned to the left. Blood matted the back of his shirt and his head, pasting his hair against his scalp. A dark stream poured from his lips.

Navarro looked up and back toward the chalky cliff looming behind him. Apparently, Charlie had fallen down the sheer rock wall, at least two hundred feet high. If he'd fallen from a place only a few feet right, he'd have landed on the higher sand slide with Dallas and Navarro.

But he hadn't, and he was dead.

Navarro ran a hand over his close-cropped scalp, draped his wrist over his knee and stared down at the seasoned tracker; deep lines of sorrow etched his dirty face. He'd met Charlie when they'd started working together at the Bar-V, but they'd grown nearly as tight as he and Tixier, who'd been together for the past twelve years.

Navarro glanced at Dallas, a vague shadow still moving away from him down the slope, the sound of his foot scuffs loud in the desert silence. No point in breaking the news to the old mestizo until they were out of this, Navarro thought. Pushing off his knees, he stood, glanced at Charlie once more.

"Sorry for leavin' like this, pard. I'll be back later to bury you proper."

Nearly losing his balance, he turned around the boulder and began moving carefully down the slope toward Dallas, who'd disappeared over the incline's brow.

Tixier was still ahead of him, and they were slipping and sliding down the last incline, when Dallas' feet slipped out from under him, and he fell backward over a yucca clump, his breath an injured bird fluttering around in his chest.

"You go, Tommy," the old mestizo wheezed. "I'm finished."

Navarro stumbled toward him, prodded his side with a boot toe. "Get your ass up, you greasy half-breed. We ain't finished yet, you son of a bitch."

"Ah, shit, Tommy . . ."

When he'd gotten Dallas on his feet again, they negotiated the last incline shoulder to shoulder, hands around waists, like lovers. They continued walking this way, holding each other up, gently guiding themselves forward.

They'd walked a half mile in what Navarro thought was the direction of their horses, when Tixier's knees bent. The mestizo slipped from Navarro's grasp and dropped to the ground, his head rolling back on his shoulders.

"Dallas," Navarro growled, holding Tixier up by his right arm. Clumsily, he dropped to a knee beside his friend, grabbed Tixier's shirt with his other hand, gave it a tug. "Don't give up. We're close to the horses." He wasn't sure that was true, but as far as they'd come, they had to be.

Setting his teeth against his own pain, Navarro squinted his eyes at Tixier and shook him hard. "Dallas, don't you fold on me!"

Tixier's sweaty head lolled to his right

shoulder. His eyes were closed, lips parted slightly.

Navarro shook him again, causing the man's head to bob. "Bastard!"

Tixier said nothing. His eyes remained closed.

Navarro eased him down onto his right shoulder. Doing so, he placed a hand on the man's lower back, feeling a sticky wetness. He brought his hand to his face. The hand was covered with blood gleaming in the starlight.

Navarro turned Tixier over slightly, saw the bullet hole over the mestizo's left kidney. Turning the man onto his back, Navarro lowered his head to his chest and turned an ear to listen.

The bird in the old mestizo's lungs had fallen silent. There was no heartbeat.

"You old bastard," Navarro wheezed, shoulders slumping. "You old son of a bitch."

Hands on his knees, he stared at Tixier. Around him, the night had fallen cool and quiet, not a breath of breeze. The branches around him were slender, crooked etchings against the star-jeweled sky. The velvet hump of Gray Rock shouldered northward — black and silent.

Navarro leaned forward, clutched Dallas'

right hand in his, gave it a squeeze. "You rest easy."

He straightened Dallas' legs and crossed his hands on his chest, then grabbed a mesquite branch and pulled himself to his feet.

He turned and stumbled off through the shrubs, arms hanging straight down at his sides.

He'd gone only a little ways before his steps grew even heavier, and he was dragging the toes of his boots in the gravel.

Finally, his knees buckled, he dropped, and his head fell back on his shoulders. His eyes closed, and he lost consciousness before he sagged sideways and hit the ground on his right arm.

"Wait a minute," the short man said. He stood before Karla at the base of Gray Rock, holding her chin in his gloved hand and running his eyes down her naked body. "You ain't one of our girls at all, are ye?"

"Please, mister." Karla drew her knees up and crossed her arms on her chest. Her heart hammered. "I need —"

"Who the hell are you? And why are you — now I ain't complainin', mind you — naked as a jaybird?" The short man chuckled.

"I'm Karla Vannorsdell, and I was —"

"Save it," the short man interrupted again. He stood and jerked her to her feet. "You can tell it to Edgar."

The paint stood fifteen yards away, reins dangling, cropping at a sage shrub. The short man pulled Karla toward the horse. Halfway there, she jerked her right hand from his grip, wheeled, and ran, leaping a sage bush and dashing between two wagon-sized boulders.

She tripped over a stone, dropped to a knee, her left foot bleeding and aching.

The short man was on her, breathing hard. "You oughtn't to do that, little miss. You're apt to make me *mad*!" Jerking her to her feet and back toward the horse, moving quickly on his short legs, he said, "What you need is for me to take you off in the brush, teach you some respect. But Edgar wouldn't like it. He don't like us messin' with his girls. You're damn lucky I follow orders!"

Holding Karla's right wrist, the short man climbed onto the paint, then pulled Karla across the saddle. She lay belly down between the short man and the horn.

She winced as the man reined the horse around and gigged it into a gallop back up through the steep, winding pass. As the horse lunged, Karla bounced across the saddle like fresh eggs in a buckboard, the horn pummeling her ribs. She tensed her neck to keep her head from slamming against the right stirrup fender. The man held her down with a firm hand on her spine.

She was going to die. She'd been so close to escaping and finding Tommy, but now she was going to die. She was certain of it. She only wished it would come quickly and relieve her of this misery.

Where the trail narrowed and doglegged, her bare feet scraped against the rock wall, evoking a moan. At the same time, she was grateful for the pain. The pain left little room for fear.

She squeezed her eyes shut and didn't open them again until she felt the horse stop. Her face crumpled as the saddle horn pinched her belly.

"Edgar," the guard said quietly.

Karla slid a look ahead of the horse. Ten yards away, at the very center of the saucer-shaped hollow, a dozen or so men lay under wool blankets, heads resting against saddles, hats tipped over their eyes. Some were curled on their sides. The fire was out, several ribbons of gray smoke rising gently from gray ashes. Bubbling, drunken snores rose toward the overhanging pine branches from which bloody black scalps had been hung to dry. The sickening smell of blood was relieved intermittently by the wafting pine smoke.

"Edgar," the guard repeated, louder this time.

A man on the left side of the fire jerked awake with a grunt and snapped a revolver up from a coiled holster, thumbing back the hammer. The sudden movement made the horse shy, and the saddle prodded Karla again painfully. Several more men came alive, then, too, cursing and reaching for weapons.

"Hold it, hold it." The rider raised his voice. "It's Ramsay. Got a present for ye, Edgar."

The man grabbed Karla's right arm and brusquely tossed her from the horse. She fell on her back. Pain shot through her left elbow. She scrambled back against a boulder and drew her knees up, folded her arms across her breasts.

She raked her gaze across the silhouetted figures staring back at her. The man called Edgar slowly rose, letting his wool blanket fall from his shoulders. His pistol fell to his side as he moved toward Karla on long, skinny legs encased in baggy broadcloth trousers, like those from a man's Sunday suit. The knees were patched with denim, and he wore red socks with holes in the toes.

Edgar dropped to a knee before Karla, and she recoiled from his cool appraisal. What she first had thought were pimples on his face were actually dried blood splatters. The face itself was long and angular, with an aquiline nose and deep-set eyes under a heavy blond brow.

His hair was blond and curly; heavy peach fuzz mantled his jaws. Karla winced at the fetor of rancid sweat, alcohol, and death wafting from his body.

"Caught her at the bottom of the mountain," the guard said, still mounted. "Ridin' like cans were tied to that horse's tail. Naked as the day she was born, just like she is now." He chuckled. "Ain't she somethin'?"

Edgar canted his head this way and that. Set against his blood-splattered face, his eyes were oddly gentle, but in a demented sort of way. Karla flinched, smacking her head against the rock, as he reached up and took her chin in his right hand. He held her gently, caressed her cheek with his thumb.

"Injuns have you?" he asked.

Karla stared at him. She wasn't sure how to answer. They must not know about

Tommy and the other Bar-V men. If they did know, would they help them or kill them?

Instinctively knowing the answer, she nodded and squeezed her shoulders against her fear.

"What's your name?" Edgar asked. Several other men had walked up behind him now, staring down at Karla. The alcohol and death smell was so strong that Karla's stomach clenched. To avoid it, she breathed through her mouth.

"Karla Vannorsdell," she said, her voice brittle. "I was captured by the Apaches." Tears boiled from her eyes. "Would you please let me go?"

"Seen where she was staked out with the other girl, Edgar," one of the men behind him said. "The other girl's dead. Tossed her on the pile with the Injuns. Damn shame. She was near as fine as this one."

Edgar nodded, his eyes glued to Karla. He gently grabbed her wrists and pulled her arms away from her chest. He stared at her.

"Please . . ." she begged.

"Karla, you are one fine-looking specimen," Edgar said. "Damn shame. I'd like you for myself, but you'll bring a nice price from Ettinger." He glanced over his shoulder. "She needs clothes so she don't freeze to death, and a hat so the sun don't fry her tomorrow. Come on, boys. Cough up your spares."

"Please . . ." Karla sobbed.

Rising, Edgar turned and walked back to his blanket, throwing his lanky arms out and yawning. "Tie her with the others. Good and tight. She's a runner, that one."

Chapter 14

When Navarro opened his eyes again, he found himself on a cot, his tightly wrapped head on a pillow. It was a flat pillow, but a pillow, just the same — the cover white and crisp and smelling like starch. The last time he'd rested his head on such a pillow, he'd been in the infirmary at Fort Apache, the stone tip of a Coyotero's arrow buried in his leg.

Squinting against the dull ache just behind his eyes — he imagined a thin but painful fissure running from his right temple down through his right jaw — he looked around the long, sunlit room he found himself in. To his right and left, cots with wool Army blankets and pillows were lined along both sides of the room. Several of the cots were occupied — blurred humps beneath the blankets. At the left end of the room, two men in white jackets and soldiers' slacks stood talking quietly, in businesslike tones.

A tall black stove stood two cots down to Navarro's right, in the aisle running the length of the room. Sun glistened off the iron from the sashed, flyspecked windows cut deep into both adobe walls. A table stood beside the stove, draped with a white sheet and piled with silver trays and medical tools. There was an alarm clock on the table, ticking loudly.

Beneath the ticking, the shouted commands and marching feet of close-order drill rose from outside. A horse whinnied. Closer by, a man laughed, and Navarro gave his aching gaze to an open window across the room and ten feet right.

A soldier in a white shirt, suspenders, and a visored forage cap stood just outside the window, smoking and laughing in the arbor shade with another man Navarro couldn't see. Tom smelled the rich aroma of their cigarettes. He took a deep breath, yearning for one himself.

He lay back against the pillow and stared at the ceiling, trying to remember what had put him here. Then he became aware again of the tight wrap around his head. He lifted his hands to it, felt the gauze strips.

It all came back to him at once, like a half-remembered dream: Karla, the Apaches, Dallas, and Charlie. There was something

176

unreal about the memory. The sun streaming through the windows was too bright, the sky too brassy blue. The world seemed too calm and orderly, for him to have lost not only Karla, but two of his best friends, as well.

Knowing it hadn't been a dream did nothing to quell the dreamlike quality. At the same time, his heart squeezed with sorrow.

Karla, Dallas, Charlie . . .

"You still kickin', Mr. Navarro?" The voice came from across the room.

Tom switched his gaze to a man stretched out on a cot on the opposite side of the aisle and two cots down on the left. His vision was still blurred. He blinked hard to clear it, until the round young face swam into focus beneath a bandage like Navarro's.

The man's right leg was in a cast and drawn up by wires and pulleys to an iron bar hanging over the end of the man's bed. The man's right arm was in a cast, as well, and looped through a sling around his neck.

"Ward?"

The captain offered a wan smile.

"Figured you dead, too," Navarro said.

The captain lifted a shoulder. His arms were crossed behind his head. His smooth sunburned cheeks were freshly shaved. "You're at Fort Huachuca."

"How long I . . . we been here?"

"Three days."

"Goddamn."

"This young man saved your life, Mr. Navarro."

Tom turned to see one of the two men who'd been speaking near the outside door now moving toward him down the center of the room. Fortyish, thick red hair carelessly parted. Beard and mustache. He wore a black tie and a white jacket with captain's bars, and a stethoscope around his neck. He held a clipboard in one hand, a gnarled quirley in the other. The cuffs of his baggy wool trousers dragged on the floor.

The medico halted near Navarro's cot. "With a broken arm and leg, he crawled a mile to the main trail, and lay there for three hours, until a patrol happened by. He directed the soldiers to you."

"Much obliged," Navarro said to Ward. "Soldiers go up the mountain?"

"Found only a bunch of dead Apaches," Ward said. "Scalped, left to rot in the sun — even Nan-dash."

"No girl?"

"No girl."

"Scalp hunters," Navarro said, remembering how the Indians had suddenly seemed distracted when he, Karla, and the others

178

were trying to get away. His brain working sluggishly, he thought it over. The soldiers hadn't found Karla's body, which meant she'd either escaped on her own, maybe down another side of the mountain, or the scalp hunters had nabbed her. If they'd nabbed her, where had they taken her? Why?

They must've been the bunch the late Cheatam and Gomez had been riding to meet. If only Tom had probed the horse thieves a little deeper, found out where they were selling the scalps. Probably the same place they were taking Karla . . .

Tom, suddenly realizing the medico was talking to him, looked up at the potbellied, stoop-shouldered man.

"I'm Dr. Sullivan, post surgeon," the man repeated louder and more slowly, as though talking to a dimwit. "How are you feeling?"

"I got a helluva headache, my lower leg feels bee-stung, I'm hungry, and I have to piss like a plowhorse. Other than that, I think I'm ready to ride."

Chuckles echoed off the adobe walls. Navarro glanced around the room. Two of the other three patients regarded him from their cots, grinning. The two soldiers who'd been talking outside now stood shoulder to shoulder at an open window, grinning at him.

"Your reputation precedes you, Mr. Navarro," the doctor said, jerking his head around to indicate the onlookers. "You're legendary. I had to post a guard on the building to keep the enlisted men from strolling through to get a peek at the famous —" He frowned thoughtfully. "What do they call you?"

" 'Taos Tommy' Navarro," said one of the near-toothless men peering through the window, with a jubilant air.

"Famed Injun tracker and gunslick," Ward added with a pensive smile. "I must be the only soldier in the Territory that hadn't heard of you."

Embarrassed by the foofaraw, Navarro returned his gaze to the doctor. "When can I get out of here?"

"You have a fractured skull," the doctor said. "For that alone, I recommend bedrest for the next two weeks. The bullet that plowed through your leg missed the bone, but I'm going to need to keep draining it to avoid infection."

"Shit!" Navarro brought his right fist down against his cot, then winced against the searing pain in his skull. If Karla was still alive in three weeks, would he be able to find her? The tracks the scalp hunters had made leaving Gray Rock would have long since disappeared.

He looked at the doctor, who was drawing deep on his quirley stub. "I need to talk to the post commander pronto."

No sooner had the words left his mouth than heavy footsteps pounded the floorboards. Looking around the doctor, Navarro saw a tall heavyset man enter the infirmary, doffing a big tan hat with half the brim pinned to the crown.

"I ain't used to takin' orders from civilians," the man said in a deep, burly voice echoing around the narrow room. "But you're in luck, Tom. I came just to get a look at ye with your eyes open."

"Well, I'll be damned," Navarro said as the big man approached. He was nearly as tall as Navarro's six-three, but his torso was round as a whiskey keg, his double chin wobbled around on his neck, and he had half as much hair as when Tom had seen him last. "Phil Bryson?"

"Don't look so damn surprised. Since they weren't promoting you rebels, I was bound to make major eventually."

Bryson held out his hand, and Navarro shook it, remembering a Lieutenant Bryson, tall and gallant, with muttonchop whiskers and a full head of hair. He'd been a junior officer most of the years Navarro had scouted off and on out of Forts Apache and Bowie. A hereditary addiction to alcohol — his father had died with a liver the size of a boar's head — had kept Bryson at the rank he'd assumed upon graduation from West Point, but despite his off-duty predilection for spiritous liquids, he'd been one of the most levelheaded officers Navarro had known. His lack of ego and his gallows humor had made him a favorite among the enlisted men and the noncoms, and a sport to carouse with.

Smelling the liquor rolling off the man now, and seeing the syphilitic white around his eyes and mouth, Navarro knew that Bryson's promotion had probably been less the result of the soldier's change of character than of the Army's lowered standards. Too many officers had simply died in the field, and as Bryson had said, the War Department Act of 1866 excluded ex-Confederates from holding commissions.

"Couldn't have happened to a better man," Navarro said, as Bryson pulled a Windsor chair out from the wall. The doctor had crossed the aisle to check on Ward.

"Ah, bullshit," Bryson said, the chair squawking as he lowered his considerable girth to it. "You and I both know they promoted me because they're short-handed, but what do I care? I'm gettin' on in years, they make the pillows softer for majors, and I get first pick at the new batches of whiskey and whores from Las Cruces. Hell with 'em if they can't take a joke." Plucking two stogies from inside his tunic and glancing at the doctor, he said, "Doc, can he have a cigar?"

"No," Sullivan said curtly as he unwrapped the bandage around Ward's head.

Bryson extended the two cigars to Navarro, who took one and bit off the end. "What in the hell were you doin' atop Gray Rock, anyway? Thought you gave up chasin' 'Paches."

"I was looking for a girl," Navarro said as Bryson lit Tom's cigar. Puffing smoke, the match flame leaping as he drew, Navarro said, "Daughter of the rancher I ride for. Nan-dash had her. Now the scalp hunters have her." He raised his eyes to Bryson. "I'd appreciate your help, Phil."

When Navarro's cigar was lit, the major dropped the match on the floor and stomped it out with his boot. "No chance, Tommy," he said regretfully, reaching for another match.

"What are you talkin' about? You're out here to protect civilians, aren't you?"

"From Apaches. At the moment, I'm

stretched too thin to go after scalp hunters and slave traders."

"Slave traders?"

"If the men who have your girl are who I think they are, they're led by Edgar Bontemps. Scalp hunter and slave trader. Ex-Army man. He and his men — mostly deserters like himself — hole up somewhere in Mexico. They raid up here for Apache scalps and young Yanqui women."

"Where do they take the women?"

Bryson scowled and puffed his cigar. "I've followed him as far as the border. Had to stop there. You know as well as I do that going any farther might be viewed as an act of war by the Mexicans, with whom our government has a very precarious relationship."

"So what you're telling me, then, Phil, is that nothing's being done about the slave trading."

"Even if I had the men, I couldn't track Bontemps into Mexico, Tommy."

"So lay for him on this side of the border." Navarro's voice rose tightly. "Capture the son of a bitch and force him to tell you *what he's done with the girls!*"

"I told you, I'm stretched too thin. Half my men patrol the mining country east and west of here, rounding up reservation-jumping Mescaleros and Chiricahuas when they can find them, and the others ride shotgun on ore shipments."

"Ore shipments?"

"There's an American- and British-owned gold mine in Sonora. The company has a special agreement with the Sonoran province. The *rurales* escort the bars to the border. My troops take it from there, have it smelted, then haul the bars to the federal shipping depot in Lordsburg. Ties up twenty men, a full third of my garrison, fourteen days out of every month. With the others out on patrols, I don't have enough men for latrine duty. The privies can get mighty smelly around here."

"Goddamn it, Phil." Drawing angrily on the cigar, Navarro lay back on the pillow and stared hard at the ceiling.

"You know how it is, Tom," Bryson said, struggling up from his chair, breathing hard. "You know how it's *always* been. We do the best we can with a smattering of green recruits. But, frankly, I'm not sure a full battalion of seasoned fighters backed up with Howitzers and a brace of Injun trackers could do anything for your girl." He squeezed Navarro's shoulder. "You rest. I'll check on you again tomorrow."

With that, Bryson turned and, boots thumping and creaking across the rough puncheons, headed for the door.

"Who's this Edgar Bontemps?" Tom asked.

Bryson turned, frowning. "Why?"

Navarro turned his head on the pillow, cigar in his teeth, and stared at Bryson.

The major sighed. "Ex-Confederate guerrilla. Rode with Mosby. After the War, he joined the frontier Army, came west to fight the Indians. Decided he didn't like galvanization, after all, so he deserted, took several other ex-Confederates with him, and began riding the owlhoot trail."

The major returned Navarro's dark stare and growled with an air of warning, "He's a killer, Tommy. Worse than the worst Apache, they say. Crazier than a tree full of owls. He's armed with stolen Army munitions, and his gang numbers in the twenties, sometimes thirties."

Navarro turned back to the ceiling, folded his arms behind his head, and thoughtfully turned the cigar in his mouth with his tongue.

"Doubtful even 'Taos Tommy' Navarro can bring this one down," Bryson warned. He turned and went out.

Navarro puffed the cigar. "We'll see."

CHAPTER 15

Navarro dictated a telegram to Paul Van-norsdell at the Bar-V, explaining the situation, then slept for the rest of that day and most of the next.

When he woke up, he began playing poker for matchsticks with Captain Ward. Several of Tom's off-duty admirers — soldiers and trackers who'd heard the "Taos Tommy" Navarro legends — drifted into the infirmary to play cards with their hero. Navarro played so much poker and cribbage over the next three days that he was holding, folding, and filling in straights in his sleep.

He didn't mind.

He'd resigned himself to a mending period before he could set off after Karla again. Just lying on his cot, grinding his teeth as he stared at the ceiling, and imagining what he was going to do to Edgar Bontemps once he caught up with the bastard would have been like cutting off his own head with a rusty saw. Wouldn't do him or Karla any good at all.

The morning of his fourth day at the fort, he asked Dr. Sullivan for a crutch and something to shoot at.

The doctor had just finished tending a rattlesnake-bit woodcutter and was heading back to his office at the north end of the infirmary. Sullivan turned around, his heavy brows knit with incredulity, the eternal brown paper cigarette protruding from the right corner of his mouth. "Something to *shoot* at?"

"A can, a little box, or a horseshoe. Hell, give me a whiskey bottle."

"Neither your leg nor you head is well enough for you to be gallivanting around the post *shooting* things, Mr. Navarro."

Wearing only his long underwear and socks, Tom hobbled out of bed and, bracing himself with one hand on the window, knelt on his good leg before the wooden footlocker beside it. He removed the lamp from the top, and lifted the lid.

"I'm gonna shoot something, Doc. *You* can decide what . . . or *I* can." He reached inside the locker and pulled out his .44 and cartridge belt.

Sullivan cursed and disappeared into his office. He returned a minute later with a crutch in one hand, a square sulphate of quinia can in the other. With pursed lips and arched brows, he extended both to Navarro sitting on the bed and buckling his cartridge belt around his waist.

Tom took the crutch and the can, pulled himself to his feet, and adjusted the .44 on his hip. He was a good distance from the washwomen of Suds' Row, so he saw no need to don more than his balbriggans. "Where's the best place to shoot without ruffling too many feathers?"

"I would suggest the ravine behind the infirmary."

"Obliged."

Navarro draped his left arm over the crutch and ambled into the aisle between the beds. The crutch caught in a floor knot, and Tom stumbled forward cursing. Rushing toward him, the doctor helped him free the crutch from the knot and position it back under Tom's right arm before he fell.

Tom shuttled his weight back to the crutch and, with a wink at Captain Ward looking up from a game of solitaire with concern, continued hop-shuffling forward. "Close one — thanks again, Doc."

"Nice to know my education wasn't wasted," Sullivan grumbled. He grabbed the can from Navarro's right arm, followed him out of the building and to the sun-blasted arroyo behind it.

On the arroyo's lip, Navarro leaned into the crutch and shucked his .44. He flipped open the loading gate, checked for pills, then flipped the gate shut and spun the cylinder.

"Chuck the can, Doc."

With a disapproving chuff, Sullivan threw the can to the opposite bank, thirty yards away, missing the lip by a foot. The can rolled down two feet and snugged up against a rock, label out, nearly perpendicular to the bank.

Navarro stared at the label, blinking. He slid his .44 from its holster, thumbed back the hammer, and extended his arm. Squinting one eye, he sighted down the Navy's barrel.

The gun popped.

Sullivan removed the quirley from his mouth and looked at the can. He turned to Navarro. "Missed it."

"Clean."

"You can't see it."

"It's some fuzzy, but I can see it," Navarro said, flipping the gate open and removing the spent shell. "As a matter of fact, I can see two of 'em." He plucked a fresh shell from his cartridge belt, thumbed it through the loading gate, spun the cylinder, and returned the .44 to its holster.

"When I can see only one, and hit the son of a bitch, I'm heading to Mexico."

That night, Major Bryson came by with a bottle and two tumblers. He did nothing to convince Navarro not to go after Bontemps. The major knew he had no jurisdiction in the matter, beyond friendship, and even if he had, convincing Navarro to give up his search would have been like trying to reroute a river with a handful of sand.

When he'd finished his cigar and had signed a requisition to supply Navarro with two Army horses — a packhorse and a saddle mount — the major raised his glass in salute. "To a safe journey, Tom. But frankly, I don't expect you'll have one."

They touched glasses, and drank.

The major ambled back to his lonely quarters feeling owly and depressed — the frontier was losing too many old salts like Tom Navarro — and turned in early with a dime novel and a bottle of cheap whiskey.

The next morning, Navarro took another shot at the medicine can. Again, he missed his target but noted there were only 1.5 cans now instead of two, and he was getting closer to blowing the Q out of QUINAE. He celebrated with a drink at the sutler's saloon, then hobbled toward the stables to see about his horses.

He was ambling along the path through the sage and saguaros, sweating in the hot sun, when two young privates — a freckle-faced towhead and a lanky kid with a limp — headed toward him from the quartermaster's barn and corrals.

The two soldiers saluted and smiled as they approached. Navarro nodded back. The path was narrow, and the two privates made way for him, but the kid with the limp moved back onto the trail too quickly, his right foot clipping Tom's crutch.

Losing the crutch and tripping over a sage bush, Tom cursed and, limbs akimbo, fell in a heap.

"Oh, gosh, oh, shit, Mr. Navarro!" the gimpy kid lamented, scrambling back and forth between Tom and the fallen crutch, not sure which one to pick up first.

"Look what ye done, Dwight, ye damn fool!" the towhead admonished. "Ye done tripped, Mr. *Navarro*!"

"Oh, jeeze!"

"Fool! Grab his crutch, for christ's sake!" The towhead crouched over Navarro. "You all right, sir? Should I send for the doc?"

Tom had propped himself on an arm. "No

need for the doc, fellas. No harm done."

"I'm sorry, Mr. Navarro," the gimpy kid said, reaching for the crutch and fumbling with his duckbilled forage hat, doffing it, dropping it, picking it up, and holding it across his chest.

"Give him the crutch, you moron!"

"Here, Mr. Navarro — and let me give ye a hand. . . ."

Navarro shook his head. "No harm done." He maneuvered the crutch beneath his arm and, as the towhead helped from the other side, levered himself to his feet.

"You sure you're okay, sir? I'd be happy to —"

"I'm fine. Fit as a fiddle. Tight as razor wire."

"Dwight here don't move along so well his ownself," the towhead explained, sliding his blue eyes toward his friend. "Since he took that 'Pache arrow last month, he's had a gait like a three-legged horse trottin' over hot coals."

"My sympathies, son. They have you on a recovery string?"

The lanky kid nodded and bunched his lips. "Yeah, can't do much. The sergeant's got me cleanin' windows some, but mostly I just whittle and hobble around chattin' up the girls over to Suds' Row."

"You could do worse than chat with the ladies on a soldier's salary," Navarro said, giving the lanky kid an encouraging shoulder pat, then turning to continue down the trail.

"See you, Mr. Navarro," the lanky kid called behind him. "Again, my apologies."

"Be well, sir," the towhead yelled.

Navarro threw his right arm up and hobbled around a dogleg in the hard-packed trail.

The two privates continued in the opposite direction, walking side by side. As they approached the parade ground where the guidon snapped and popped in the breeze and a sergeant dressed down a corporal for drunkenness, the lanky kid suddenly lost his limp.

He snickered. "Did you see the old bastard fall?"

The towhead laughed and exclaimed in a mocking rasp, "So sorry, Mr. Navarro!"

"How good you think he can shoot with only one leg to balance on?"

" 'Bout as well as he could outrun a jackrabbit."

The soldiers chuckled.

The lanky kid sobered. "Tonight, we see how well he can outrun a bullet."

■ ■ ■ ■

When Navarro had picked out a long-legged bay for riding and a thick-hammed, white-socked dun for packing, he spent some time buttering up the remount duty noncom, a prickly, red-bearded Norwegian named Jasper Dahl, by complimenting the man on the cleanliness and orderliness of the barn, hayloft, and tack room.

"A place for everything and everything in its place," Navarro commented, nodding with approval. "Why, hell, I'd drink out of those water troughs myself!"

"Horses perform better when they're well-cared for," Dahl said. A fuzzy kitten was crawling on his broad shoulders. "It's the Army way. You seen the barns at Fort Bowie? I don't mean to stab no one in the back, but the quartermaster over there has gotten a little sloppy. These horses shit, and I or my boys is right there with the shovel."

They chatted over a cup of coffee, Navarro offering his appreciation for the horses, buttering the man up further. Though the middle-aged Norski didn't actually own the animals himself, Navarro had never known a remount man who didn't consider the horses his own. Besides,

Navarro wanted the bay and the dun fed plenty of oats and corn tonight and ready to ride at dawn the next day, when he hoped to leave.

"That won't be a problem, Mr. Navarro," Dahl said, shaking Tom's hand when he'd grabbed his crutch and stood up from the sergeant's battered card table. "I'll give 'em a little extra and throw a few pounds in a feed pouch."

"Much obliged, Mr. Dahl."

"Oh, watch that dun's right forefoot if you're on a narrow trace somewheres — in the mountains, say. He tends to throw it out to the side. Hate to see him end up in a canyon. That's the best packhorse in my remuda."

Navarro waved and thanked the man again as, leaning into the crutch, he split the barn doors and headed back to the parade ground, where he bought a shave and a haircut in the post barbershop.

After stripping and removing the bandage from his lower right leg, he lounged in a tub in the barber's back room. Lifting the leg from the soapy water, he ran his right thumb across the wound, probing and inspecting it.

The entry and exit holes looked like hell, stitched and swollen, but the wound looked a lot better since the last time Sullivan had lanced it. The puss had dried up. More important, Tom could put full weight on his calf. He'd mostly been using the crutch to hasten the healing, so it wouldn't be as apt to open up once he was on the trail.

It was his head that had grieved Navarro the most, but while the frequent headaches were still blinding, they were short-lived, and his vision was only occasionally blurry. He hoped riding wouldn't set him back, but he had to chance it.

Every hour took Karla another hour beyond his reach. . . .

"Hear you're goin' after Edgar Bontemps," the barber said as Navarro was leaving. The man shook his bald head and clipped away at the auburn-curled lieutenant in his chair. "Only a polecat woulda mammied that skunk."

As Navarro turned left on the boardwalk outside the barbershop, he caught someone staring at him out of the corner of his eye. Shuttling his gaze across the hard-packed, hoof-pocked parade ground, he saw the towhead who'd run into him earlier, standing with several other soldiers around a Murphy freight supply wagon before the officers' adobe duplexes.

The soldiers were taking a smoke break.

Leaning against the massive left rear wheel, the towhead looked quickly away from Tom. Seeing that Navarro had spotted him, the kid turned back and flicked a hand in a halfhearted wave, flushing and showing his teeth through a grin.

Navarro returned the wave and maneuvered his crutch toward the post trader's store, where he bought food, coffee, tobacco, and new trail duds — including a hat, to replace the one he lost on Gray Rock.

When he'd picked out a new Winchester rifle and had stocked up on ammo, he arranged for the trader's son to deliver the goods to the infirmary. Heading that way himself, feeling fatigued, he promptly collapsed on his cot for a nap.

That night, after taps, Tom played a final game of poker with Captain Ward and Doc Sullivan on a small table beside Captain Ward's cot. A hanging lamp offered a murky light made murkier by the men's cigar and cigarette smoke. The building's shutters were open, awaiting a breeze to stir the heavy desert heat.

Navarro and Ward were the only two patients left in the infirmary, one wounded soldier having died from the Apache lance he'd taken through his spleen. Having mended, the others had been sent back to their platoons.

Ward would have to spend another two weeks in the infirmary before he could be sent back to his company at Fort Bowie.

"You still hitting the trail tomorrow, Mr. Navarro?" Ward asked as he studied his cards, his right leg inclined. The captain sounded disappointed.

Navarro nodded and shoved three matchsticks toward the center of the table.

"Only if he can blow the 'Q' out of the quinine can," Sullivan said.

"I'll hit the sumbitch," Navarro growled, wishing he'd never mentioned the personal challenge. He intended to leave in the morning, blown "Q" or no blown "Q."

"What about your leg?" the doctor asked.

"If my head's goin', the leg doesn't have any choice but to tag along."

After lights out, and after Ward had gone to sleep, snoring softly on the other side of the aisle, Navarro slipped out of bed and wrapped his cartridge belt around his waist. He left his boots under the cot and the crutch propped against the wall. He padded barefoot to the door, cracked it, and peered outside.

The parade ground was dark, the windows of the encircling buildings unlit. Nothing moved but a silk streamer hanging from a nearby porch beam, stirred by a subtle breeze.

Satisfied the coast was clear, Navarro stepped through the door, closed it softly, listening for the click, then slipped to his right along the boardwalk and hunkered down in the shadows on the other side of an iron-banded rain barrel.

Navarro unholstered his .44 and held it between his knees, curling his right index finger through the trigger guard.

He waited.

CHAPTER 16

Navarro didn't have long to wait.

Twenty minutes later, he heard running feet on his left. He leaned back and stole a look between the rain barrel and the building, toward the front door, but he couldn't see anything. The sounds had come from off the north end of the infirmary, out of sight.

Navarro held the pistol. He waited, listening to the crickets and the yammers of a lone coyote somewhere south of the fort.

Finally, a strained breath. A movement at the northeast corner of the building, on the other side of the barrel. A tap of a heel, then the squawk of a floorboard as a man mounted the porch. Boots thudded softly. Breaths roiled out from tensed lungs.

The doorknob turned with a faint chirp.

Navarro looked over the rain barrel's lip, saw the infirmary's front door squeak slowly open. A tall figure passed into the building.

From this angle, Navarro could see only a billed forage cap. Another, shorter figure followed, leaving the door open behind him.

Navarro remained behind the barrel, holding his .44 in both hands. Staring across the parade ground before him, he yawned, stretched the kinks out of his neck.

He heard the two men approach the door again, walking on the balls of their Army-issue brogans. When they'd both slipped onto the porch and pulled the door closed behind them, one whispered to the other, "Where the hell is he?"

"The privy?"

"Let's check."

Navarro rose slowly and extended his .44 over the barrel. The men had turned their backs as, moving left of the door, they were about to swing around the side of the infirmary, heading for the privy out back.

"I got you both dead to rights," Navarro said tightly. "Any sudden move, and they'll be throwin' dirt over you come sunup."

The towhead and the taller soldier, who didn't seem to have the limp anymore, both froze. The tall one stood just off the end of the boardwalk, half turned left. The towhead was still standing at the edge of the boards. They both held Army-issue .44s in their right hands hanging low at their sides.

Both men tensed, turning their heads slightly to get a glimpse of the man behind them.

"Stand still. You two little jiggers know what I look like." Navarro stepped to the barrel's right side and place his left hand on it for support; his left leg was weak from nonuse. "Toss those pistols down."

When the soldiers hesitated, Tom thumbed his .44's hammer back. The ratcheting click was loud in the silence.

The towhead tossed his Colt Army into the yard ahead and right of the taller kid, who followed suit.

With both pistols in the dust, Tom asked, "Why you boys lookin' to pull my picket pin?"

After a brief hesitation, the towhead said, "Don't know what you're talkin' about, Mr. Navarro. We were just comin' over to chat."

"We couldn't sleep," the other one added. "We wanted to hear some stories about gunfights and such."

"Boys, if you don't give it to me straight, I'm gonna back shoot you both, which is hell of a lot more than you deserve for trying to bushwack me while I slept."

Neither one said anything. The coyote was giving his vocal cords a rest, but the crickets continued their raucous serenade.

"You killed my brother," the tall soldier blurted, his voice tense. "Three years ago . . . in Abilene."

Navarro studied the kid's back, trying to remember. Abilene. Three years ago, Vannorsdell had sent him and Tixier to Abilene to pick up some breed bulls. While there, a kid wanting to make a name for himself had slapped leather on him in a general store. Tixier had seen it coming, yelled a warning, and Navarro had drilled three pills through the kid's chest.

The kid's younger brother had been in the bawdy house next door, but he'd run over when he'd heard the shooting. The kid had said nothing to Navarro, but Tom knew from the look in the kid's eyes, as he'd crouched over the body, that he'd be trouble one day.

That day had arrived.

"Your brother made a mistake, boy. Don't you do the same."

"You didn't have to kill him."

"No, I reckon I didn't have to. But if I hadn't, I'd be pushing up Texas wildflowers."

"He just wanted to see how fast you were. He didn't want to shoot."

"Bullshit." Navarro looked at the towhead. "What's your stake in this, private?"

"Me?" the towhead said, turning a grin over his right shoulder. "I just want the honor of turning you under, Mr. Navarro. You know — somethin' to tell my grandkids about."

Footfalls sounded within the infirmary. Lantern light spilled onto the porch. The doctor poked his head through the door, between Navarro and the would-be assassins, holding a shimmering bracket lamp high above the boards. "What in the name of Christ is going on here?"

The light momentarily blinded Navarro. He blinked against the glare, leaned his head to the right, trying to see around the lamp. "Go back inside, Doc!"

Sullivan jerked the lamp back, retreating, but the young shooters had already taken advantage of the distraction. They'd leapt for their guns, both pivoting at their hips and throwing themselves groundward — one right, one left.

"Shit!" Navarro railed, leveling his revolver on the two flying shadows. "Boys, don't do it."

It was too late. Light shimmered on the weapon the lanky kid raised from a crouch. The gun exploded, stabbing flames. Navarro had thrown himself right, and the bullet barked into the porch post in front of him.

Navarro's own Colt jumped. The lanky kid grunted and stumbled backward. Navarro turned left and peered through the smoke. The towhead was hunkered on his heels, thrusting his revolver out from his chest and yelling, "Die, you — !"

Navarro's Colt exploded once more.

From the way the kid's head snapped back, knocking his forage cap off, Tom knew the bullet had plowed through his forehead. The towhead triggered his revolver into the ground as he fell straight back in the dust and lay stone-still, not even twitching.

Men yelled to Navarro's right, and he turned to see two sentries running toward him, Springfield rifles raised. Several windows surrounding the parade ground were lit, and more soldiers were spilling out of the barracks in various stages of dress.

"Drop the gun, ye son of a bitch!" the sergeant of the guard yelled as he approached the infirmary's north end — a stocky Swede in a tan kepi with a pinned-up brim. His gold chevrons shone in the light from the doctor's lamp, once again hovering over the smoky porch.

Tom holstered his pistol and raised his hands. "It's Tom Navarro, Sergeant. These privates tried to ambush me."

The sergeant lowered his pistol slightly as

he approached the two dead soldiers sprawled in the dust. The two sentries marched up on Tom's right, flanked by a dozen or so soldiers rousted by the gunfire, several looking panicked and wielding firearms. As this was Apache country, they'd probably expected to find themselves under Indian attack.

"Schultz and Ball," the sergeant muttered, glancing over the bodies while keeping his pistol half trained on Tom. "What the hell happened here, Navarro?"

"Yes, what the hell's going on?" Tom turned to see Phil Bryson wedging through the crowd of half-dressed soldiers, ignoring the obligatory salutes as he knotted the belt around his robe and ambled up to the edge of the porch. Navarro still stood by the bullet-pocked post, hands half raised, in his long johns and pistol belt.

Tom shuttled his gaze from the major, looking over the dead men one more time, a look of distaste lifting his weathered cheeks. "Same ole, same ole, Phil. The past came a-gunnin'. Two more dead."

"They're dead, all right," Sullivan said, crouched over the lanky kid's sprawled carcass. Dressed in striped pajamas and leather slippers, he looked at Bryson. "He had no choice, Major."

Navarro saw the look on Bryson's face. He'd seen the same look before, on the faces of lawmen in whose towns he'd been prodded to defend himself against those seeking fame. Regret. Disgust. Scorn tempered by a general liking for the man at the trouble's heart, knowing it wasn't Tom's fault, but wishing he'd saddle a horse and ride, after all.

"Well, I reckon you as good as plugged that 'Q,' " the doctor said.

He turned, went inside, and sat down on his cot. Captain Ward had lighted the candle on his footlocker. He lay propped on his pillow, arms crossed behind his head, watching Navarro sitting on the edge of his own cot, his face in his hands.

The captain didn't say anything to the lean, silver-headed tracker, but he watched him for a long time.

Navarro removed his gun belt, coiled it on his locker, lay back on his cot with a long, weary sigh, and closed his eyes.

Ward blew out the candle and listened to the crowd disperse outside his window.

Around eleven the next morning, Karla rode slumped in her saddle, her hands snubbed to the horn. Her head hung low, pressed down by the heavy weight of the interminable desert sun and by the deadening fatigue of the trail.

The hat and clothes the bandits had given her protected the top of her head and her body from the brassy orb seemingly hanging just a few feet above. But the intense light and the dust-laden wind had managed to burn her face, hands, and unprotected feet, causing the skin to blister and peel. Long miles from home, tied and prodded like an animal by fifteen of the most savage men Karla had ever seen, she was being herded even farther into the bowels of remote, lawless Mexico — with eight other girls even unluckier than she, because they'd endured the slavers' abuse even longer.

Karla thought of Juan, Tommy, Dallas, and Charlie — and her chin dipped even lower, eyelids pinching down below the brim of her tattered hat. For Juan she felt a deep, relentless grief. For Tommy and the other ranchmen, grief as well as guilt. If she hadn't made the impetuous decision to ride out after Juan, the Bar-V men wouldn't have had to ride after her . . . and die needlessly.

As the procession rode single-file through a brush-clogged break in the rock wall of a sandstone ridge, six hardcases rode ahead of the eight girls, while six others rode behind. This country was honeycombed with Indians and other men just as bad as the slavers, and worse, so two scouted ahead while another rode behind, watching the group's flank.

At noon, the leader, whose name Karla had learned was Edgar Bontemps, called a halt at the base of a pine-clad slope, where a shallow creek trickled across alluviated sand. The girls were untied from their saddles and allowed, one by one, to wander off behind nearby shrubs for nature tending. The men peered through the branches, hooting and laughing.

When the girls returned, they were tied ankle to ankle along the shaded stream and tossed moldy jerky and stale crackers as though they were dogs. Several avoided the food, choosing only the cool springwater, sprawling prone and dipping their faces or cupping the water to their lips with their hands.

Karla drank deeply, then sat up and regarded the strip of jerky near her knee. She took a bite, wrinkling her nose against the rancid taste, and stuffed the rest in her shirt for later. She hadn't eaten since the slavers had tossed the girls scanty pieces of prairie chicken last night. She'd eaten only a wing, but she still wasn't hungry. She wondered if she'd ever be hungry again. She felt so defeated that part of her wanted to just curl up and die.

"All right, ladies," Bontemps said when the men were finishing their coffee and kicking dirt on the lunch fire. "I know how eager you are to get goin', so let's ride!"

A couple of the hardcases brought up the girls' horses, from where they'd been tied in a grove of desert willows a few yards downstream. Three of the girls had been set atop their saddles, two of the bandits tying their wrists to the horns, when a short hardcase named Dupree — thin and dark, wearing a ragged black beard on his sharp-featured face — reached for the skinny little fourteen-year-old whose name Karla had learned was Marlene.

The girls who hadn't mounted their horses yet had been untied and ordered to stand. Marlene, however, had remained on her knees, silently sobbing, her chin on her chest.

Dupree prodded the girl's thigh with his boot toe. "Come on, girl. On your feet."

Marlene continued sobbing. When the man kicked her again, harder this time, she sagged sideways in the sand and drew her knees up to her chest. Her sunburned cheeks were pinched, her eyes tightly closed. Tears squeezed out from beneath the lids, staining the sand under her face.

"Goddamn you, girl, I told you to stand!" Dupree shouted, reaching down and jerking the girl to her knees by a handful of hair.

Before Karla knew what she was doing, she'd bolted forward and slammed her left shoulder into Dupree's chest, knocking the hardcase backward. "Leave her alone, you son of a bitch!"

CHAPTER 17

Setting his feet beneath him, Dupree looked at Karla with wild-eyed rage. The men who'd been resetting the saddles had turned to watch the show, chuckling.

"That girl there — she's got spunk," one remarked.

Dupree's face turned even redder. He drew his right arm back, then suddenly forward, slamming the back of his hand against Karla's face. Karla spun and flew, falling on her stomach. She heaved herself up on her arms. Her right cheek burning, her lower lip split and beginning to bleed, she turned quickly to see Dupree glaring at her as he moved toward her slowly, hands balled into tight fists, eyes glassy with rage. Karla scooted back on her seat and drew her knees up to protect herself from another blow.

"No one pushes Derrold Dupree. *You hear?*"

"Hold it, Dee."

The voice had come from behind Dupree. The leader, Edgar Bontemps, stood beside his horse — a tall Chickasaw with two black socks and two white. One hand shoved down in his left saddlebag, he frowned across his horse's rump at Dupree.

Dupree stopped in his tracks, staring furiously down at Karla. Bontemps grimaced, pulled his hand out of the saddlebag, and walked around his horse. As he strolled up to Dupree, his liquid blue eyes softened, and he laid a casual hand on the man's thin shoulder.

"You know we don't hit the girls," Bontemps said, keeping his voice low and mild, one friend speaking to another. "Those are the rules, Dee. You understand the rules, right? We don't get paid for damaged merchandise."

Dupree stared hard at Karla for several more seconds. Then his shoulders loosened, and some of the flintiness left his colorless eyes. "Right, Edgar."

Bontemps looked over his shoulder, where the other men were cinching their saddles and removing the feedbags from their horses' snouts. Karla's Arabian stood among the other horses, the hardcases having picked it up somewhere along the trail.

"Willis, come over here and tend the women, will you?" Bontemps said. "Dee's a mite frustrated and needs a break."

"You got it, Edgar," Willis said, grinning and waving his coffeepot in the air, drying it before dropping it into a telescoping leather travel bag. "Be happy to."

Bontemps smiled at Dupree. "Go tend your own mount. I want you and Granger to scout ahead this afternoon." He slapped the man's shoulder twice, puffing dust from Dupree's black shirt and dyed hemp vest. "Best get a move on."

When Dupree had gone, Bontemps jerked his trousers up his thighs and squatted over Karla. She removed her fingers from her swollen lip and peered reluctantly up at the grotesque man.

His oily, wildly curly hair made his bowler hat sit unevenly upon his head. He had curious and disturbing dark rings around his eyes, and gold earrings in both ears, which caused the lobes to droop grotesquely. On his arms, below the folded sleeves of an orange silk shirt with ruffled sleeves, were tattoos of snakes and trees and naked women. Karla had seen earlier that the palms of both his hands had been tattooed with bright red apples, each missing a bite.

With exaggerated tolerance, drawing out

215

his Southern accent, he said, "Don't make my boys mad, young lady. As you can see, you won't like 'em when they're mad."

Karla brushed at the blood trickling down her lip.

Bontemps reached out, thumbed some of the blood from her chin, then looked at his thumb as though he'd never seen blood before. Rubbing his thumb on a patched trouser knee, he glanced at the sobbing Marlene and said to Karla, "Now get that cryin' brat on her horse before I shoot her and throw her in a ravine. That girl'll bring a nice sum, all young and smooth, but I don't put up with bullshit."

With that, Bontemps rose and walked away.

When Willis came over, stood before Karla, and crossed his big arms on his chest, threatening, Karla knelt down beside Marlene. The girl had stopped crying. She lay on her side, shivering and staring at the ground, her skirts and petticoats fanned out around her legs.

Karla swept a lock of copper blond hair back from the girl's cheek. "Come on, Marlene. You have to get up now."

The girl said nothing. A shiver racked her like an electrical charge. The desert air had dried the tears on her cheeks, leaving a salty patina.

"Please, Marlene." Karla was surprised by the sudden resolve she was feeling. She'd thought she'd given up, but the prospect of the girl being killed forced her to put some steel into her voice as she spoke into the girl's right ear. "If you don't get up, Marlene, they're going to kill you, and you'll never see your family again."

Thinly, the girl said, "I won't see them again, anyway."

"Yes, you will," Karla whispered in the girl's ear. "I promise you will." She knew she had no grounds to make such a promise, but the words were out before she could take them back. She'd spoken them with such quiet force that she found herself strangely buoyed by them. It was almost as if she'd heard them spoken by someone else.

All the other girls were mounted now, and looking wanly down at Karla and Marlene. One of them — a sixteen-year-old, Billie, who'd worked at a stage station near Benson — had tears in her hazel eyes. "Come on, Marlene. Listen to Karla. We'll be all right."

"Come on, come on," Willis growled. "We ain't got all goddamn day!"

Marlene lifted her head and looked at

217

Karla, hope showing in her eyes. Karla gave the girl her floppy black hat, which had been lying nearby, and tugged on the girl's arm. Marlene snugged her hat on her head and slowly gained her feet. Karla led her over to her horse, helped her poke a dirty bare foot into a stirrup, then lifted her up into the saddle.

Stoically, Marlene stared down at Karla as Willis tied the girl's hands to the saddle horn, the slaver muttering and shaking his head as he worked. Karla patted Marlene's thigh encouragingly.

When Willis finished tying Marlene's hands, he turned to Karla and gave her a brusque shove toward the pinto she'd been riding. "Come on, Mother," he said with dry mockery. "Climb into the saddle. I'm tired of this foolishness."

As Karla stumbled back toward the paint, she glanced at the skinning knife riding in the beaded leather sheath on the man's left hip. As she reached up for her saddle horn and poked a bare foot through the left stirrup, the image remained in her vision, as if burned into her retina.

Having fought off her inertia, she began turning a plan in her mind.

If she could only get her hands on a knife . . .

Later, as the group rode across a cedar-pocked flat, Karla found herself positioned off the left rear hip of Marlene's mare.

"How are you doing, Marlene?"

Marlene turned to her, the floppy black hat shading the girl's small face. She glanced at Willis riding several yards behind Karla, trimming his fingernails with a folding knife, whistling and swaying lazily in his saddle.

"Am I really gonna see my folks again, Karla . . . or were you just saying that?"

"I meant every word of it, Marlene," Karla said, keeping her voice low. As she stared straight ahead, her eyes were resolute. "We're going to get away from these men."

As they continued riding the rest of that day, Karla kept eyeing the knives her captors wore in belt sheaths, ankle sheaths, sheaths hanging from leather lanyards around their necks, down their backs, or protruding from boot tops. One man even wore a small bone-handled knife in his hat, Karla noticed when he'd doffed the low-crowned sombrero to wipe sweat from the band.

Most of the men wore at least two knives, prominently displayed. Who knew how many more they were wearing, secreted away in their clothes?

With that many knives around, Karla should be able to get her hands on at least one.

She mulled the idea until the group stopped at noon the next day. She was freed to tend to nature and, squatting down behind rocks, saw something bright lying in the red gravel ten feet away, between two scraggly pinions. When she finished her business, she glanced around and, seeing that the man instructed to keep his eye on her was smoking and talking to another man to his right, stole over to the object and looked down.

Her heart skipped a beat.

What she found herself staring at was an Indian arrow — sun-bleached and cracked but with a razor sharp, flatiron head. She glanced around again. The two men behind the rocks were still talking. Quickly, she crouched down, plucked the arrow off the ground, and broke it over her knee, making the break as close to the head as she could.

She stood, slipped the sharp tip and four-inch length of broken arrow into her right front pocket, pulled the long shirttails from her jeans, and arranged them over the pocket, concealing the elongated lump. Turning, she strode back to the horses.

The chinless, stubby-nosed man assigned

to watch her stared at her suspiciously, his carbine crossed in his arms. "What were you doing over there?"

"What do you think?"

"What was that cracking noise?"

"I stepped on a twig," Karla said, rolling her eyes as she brushed past the man, whom she'd overheard being called Snipe. "Don't get your shorts all in a knot."

When the group stopped again that night, bivouacking in a deep sand gorge, the girls were again tied in a string at least a hundred feet away from the men. As the altitude was higher here, the nights colder, Willis had been ordered to build them a small fire. Water was more plentiful here, too, so each girl was given a cup of coffee to wash down her serving of the antelope, which a couple of the scouts had shot earlier.

After they'd each been freed to tend to nature, and when their fire had been banked and they'd each been given a blanket, they all curled up and went to sleep. All except Karla.

She lay awake listening to the men getting drunk and singing and laughing around their fire on the other side of the gorge, just beyond some rocks and brush. They'd run into more whiskey traders earlier, so if things went like the last time they'd traded scalps for whiskey, they'd probably all be sleeping like March lambs within a few hours. One man had been sent to guard the girls, but he'd apparently had a good portion of mescal over supper. Sitting against the high rock wall to Karla's right, he was having trouble keeping his head up. He took frequent sips from a small flask he'd produced from his boot well.

Lying on her side, curled beneath her single blanket, Karla watched him through slitted lids. Even before the other men had turned in for the night, the guard was sound asleep, chin on his chest, hat fallen onto the rifle resting across his thighs.

When both fires had burned down, and the men's snores competed with the coyotes' yammering, Karla rolled onto her left side. During the last time the men had untied her, she'd hidden the arrowhead up her right shirtsleeve. Jostling her arm until the arrow fell into her palm, she nudged Billie with her other elbow.

The girl groaned but remained asleep.

"Billie," Karla whispered, nudging her again, "wake up."

The girl's eyes opened, and she tensed with alarm. "What?"

"Shhh," Karla said. "I have a plan to get

us out of here. Are you awake enough to listen?"

Billie turned to face her, blinking. "What're you talking about?"

"I promised Marlene I'd get her back to her family, and I aim to keep my promise. Are you ready?"

"What . . . how . . . ?"

"I found an arrow sharp enough to cut through the ropes." Karla turned a glance at the guard, who had now rolled onto his right shoulder, snoring.

Turning to Billie again, and keeping her voice down, Karla said, "They're all drunk. Once we get all the girls untied, we can put bridles on the horses and ride out of here. If we're very quiet, I think we can do it."

Billie rose up on her left elbow. "How will we know where to go?"

"We'll head north until we find a ranch or a town . . . anyone who'll help us get back to the border." Karla spared another glance at the guard. "These drunks'll probably sleep until dawn. By the time they find us gone, we'll be a good five or six hours away."

Billie turned from Karla to regard the camp beyond the brush and the rocks. The fire had died down, but enough flickering light remained to silhouette the men slumped along the base of the rock wall.

Not far from the firelight, the towering walls enshrouded the gorge in chill velvety darkness.

Billie turned to Karla. "All right."

"Roll over," Karla said, "and extend your wrists as far back as you can."

As Billie rolled one way, giving her back and tied wrists to Karla, Karla rolled the other way, giving her own back and tied wrists to the girl. Sliding as close to Billie as she could, Karla took the girls hands in her own, traced the rope with her fingers, then took the arrowhead between the thumb and index finger of her right hand, and began sawing at the rope.

It was a long, tedious process, for the rope was stout, and the arrow wasn't as sharp as a good bowie or skinning knife, like those worn by the hardcases. Lying with her back to what she was cutting, with her hands tied, cut off the blood flow. Her fingers stiffened quickly and she had to clasp the arrowhead in her palm several times, and rest. Precious time was wasting. She hadn't thought it would take this long.

She was about two-thirds through the rope when the guard snorted suddenly. Karla had been staring at the ground as she worked, jaw tensed, but she lifted her gaze to the man now. He'd lifted his head and seemed to be looking this way. It was too dark for her to see him clearly, but she thought his mouth opened.

"I told you the money was good in that little bank," he grumbled thickly. "Didn't I tell you, boys?"

Karla lay still, clasping Billie's hands in her own to keep her quiet. Karla could hear her heart beating. She stared at the hardcase. A minute later, his head collapsed, and a half minute after that, his snores resumed, blending with the others on the other side of the canyon.

Karla went back to work on Billie's rope, and a minute later, her fingers stiff and swollen, she sawed through the last of the hemp strands. The rope gave, and Billie's wrists sprang free.

"You did it!" Billie whispered.

Karla relaxed her tired muscles, resting her head on the ground, catching her breath. "Now free me," she whispered to the girl behind her. "The arrow's in my hand."

Billie scrambled onto her knees and plucked the arrowhead from Karla's right palm. Billie placed one hand on Karla's shoulder and sawed at the rope with the other — choppy, uneven strokes. The knots were too tight for even the hardcases to work loose with their fingers; they always cut the rope. Billie grunted and gasped with effort, jerking Karla's shoulders back and forth. But since she had full use of her hands, it wasn't long before Karla felt the rope give.

Scrambling onto her knees, she ripped off the remaining rope from both wrists, then tugged and pulled and squeezed until she had her ankles free, as well. She squeezed Billie's arm. "I'll be right back."

"Where are you going?"

Silently, Karla stood and tiptoed over to the unconscious guard. She crouched beside him, placed her hand on the bone-handled knife poking up from a sheath on his right hip, and slowly slipped it out.

Holding the knife in both hands, she turned slowly and tiptoed back to Billie kneeling and watching her, the girl's wide eyes shadowed by the dying umber fire. Karla knelt and put the knife's sharp edge to the ropes tying Billie's ankles together. One flick of the knife, and Billie's feet were free.

"Let's free the rest of the girls," Karla whispered, rising.

She turned away from Billie, then turned quickly back. A shadow moved just behind the girl, a high-crowned hat taking shape in the dull light. Karla's blood turned to ice.

Before she could move or think or do anything, an arm snaked around her from behind.

A hand closed brusquely over her mouth, pinching off her wind, lifting her off her feet, and jerking her back, half carrying, half dragging her off down the canyon.

CHAPTER 18

Karla flailed with the knife until an arm smashed down on her wrist. Her hand opened, and the knife fell as she was pulled quickly backward, stumbling over rocks and shrubs. She fell and was dragged over sand and gravel, the bottoms of her feet and the backs of her heels rubbed raw.

She must have been carried sixty or seventy yards down the canyon before the man suddenly released her. She fell hard on her back, the air slammed from her lungs.

"Got yourself free, uh, pretty gringa?" the man said in a heavy Mexican accent, catching his breath. "Good. That makes less work for me and Weelis."

Karla was too out of breath to say anything. She looked back the way she'd come. A shadow moved toward her. Two figures, in fact — the man called Willis manhandling Billie the way Karla had been wrenched and dragged down the canyon. Willis had one arm around the girl's waist, his other hand cupped over her mouth.

Approaching, he twisted around and flung Billie down beside Karla, then brought his hat to his mouth, sucking a finger. "Little bitch bit me!"

Billie gasped and sobbed, her hair splayed across her face.

Gaining her breath at last, Karla rose up on her elbows and snarled at the Mexican, whom she'd heard called Pancho, "What do you think you're doing?"

Pancho flung his hat aside and grinned down at her, showing his pointed brown teeth buried within his thin, drooping mustaches. "Weelis and I decided we have gone without female companionship long enough."

With that, he chuckled and threw himself atop Karla, pinning her hands down with his own and nuzzling her neck. Karla recoiled from the oily, bristly feel of the man, and from the ripe stench of the mescal on his breath. Gritting her teeth, she struggled, scissoring her legs and trying to free her hands.

As she fought, she heard Billie struggling to her left, pleading and sobbing. Clothing ripped. Billie started to scream, but it was cut short by a hand on her mouth.

"Shut up, you little bitch," Willis growled at the girl. "One word of this to Edgar, and Pancho and I'll skin you both alive!"

Karla slipped her right hand out from under Pancho's left, and slapped the wiry Mexican hard across his face. Laughing, he grabbed her wrist, squeezing until she thought the bone was being pulverized, and slammed it back down in the gravel beside her head.

He was lowering his head once more to hers when he suddenly froze. Keeping his hand clamped down on hers, he jolted upright and looked around, listening.

"Weelis," he whispered.

Willis was too involved to reply until Pancho had called his name two more times. Willis raised his head from Billie's chest and turned to his cohort, frowning incredulously, his hair in his eyes.

Pancho opened his mouth to speak but stopped when something thrashed in the brush on the south side of the canyon, to Karla's right. Both men turned sharply that way. An instant later, Pancho released Karla's left hand, and slipped his revolver from his holster, thumbing back the hammer.

"What the hell was that?" Willis said, rising on his knees and unholstering his own pistol.

The brush on the other opposite of the canyon thrashed, as though something large were on the prod. Both men whipped their heads that way.

" 'Paches," Willis said, a trill in his voice. He stood, stumbling back a step. "Shit . . ."

"Madre Maria!" Pancho cried, standing over Karla and extending his pistol toward the right side of the canyon.

Karla turned her face to the ground and crossed her arms over her head as the bark of Pancho's revolver echoed like a cannon in the narrow cleft. The man fired again. Willis did, as well, both men firing until the chasm filled with one continuous roar, making Karla's ears ring and her nostrils fill with the rotten-egg smell of cordite.

The din died suddenly, punctuated by both gun hammers snapping on empty chambers.

"What the hell . . . ?" Willis whispered.

Karla lowered her arms and turned to look up at the two men. They stood ten feet away, back to back, facing opposite sides of the canyon. The darkness was relieved by only the few stars that shone between the towering rock walls. Billie lay huddled to

Karla's right, facedown, head buried in her arms.

On the right side of the canyon, the brush popped and rattled, as though someone were thrashing around with a stick.

"Sheet," Pancho muttered. "They're still there — reload!"

Both men had just begun ripping fresh shells from their cartridge belts when a gun popped on the right side of the canyon, the flash like a sudden lightning bolt lashing parallel to the ground.

"*Madre!*" Pancho cried, both knees buckling as he grabbed his left thigh.

Willis flipped opened his revolver's loading gate and tried shoving a bullet into a chamber. The bullet clicked against the cylinder and dropped from his shaking hands, plunking off his right boot toe.

The gun in the brush popped again.

Willis' right leg snapped back. The man grunted sharply and fell, clutching his knee and cursing.

Silence thickened, relieved only by the sighs and groans of the two wounded men shuffling around in the darkness before Karla, who lay on her side beside Billie, one hand on the girl's back.

For a time, she'd been certain she was about to die. Now she wasn't so certain. . . .

The brush on the right side of the canyon thrashed. A man chuckled. Karla turned from the wounded men to see a tall shadow move out from the canyon wall. The brush on the opposite side of the canyon crackled, and another shadow walked out to meet the first one in the canyon's center, where Pancho and Willis clutched their wounded limbs and rolled on their backs in agony.

"Does that hurt terribly, Pancho?" Edgar Bontemps asked. "It should." He slid his foot toward the wounded Mexican.

Pancho screamed. *"Ah, madre, please . . . !"*

Sensing what was coming, Karla closed her hands over Billie's ears and steeled herself, wincing.

"What have I told you men about playing with the girls? Huh, Willis? What have I told you about damaging the trade goods?"

"Please, Edgar," Willis said in a pinched voice. "Don't do this. You can't expect us to ride with these girls for days without tryin' to get a little. That ain't *reasonable.* It just ain't *reasonable."* He panted. "Oh, Lord. You blew out my *knee,* Edgar!"

The gun exploded again, flames stabbing down from Bontemps' silhouette. Willis screamed. It did not sound like a human scream at all, as it spiraled and echoed toward the canyon's rim, charging the darkness with an enervated fever.

"There!" the man raged. "I blew out the other!"

Willis cried and panted. He whimpered like a small child.

"Just 'cause you," Willis managed to squeak out accusingly, "just 'cause you can't take no pleasure . . . since the war . . ."

Another gun blast silenced him.

"And now for you, Pancho . . . a lesson to take to the next world."

"No, por favor!"

Pop! Pop!

Silence except the distant murmurs of the other men spilling out from the camp.

"Should I bury 'em, Edgar?" Dupree asked.

"No," Bontemps said. "Drag 'em back to camp so the others get a good look at what happens to those that fool with the merchandise." Walking away, he holstered his pistol and grumbled, "And tie those girls with the others."

Two days later, Mordecai Hawkins — chief wrangler for the Butterfield stage station at Benson, Arizona — halted his horse along a rocky saddle high in pine-clad Sonoran mountains. Holding his Henry rifle in his right hand, he leaned out over his left stirrup and scoured the ground with his gaze.

After a minute, Hawkins straightened, slammed his left fist down on his saddle horn so hard that the claybank spooked, flicking its ears and tossing its head. The old wrangler loosed a spiel of epithets that would have colored the cheeks of the woolliest St. Louis grogshop proprietor.

"What is it, Mr. Hawkins?" a woman said behind him.

The wrangler broke off the tirade midsentence and whipped around in his saddle, startled. "Uh . . . sorry, Mrs. Talon," the old wrangler said meekly. "Didn't hear ye ride up."

"Have we lost the trail again?" Louise Talon asked.

She sat a tall paint mare — a regal brown-eyed woman of early middle-age, with long cherry blond hair pulled back in a ponytail held fast with a bone clasp at the nape of her neck. She wore black gloves, a felt hat, a cream blouse that accented the full breasts and slender waist, and a belted wool skirt with a slit for riding astride.

Louise Talon had what Hawkins had heard described as classical beauty, with a prominent chin, straight nose, and salty Irish humor lines around her wide-set eyes, which shone like pennies at certain times of the day. Hawkins thought the woman could pass for an Irish queen, but she was no fainting Fianna. She had run the swing station at Benson since her husband, a freight contractor, died six years ago, leaving her with one swaybacked gelding and a file drawer swollen with unpaid bills.

At first, Hawkins had scoffed at working for a woman. But having seen Mrs. Talon fight off marauding Apaches and horse thieves with a Winchester rifle, in addition to cooking, cleaning, serving stage passengers, and tending an irrigated kitchen garden, he'd deemed her as tough or tougher than many of the men he'd once trapped with up along the Green River in Wyoming — high praise from an old hardtack frontiersman like Hawkins.

" 'Pears the rain washed it out," Hawkins told her with a faint edge of annoyance. "Why don't you wait here, give the horses a blow? I'll cross that creek yonder. See if I can cut the sign again in them trees."

Without waiting for her reply, he dismounted, handed her his reins and the packhorse's lead rope, then ambled down the gravelly hill tufted in short tough grasses with a sprinkling of blue and purple wildflowers. He crossed the creek and tramped along the pine-clad shoulder of the opposite hill, lowering his head to scour the ground with his gaze.

Finally, he hunkered down on his haunches. He took his Henry rifle in his left hand, removed the worn glove from his right, and ran his fingers over a shoe print clearly defined in the needle-flecked black dirt of the forest.

He probed the soil around and within the print the way a doctor would feel for a patient's pulse.

A crow cawed in the tree crowns. Closer by, a black squirrel berated Hawkins from a rotten nook in a lightning-split lodgepole.

Ignoring the din, the old wrangler straightened. He removed his broad-brimmed hat, ran his hands through thinning salt-and-pepper hair combed back from a prominent widow's peak, and peered along the shoulder of the hill, following the tracks with his gray-eyed gaze.

Finally, snugging the hat back down on his head, its thong hanging free beneath his chin, Hawkins turned and ambled back the way he had come. He waded the stream and approached the three horses and the woman waiting for him on the other side.

"It's right where I figured it would be, ma'am," Hawkins said as he slid his Henry into his saddle boot. "The forest kept the

237

rain off it. Looks like they crossed the stream and rode along the shoulder of the hill yonder."

"They're avoiding the main trails again."

"Looks that way. Cautious son o' bitches, pardon my French."

"How far ahead?"

Hawkins took the reins from her and swung up onto his claybank. "I'd say about two days, ma'am. Maybe three. Even where the tracks are protected from the weather, they've disintegrated some."

"Damn," Louise said. "I was hoping we were gaining on them."

Hawkins heeled the claybank forward, tugging on the lead rope attached to the steeldust packhorse. "It's gonna be tough catchin' up to those skanks. They been through this country more than once, know it well, and what's more, they know where they're headed. All we can do is follow, read their sign . . . where we can *find* sign."

They'd been on the trail for the past week and a half, since Billie Brennan, the girl who worked for Mrs. Talon at the swing station, didn't return from doing laundry down at the creek one afternoon. When Mordecai had gone to check on her, he'd found the laundry strewn across the brush and in the water, and the prints of a dozen horses. Not barefoot horses, like the ones Indians rode, but horses, like the ones white men rode.

Word was out that Edgar Bontemps' crew of slave-trading scalp hunters was working the country.

Mordecai had saddled a horse and followed the slavers' trail, slowly arcing south toward Mexico, till it was too dark to see. He'd returned to the swing station to find Mrs. Talon standing before the cabin's lighted windows, hands on her hips, waiting. He'd ridden up to her and, in response to the question in her brown eyes, slowly shook his head.

"I'll pack provisions." Turning on a heel, the woman headed inside. "We'll ride at first light."

"Mrs. Tal—"

"That girl's like a daughter to me, Mordecai," she'd said, swinging back around to face him, her hourglass figure silhouetted by the lantern-lit windows behind her. "I intend to get her back. I'll *buy* her back from those savages, if I have to."

Now Hawkins shook his head as he urged the claybank into the stream, then up the bank on the other side, and up the hill beyond, following the fading tracks of nearly two dozen shod horses. "We're just lucky we ain't run into bandits yet, or worse," he grumbled half under his breath.

Urging her horse up the hill behind the plodding packhorse, through the forest of columned sun and shadow, Louise stared at the old wrangler's slouched shoulders and the back of his sun-cracked vest. "You think I'm wrong, going after them?"

Hawkins didn't turn to her. "I don't think you're *wrong*, necessarily, ma'am. I think it would've been *better* if we'd waited till I could throw together a *posse*, track the scallawags with a bit more *fightin'* force."

"Forming a posse might've taken a week or more, spread out the way the ranches are around here. We know we can't depend on the lawmen or the Army."

Hawkins conceded the point with a nod. "I'm just wonderin' what we're gonna do once we've caught up to this bunch."

Mrs. Talon's voice betrayed strained patience. "We're going to *buy* Billie *back*."

"I ain't sure five hundred dollars is gonna do it, ma'am."

"Then we'll *take* her back . . . one way or another."

Hawkins sighed and said without enthusiasm, "Yes, ma'am."

"Mr. Hawkins, you are an infuriating old pessimist!" Louise reined the mare off the trail, overtaking the packhorse and Hawkins' claybank. "If we're going to make any headway at all, we'd better pick up the pace."

She galloped the mare out ahead of him, over the brow of the hill and into a grassy hollow between slopes. A big magpie flew up from a single gnarled cedar left of the trail, screeching.

Hawkins stared after the woman, shaking his head. "We been pushin' hard enough. These horses need a rest." She'd dropped from view, but he scowled and raised his chin to add, "These're the only horses we got — best treat 'em right!"

Later that day, they came upon two bodies in a narrow canyon, about fifty yards from where others had camped. Both men had been shot first in the legs, then finished off with bullets to the head. Hawkins and Mrs. Talon stared down at them. Scavengers had been having a feast.

"Look at that," Hawkins said. "Take you a good look. Men who would do that to each other would —"

Hooves thudded behind him. He turned to see Mrs. Talon galloping off down the canyon, following the outlaws' path.

Hawkins cursed, dug a tobacco twist from his jeans pocket, and angrily bit off a sizable chunk. Chewing, he stared after the woman,

her back defiantly straight, her saddlebags
and rifle boot flapping like wings.

Hawkins cursed again. It wasn't easy
working for a woman who had bigger *ca-
jones* than he had.

CHAPTER 19

The morning after the two privates had tried to perforate his hide, Tom Navarro rose early, dressed quickly, and bid farewell to Sullivan, Ward, and Bryson. Riding through the fort's open front gates, he saluted the two sentries and gigged the horse into a lope, the dun packhorse following on its ten-foot lead.

The morning began desert-fresh, but the sun rose, blistering, the mountains receding and cowering behind a brassy haze. Soon the Bar-V segundo's new denims and chambray shirt were sweat-stained, and his broad-brimmed black hat was coated with a fine sheen of adobe-colored dust. The only old accoutrements he had were his gun belt and .44, the undershot Justins on his feet, and the red bandanna knotted around his neck.

Navarro preferred familiar mounts for treks into strange country, but his own horse had probably either been taken by the same scalp hunters who'd nabbed Karla, or was still wandering the cuts around Gray Rock, foraging and looking for water. The bay stepped out smartly, and as he wended his way into the rough country near the peak, the bay as well as the dun proved sure-footed and deep-bottomed.

Good stayers both, and they seemed forgiving of long stretches without water. Not bad for Army remounts, which, like most soldiers, often proved overtrained and underexperienced.

The trek back to Gray Rock proved futile. The slavers' sign had been obliterated by isolated rain squalls, wind, and animals. All that remained atop the mountain was dry horse apples, dirt-caked carnage, and the sickly sweet fetor of death.

The Army had buried the bodies in graves too shallow to thwart predators. Bloody limbs and viscera were strewn about the dust and rocks.

Without tracks, he had no choice but to head south and try to cut the scalp hunters' trail somewhere along the way, or hope to hear word of where the renegades might be headed.

He camped at the butte's base, having a few drinks that night in honor of Dallas and

Charlie, noting how lonely it felt without either or both at his side. He started south so early the next morning that a mountain lion was still keening and whining atop the peak above him, probably warning wolves or coyotes away from its breakfast.

Two nights later, Navarro rode into Tombstone amid the patter of tin-panny music and the blasts of jubilant gunfire, soiled doves beckoning from cathouse balconies. After stabling his horses, he consulted Sheriff Johnny Behan, who offered no information about a slaver named Bontemps, which didn't surprise Navarro. Johnny Behan was better known for gambling and carousing than for fogging owlhoot trails.

Not wanting trouble from long-memoried enemies or prospective gunslicks, Navarro drank and ate alone in his Russ House hotel room, then slept with his pillow over his head to blot out the noise from the street below his room, including fiddle music and several bursts of gunfire.

Up with the dung shovelers the next dawn, he saddled his grained and curried mounts, and followed the river courses into Sonora. Combing such vast, rugged terrain was akin to cleaning a buffalo rug one hair at a time. Sitting a ridge and gazing over the thrusting barrancas and pillared rim-rocks stretched out between distant, blue snow-mantled peaks, he felt overwhelmed with futility.

He rode on, however. He would not give up his search until he'd either found Karla or settled her score.

He'd been scouring river basins, inquiring in little towns and at farms for two weeks, learning nothing about slave traders or Yanqui girls. Then, one morning, in the sandy creekbed in which he'd camped the night before, he came upon the sign of four shod horses.

One of the track sets caught his eye.

There was something in the horse's gate, shoe fit, or nail pattern that seemed familiar. He'd tracked many horses over the years, and thousands of prints had been seared into his brain. Maybe he only imagined something familiar about this set, but he followed them, anyway.

He'd trailed the four riders for two hours, and was plodding along a deep-rutted cart trail, with an alkali flat on his left, when a shot sounded to his right and slightly behind. He reined the bay to a halt and, shucking his Winchester from the saddle boot, whipped his head toward the sound.

A rocky ridge heaved a hundred feet off

246

the trail, paralleling it. As he studied the formation, three more rifle shots rang out. They'd seemed muffled, as though fired from inside a building.

A faint yell rose on the breeze.

Navarro reined the bay to the base of the ridge, dismounted, and tied both horses to a spindly shrub. His Winchester in his right hand, he climbed the slope, weaving around rocks and yucca. Removing his hat, he hunkered down behind a cracked, cart-sized boulder at the ridge's brow, and peered into the shallow draw on the other side.

A sun-bleached adobe stood against the draw's opposite ridge, which shelved gently back, spiked with yucca, short grass, and mesquite shrubs. Several brown and cream-colored goats milled along the rocks, pulling at the brush.

Inside the cabin, another shot barked, the slug blasting open a shutter on the other side of the house. The ricochet sliced off a rock with a metallic zing, puffing dust and narrowly missing a goat, which craned its head to stare at the bullet-scarred rock for several seconds before turning again to graze.

Ignoring the gunfire, Navarro turned his attention to the brush corral, where four horses and a mule stood statue-still, facing the rear fence and the spindly cottonwood partially shading it. Two horses were duns, one a black barb, the other a white Arabian.

Navarro stared at the Arabian, his spine tensing, his flinty blue eyes keen.

He had little doubt it was Karla's horse. Not many Mexicans could afford a white Arabian. What it was doing here, he had no idea. Maybe these people knew nothing about the slavers. Maybe they did.

"Santa Madre!" a voice cried within the weathered adobe walls.

A shot barked.

Laughter rose.

Navarro had just shifted his gaze from Karla's horse to the cabin when the front door opened. A man came half stumbling, half running into the yard. He tripped over a rock and dropped to a knee — a lanky Mexican in pajama bottoms but no shirt or hat. A burly man stepped through the door, staggering, a bottle in his right hand.

He extended the bottle at the man on the ground and berated the skinny gent in Spanish, warning him to hurry or he'd kill his brother. The stout man in the doorway, wearing a dark brown poncho with bandoliers crossed on his chest, turned drunkenly. He bounced off the doorframe, then disappeared back inside the adobe, leaving the door open behind him.

Peering around the rock, Navarro watched the slender man climb to his feet, and limp across the yard to the covered wagon parked before the corral. He reached through the back flap and pulled three bottles out of the wagon. Cradling the bottles carefully in his arms, he hurried back to the cabin and disappeared through the door.

Another shot erupted inside, followed by the sound of breaking glass . . . followed by angry shouts and another pistol blast.

Navarro studied the draw, arranging a plan for approaching the cabin without being seen. He stood, retraced his steps down the ridge, stubbornly refusing to limp on his healing right leg, then made sure his horses were both tied fast. Rifle in hand, he left the horses tied to the shrubs and scrambled along the ridge's base, heading east.

After a hundred yards, he climbed the ridge again and scrambled down the other side, then along a shallow ravine that led around behind the cabin, to the ridge on the opposite side.

He climbed halfway to the ridge's crest and hunkered down in the rocks behind the adobe, amid the goats. The animals stopped foraging to eye the stranger warily.

From here, Navarro had a clean view of

the cabin's rear. There were a door and a window on this end, but mesquite logs and brush had been piled high around the window. If he approached the adobe from the southeast corner, he should be able to make the hovel's rear door without being seen.

That was what he did, ignoring the pain in his right calf. He pressed his back to the hot, bright adobe wall left of the rear door hammered together from thin planks and cheap nails.

Inside, a gun continued its intermittent bark, followed by raucous laughter. Whoever had come calling on the poor goat herders was having one hell of a time — at the goat herders' expense. Probably whiskey peddlers or scalp hunters. The wagon he'd seen parked beside the corral had looked like those run by that brand of border tough, as thick in this country as flies on a fresh dog plop.

Laughter and pleas spewed from the adobe walls and windows, punctuated by pistol shots.

Navarro stole around the building's northeast corner and sidled up to a chest-high window in the north wall. Crouching, he slid a quick glance into the room, where six men and one young woman milled. Four of the men, sitting at a small wooden table, were tangle haired, bushy bearded, and armed with prominently displayed guns and knives. Bottles, glasses, and coins littered the table.

One man held an Indian-dark, round-faced woman on his lap and was nuzzling her neck and squeezing her breasts through a loose-fitting doeskin shift. The woman sat stiffly enduring the assault, looking away from the man, her face taut with disgust and anger.

Navarro's glance was so quick that he wasn't sure what the other two at the table were doing, but the third was aiming a Merwin and Hulbert .44 at a gray-haired Mexican man tied to a chair before a window on the other side of the room. The man wore no shirt, and his lean, muscular arms and birdlike chest bore the scars of a dozen old knife wounds.

An empty, dented vegetable tin stood atop the man's gray head. The man aiming the .44 — his elbow propped on the table, head lolling drunkenly — was the hombre who'd sent the other goat herder out to fetch more whiskey.

The young man who'd done the fetching was crouched before the stone fireplace in the back wall, stirring beans in a bubbling pot with an air of desperation and casting wild-eyed glances over his right shoulder. His black hair hung in his eyes, one of which was noticeably lower than the other.

Navarro slid his head back from the window as the older Mexican tied to the chair screamed in Spanish, "Please . . . in the name of all the sain—"

The .44 barked. A tinny thud, followed by a squeal. Shrill laughter rose.

In Spanish, a man at the table yelled, "Miguel, that's another centavo you owe me, you son of a three-legged nanny goat!"

Navarro inched his right eye once more across the window's edge. From this pinched angle, he could see only the right side of the room. The gray-haired man screamed and cursed and fought against the ropes tying his hands behind the chair back. His right temple shone with a three-inch line of bright red blood. The can lay on the floor behind his chair. He was as angry now as frightened, and his pleas were laced with curses salty enough to make the Devil take note.

Navarro slid his head back, dropped to his knees, crawled forward along the wall below the window, then rose and stalked around the adobe's northwest corner and sidled up to the open front door. He raised the Winchester in both hands.

Just beyond the door, the gray-haired man was pleading for his life while the man with the gun ordered the cook to replace the can.

One of the other traders laughed as though at the funniest joke he'd ever heard. The girl squealed and struggled, the chair creaking as though it were about to break.

The smell of fresh tortillas, frijoles, and gunsmoke wafted through the door beside Navarro's right shoulder. He waited, listening. A chair scraped back. Boots scuffed across the hard-packed floor, moving toward him.

When Tom heard them moving back toward the table, he waited until the gray-haired man began pleading again in earnest, then jacked a round into his Winchester's breech. He turned through the door and snapped the Winchester up. He drew a bead on the big man taking rheumy-eyed aim at the older man with the can on his head, and fired.

Blood burst in a fine spray from the big man's shoulder. He flew back in his chair, dropping the pistol, his beard-enshrouded lips making a broad "O" as he raged.

Two of the other three men had been sitting in a near-catatonic state of drunkenness while the fourth pawed the round-faced woman. Now, seeing Tom burst into the room, the woman howled. The man whose lap she adorned bolted up and forward, throwing the woman to the floor in a squealing heap and clawing his pistol off the table.

Tom yelled, "Stop!"

When the man kept coming toward him, raising the pistol and thumbing back the hammer, Tom drilled a round through his left thigh, just above the knee. The man dropped to that knee, his own screams joining those of the big man as he rolled onto his left hip, dropping the pistol and wrapping both hands around his leg.

Ejecting the smoking shell casing, Navarro took another step forward and raised his rifle to the other two men at the table. One froze with his right hand on his right hip. The other sat to his left, both hands lying flat on the table, fingers splayed and digging into the wood as if to gouge a sliver. Both stared at Tom fearfully, their jaws hanging.

The man on the floor before the table snapped his gun off the floor, cursing. He raised it toward Tom. Tom dropped the Winchester's barrel and shot him through the right temple, spraying the floor with blood, brains, and bone.

Navarro jacked another shell and raised

the rifle in the general direction of the two men sitting frozen behind the table. "You hombres want daisies growin' out of your jaws, or do you think we can palaver like civilized folk?"

The man with his hands splayed on the table squinted at Tom and grumbled thickly in Spanish, "What do you want to talk about, amigo?"

The big man lay propped against the far wall, clutching his bloody shoulder and breathing hard as he stared at Navarro. Tom glanced right. The man who'd been cooking was now on both knees before the fire, his arms around the woman who lay at his feet. Her round eyes in her round, dark face regarded Tom cautiously.

"You own this place?" Tom asked the young man who'd been cooking.

"*Sí.*" He looked at the man tied to the chair behind Tom. "With my brother."

"That your wife?"

"*Sí.*"

"Untie your brother. Then all of you go outside and get yourselves cleaned up."

"Amigo," said the Mexican with his hands on the table, lifting them and shrugging reasonably, "we are only settling a debt. Vincente and Alonzo bought whiskey from us last month on credit. We came for our

255

money, and they didn't have it. . . ."

Navarro glanced at the young man again, jerked his head at the gray-haired man. When the young man had untied his older brother, and they and the girl had gone outside, Navarro walked over to the table, Winchester extended from his hip. He looked at both drunk Mexicans sitting before him, still frozen in their chairs, bloodshot eyes rolling around in their sockets.

"Toss your guns in that corner. All of 'em — hideouts included."

When the two men at the table had tossed five pistols into the corner behind the door, Navarro walked over to the man lying behind them. He removed a pistol from his cartridge belt, one from a shoulder holster, and a bowie from a boot sheath. He tossed the weapons into the corner with the others, then regarded the three whiskey traders coldly. They stared back at him in kind.

"Who belongs to that white Arabian out in the corral yonder?" Navarro asked.

When none said a word, Navarro approached the table. He swung the rifle back and forward, laying the barrel soundly against the head of the man on the left. The man was nearly thrown from his chair. He clutched his ear, drew the hand away, and looked at the blood smeared on his fingers. "Son of a whore!"

"I'm gonna ask you one more time, and I better get a straight answer. Who bel—"

"It's his!" cried the man with the torn ear, jerking his head back to indicate the man lying against the wall.

The big man lay glaring up at Tom with flared nostrils. Blood puddled the floor beneath his shoulder.

"Where'd you get it?" Tom asked.

The wounded man shrugged his good shoulder. *"Cabelludo cazadores."*

"Where'd you run into these scalpers?"

"Rio Bavispe."

"Which way were they heading?"

"They head south. Traded the horse for whiskey."

"They have Yanqui girls, gringas, with 'em?"

The wounded man nodded slowly. "They have gringas." He made a lewd gesture and spread a grin. *"Bonita gringas."*

A half hour later, when Navarro had learned the direction Bontemp's men were headed, he sent the whiskey traders off in their wagon.

He left their guns with the goat herders

and headed south. Karla's Arabian followed
on a lead line.

Chapter 20

Two hours after good dark, Bontemps'
slavers herded their captives single-file
through high, pinion-studded buttes and
deep-scored canyons. Hooves clipped rocks,
saddles squeaked, bridle chains jingled.
Gassing to kill time, the men snorted occasional laughs and were shushed by Bontemps, wary of Indians or bandits having
spied the female flesh.

They'd been riding ten hours since sunup
when the renegade leader called a halt at
the lip of a wide, deep valley. Karla lifted
her head from a doze, and glanced below,
where stars shimmered off a stream curving
at the valley's bottom. Loud booms sounded
in the distance, like giant hammers pulver-
izing rock.

"Home, sweet home." Bontemps rode
among the girls clumped at the lip of the
ridge, slumped in their saddles, hands tied
to the horns. "Boys, give our girls a long

drink of water. I want 'em lookin' fresh for Sister Mary Francis."

"You got it, Edgar," one of the men said. He and two others kneed their mounts up to the girls and held canteens to their parched lips.

Karla was too fatigued to be thirsty, but she drank the warm water, anyway. Strange as the name sounded, she didn't ask who this Sister Mary Francis was. She was too dispirited to care about anything except curling into a ball and drifting into dreamless sleep.

When she and the other girls had finished drinking, Bontemps turned his horse to the ridge, throwing an arm forward. "Let's go down and turn our booty in, then see about some women and panther juice!"

The others whooped and yelled as, tugging and kicking at the girls' mounts, they followed their leader over the ridge and down the valley's steep wall. Karla leaned back in her saddle to keep from being thrown over the horn. Her horse followed Billie's, switchbacking along the slope toward the lights of a town twinkling at the bottom, spread out along both sides of the stream.

When the trail finally leveled and widened into a road, Billie glanced at Karla riding up on her right. It was too dark for Karla to see much of the girl's face, but she sensed Billie's terror. Her own fear sparked beneath her fatigue, her heartbeat quickening, nudging away her dolor.

What awaited her and the other girls at trail's end?

The eager slavers urged their mounts into a jog as they headed toward the lights clumped ahead along the stream. They met several heavy wagons, with wheels taller than most men, clattering over the potholes. As they passed, the bearded wagoneers shouted jubilant greetings while raking their glances across Karla and the other girls and yelling bawdy epithets to Bontemps' men, who responded in kind.

"Nice bunch you got there, Edgar," a driver called as the group traced a slow bend in the trail, passing an old mine portal yawning from a slope. "A very nice bunch indeed!"

"Glad you're pleased, Aldo!" Bontemps returned, waving his battered bowler.

The procession passed several shacks and corrals buried in the rocks and sage, then split two lines of adobes and false-fronted clapboard establishments throwing lantern light onto boardwalks and the dung-littered street.

Pianos clattered behind brightly lit saloon windows. Two dogs ran out from an alley to bark and nip at the horses. Men standing along the boardwalks — broad, bearded men in cloth caps and low-heeled boots and suspenders — held out their drinks and cheered.

"Nice to see white girls again, Edgar!" one man shouted in a heavy German accent. "Ole Chris here has started lookin' as purty as a Frisco dove. Ha!"

Karla's horse followed Billie's around a dry fountain. A few seconds later, she found herself sitting before a vast stone church standing dark against the sky. There was a seven-foot-high wall around the church, with several saddled horses tied to hitch-racks.

Beyond a wrought-iron gate, a man holding a rifle rose from a chair. The man opened a door and disappeared inside the church. A minute later, the door opened again. A stocky woman in a long dress stepped out, silhouetted by the lantern light behind her. The first man and two others, with pistols on their hips, stepped out behind her.

The three men dwarfed the woman in height but not in girth. She paused before the open door. Dark hair was piled atop her head. A cigarette smoldered in her right hand. She took a puff and blew out the smoke. Then she and the three guards moved down the flagstone path and out the squeaky gate.

"It's about time you're gettin' in," the woman said to Bontemps, who was sitting his horse ahead of the others.

"Nice to see you, too, Sister Mary Francis," the renegade leader returned, his voice thick with irony.

The stubby woman took another puff from her cigarette as she strolled before Karla and the other girls still sitting their horses, dusty hair hanging in their eyes. While the three guards waited in the shadows of the adobe wall, she strolled back over to Bontemps, planted her fists on her hips, and glared up at the man.

"I told you not to run the damn fat off of 'em. They're skinnier than the last bunch you brought in. These Germans and Micks like their women with a little tallow. I done told you that, Edgar."

"It's a damn long ride, Sister."

"And what is that smell?"

"What smell?"

Sniffing, Sister Mary Francis turned to the horse of the man sitting just behind and to the right of Bontemps. Scowling, she pointed her cigarette at the scalps hanging from the saddle. "Jesus H. Christ!" the woman exclaimed, her shrill voice echoing off the church's stone walls. "You took scalps again!"

Bontemps said nothing.

"I thought I told you not to take any more scalps when you were trailin' girls. You know how hard it is to get that stink from a girl's hair? The miners may not mind, but the high-stakes gamblers don't pay for stink. They getta whiff o' that just once, and that's all they smell — *ever!*"

"Mr. Ettinger pays just about as much for scalps as he does for wimen."

"I told *him* like I told *you.*"

"Well, he didn't tell me," Bontemps said, leaning out from his saddle and giving the woman a caustic glare. "And *he's* who I work for. Not *you.*"

Sister Mary Francis balled her fists at her sides and returned the renegade's glare. Karla could hear her labored breath, but the woman said nothing.

"Come on, boys," Bontemps said, reining his horse around. "Let's get us a drink."

When the eight slavers had turned back toward the saloons, their horses clip-clopping down the hard-packed street, Sister Mary Francis stood scrutinizing the eight captive girls, fists on her hips. Her cigarette smoldered in her right hand. Flanking her was the man with the rifle. He was tall and balding, with curly hair tufted above his ears.

"Lyle, cut these girls free of their saddles."

"You got it, Sister Mary Francis," the man said slowly, his words slightly garbled.

As he plucked a knife from his belt and ambled over to the girl on Karla's right, the stout woman announced, "I'm Sister Mary Francis. You girls have been brought here to pleasure the miners who work for Mr. Ettinger. Pleasure means whatever they want you to do, you do it. You don't do it willingly and act like you're enjoyin' it, you'll get your skinny asses sent down to Hermosillo or Mexico City." Sister Mary Francis nodded. "Take my word, you'll like it a lot less down there."

The man with the knife had cut Karla's ropes, then stepped over to Billie. Stiffly, Karla climbed down from the saddle and turned to the woman called Sister Mary Francis, rage steeling her spine and making her voice tremble. "Who are you? And what in *hell* gives you the right to bring us here against our wills?"

The broad woman turned to her. As far as Karla could tell in the dim light, the wom-

265

an's face was expressionless. She stepped toward Karla. "You got spunk. I like that."

"You didn't answer my question."

The woman's right hand came up so fast that Karla didn't see it before it connected with her right cheek — an ear-ringing blow that knocked the girl back against her sweat-lathered horse. Her legs were so weak from the long ride that her knees buckled. She fell, clutching her cheek. Hating herself for showing weakness, she sobbed.

"I like spunk, but I'll have no truck with backtalk." Sister Mary Francis raised her voice to the others. "Let that be a lesson to you all. You'll be treated right if you do your jobs. But I don't cotton to backtalk. Never have, never will." She turned to the three armed men ushering the other girls out in front of the horses. "Bring 'em on upstairs so we can get 'em cleaned up and in bed."

When the woman turned and disappeared into the courtyard, Billie appeared at Karla's side. "You all right, Karla?"

Karla nodded as Billie helped her stand. Her right cheek was aflame but the ringing in her ears was subsiding. The stout woman packed a punch. "I'll be all right." Her voice was thin, quaking. She had to get ahold of herself.

"You two shut up and get movin'," one of

the armed men growled, taking both Karla's and Billie's arms in his big hands and shoving the girls forward.

One man led the way through the wrought-iron gate and into the stone courtyard, while the two others brought up the rear, making sure none of the girls broke and ran. A few seconds later, Karla found herself standing beside Billie inside the church.

Only it was no longer a church.

All the pews had been replaced with square tables and Windsor chairs. Here and there, plush sofas and coffee tables had been arranged in isolated, intimate sitting areas complete with brass spittoons, silver ash trays, and bear, wolf, or panther rugs. Bawdy paintings lined the thick walls between the arched stained-glass windows. Chinese lanterns hung from square-hewn joists and the low wainscoted ceiling.

"Get movin', honey," urged one of the men behind Karla, giving her a brusque shove.

As she moved forward, following Billie and the man with the rifle, she turned her gaze left, where a black-haired, black-mustached man in a dove gray uniform sat on a dark blue couch, a young girl on his knee. The brown-eyed redhead, dressed in a low-cut cream gown, was leaning back against the man's right shoulder, nuzzling his neck and fingering the gold buttons on his tunic.

When he'd spied Karla and the other captives moving down the room's center, he glanced at the other men in the room and yelled something in Spanish. Several others cheered and clapped. Eyes glassy from drink, the man with the redhead raised the goblet in his right hand. *"Salud!"*

The redhead turned to Karla and smiled, then turned her head sideways on the man's chest and resumed talking in his ear and playing with his buttons.

Karla regarded the back of the room, where the original church altar served as a bar, with heavy plank extensions winging out from both sides. Several other dark, uniformed men stood at the bar, drinking, smoking, and regarding the girls lewdly as they turned and followed the man with the rifle up a red-carpeted staircase.

Karla was so tired and sore from riding that, with each step, her legs shrieked with pain.

"Two to a room," the man with the rifle said dully, when they'd all reached the dimly lit, second-story hall.

Doors opened off each side. Kerosene

268

bracket lamps, shaded by deep red glass to make the hall even dimmer, guttered and smoked, revealing the shag carpet runner beneath their feet. The girls just stood there, hesitating. Like Karla, they sensed that once inside those rooms, they were doomed.

"Two to a room, damn it," boomed one of the two men marching up the stairs. "Come on, pair off, damn it! We ain't got all night."

A door opened to Karla's right, and she was thrust inside. Because Billie had been standing beside her, Billie was thrust into the same room.

"Strip down and get ready for baths," ordered the man, closing the door behind them. From the outside, a key clicked in the lock.

On the door hung a small placard:

GENTLEMAN, PLEASE USE THE SPITTOON AND ASH TRAY.

Wearily, Karla shuttled her gaze from the door, looking around the room, with its big brass bed, mirrored dresser, washstand, and armoire. Small containers of face paint sat in a silver tray atop the dresser. There were two chairs positioned on either side of a small table, and a scroll-backed fainting couch along the wall right of the door. A copper tub lay on the floor near the bed and a glistening brass spittoon. On the bed itself were towels and nightgowns.

Karla turned back to Billie standing beside her. The girl regarded her fearfully, lips trembling. Billie clutched Karla's hand. "What are we gonna do?"

Saying nothing, Karla gently led Billie over to the fainting couch, and pulled the girl down beside her. She wrapped her arm around Billie's shoulders, drew the girl to her breast, and held her as she sobbed.

"I don't know," Karla said, staring at the floor. "I'll think of something."

A few minutes later, several Chinese boys in dungarees and rope sandals hauled water to the four rooms occupied by the captive girls. The copper tubs were filled. Sister Mary Francis supervised the baths, letting no girl leave the tub before the death smell had been scrubbed away.

The smirking guards were allowed to watch from the open doorways.

Later, when Karla and Billie were in bed, the lock clicked. The door opened. Karla lifted her head. Five shadowy figures entered, silhouetted by the hall light behind them.

Two grabbed her and held her down. Her heart pounded; she gasped for air against her fear. Two other men grabbed Billie, who squealed against their grips.

The third man leaned over Billie. Light from the hall reflected on the syringe in his hands.

"You sons of bitches!" Karla spat.

When Billie had collapsed, the man walked around the bed to Karla. She tried to fight them, but they held her fast to the bed.

"Bastard!" she cried as the needle moved toward her.

The needle stabbed her flesh, burned as the liquid spurted into a vein. The men held her down until her muscles relaxed. Her head spun once. She had a falling sensation.

Her head hit the pillow, and everything went black.

CHAPTER 21

In the late afternoon, Tom Navarro descended the ridge of a deep canyon about a mile or so wide, with a creek running down the middle and sheathed by ironwood, paloverde, and desert hackberry shrubs.

It was dry country he was traversing, heading generally southeast, and he hadn't run across a water source since early yesterday afternoon.

Near the canyon's bottom, he found a game path. He followed the trace around several rocky scarps and cedar snags, gradually descending the slope as he headed for the cottonwoods lined out along the cutbank. Rounding a hillock and hearing water, he turned to the creek on his left.

He looked away, then turned back quickly, jerking the dun's reins taut, his right hand dropping automatically to the butt of his .44.

He left the gun in its holster as he peered

over the cutbank. In the dark water dappled with sunlight filtering through the dusty cottonwoods, just this side of a low beaver dam, stood a naked woman. A medium-height, slender woman — tanned and full-breasted, with long red hair dripping wet and falling down her shoulders. Crouching, she was scooping water over her breasts.

Tom wasn't a man to ogle naked women he happened upon out in the wild. But he hadn't expected to see her here, and since she was only about fifteen yards away, it was really too late to turn his horses around and disappear without being seen or heard.

He'd opened his mouth to address the woman, but before he could get any words out, she glanced up. When she saw him, her eyes snapped wide. With a shocked exclamation, she straightened, crossed her arms over her chest, and stumbled back in the water, nearly falling.

"Didn't mean to intrude," Navarro grumbled, throwing up his right hand and turning his eyes discreetly away. "I didn't know —"

A gun hammer clicked.

He slanted his gaze back to the woman. She'd grabbed a pistol from the clothes and the blue-striped Indian blanket piled atop the embankment on her left, and was aiming it now at Tom while covering her chest with a red plaid shirt.

"Who are you and what in the *hell* do you want?"

Before Tom could answer, the woman glanced over her right shoulder and called, "Mr. Hawkins!"

When she turned back to Navarro, she raised the pistol — an octagonal-barreled Thomas .45 revolver — even higher, aimed at Tom's head. Presently, a man appeared, jogging around a bluff on the other side of the stream. He was ten or fifteen years older than Tom. Bearded, stoop-shouldered, and bandy-legged, with a weathered hide vest over a smoke-blackened buckskin shirt, duck pants, and an ancient pistol belt. Holding a revolver up near his shoulder, he halted on the lip of the bank, frowning across the creek at Navarro.

"This man's been watching me bathe," the woman said. "A bandit, no doubt. Or worse."

"Some would say worse," Tom said, "but I didn't see you until it was too late to do much but apologize and turn around. Since you haven't seen fit to let me do either, why don't you put away that blunderbuss and let me introduce myself?"

The woman's eyes softened ever so slightly

and she lowered the pistol while still keeping it aimed in Navarro's direction.

"I'm Tom Navarro," he said. "Segundo for the Vannorsdell Bar-V brand, northeast of Tucson."

"Hell, I knew it was you!" said the oldster on the bank. He glanced at the woman and lowered his own revolver to his side, pointing with his other hand. "Why, that's 'Taos Tommy,' the gunslick and Army tracker!"

"A gunslick?"

"It's okay, ma'am," the old man assured her. "He's never been known to shoot a man in cold blood."

Tom glanced at the oldster. "Have we met?"

"No, I don't reckon we ever have. But I was in Taos, muleskinnin' for a freight outfit, that day you acquired the name. Those two deputies had it comin', though, I'll give ye that. They'd been raisin' hob with the locals for months and it weren't gettin' no better." He paused, smiling with admiration. "Where you headed? If you don't mind me askin'."

"Perhaps we could continue this conversation elsewhere . . ." said the woman, sliding sarcastic glances between the two men. The light glowed crimson in her wet red hair as she hunkered low in the water and held the shirt to her chest.

"You're welcome to join us fer coffee," the man said. Jerking a thumb over his right shoulder, he added, "Our camp's back here, under the cottonwoods, well hidden from both ridges, good water and grass for the horses."

It was only about four thirty, with several hours of good light left. Tom hadn't planned to hole up until sunset. A cup of coffee wouldn't hurt, however. The horses were also ready for a rest. Besides, the woman was handsome, and he couldn't help wonder what she and the codger were doing out here.

The old man said, "There's a ford up yonder, on the other side of the dam."

With an acknowledging grunt, Tom gigged the bay forward along the game path, the dun packhorse and the Arabian following, swishing their tails at the blackflies milling about the water. He tried to keep his eyes off the woman, but when he'd passed her still standing in the creek, he glanced back over his left shoulder.

Yes, a handsome woman, in her mid- to late-thirties, he figured. Still covering herself with the shirt and the gun, she'd quarter-turned to face him, offering as little bare flesh as possible, in water reaching only to her thighs. Flushing, Navarro turned back around.

When he'd crossed the creek and staked his horses in the grass along the bank, he walked over to the strangers' fire and accepted a cup of coffee from the old man.

"Mordecai Hawkins is my handle." He poured a cup of the oily, black brew for himself. "Hostler for the Butterfield station at Benson. Mrs. Talon, she runs the place."

"Louise Talon," the woman said as she approached through the cottonwoods, taking long, graceful strides. She was dressed now in the red plaid shirt and dark brown riding skirt, the colors matching her damp hair, which she'd pinned behind her neck, several strands curling about her cheeks. "I'm sorry I was short with you, Mr. Navarro. This country makes me a little jumpy."

"No harm done," Tom said, as Hawkins tipped the charred pot over his cup again. Louise Talon had a firm but feminine handshake. "You folks are a little off the beaten path, aren't you?"

"Might say the same thing about you," the woman said, tempering her steady gaze with a smile.

"I'm looking for a young lady nabbed by slave traders in Arizona. I was told they were heading southeast."

Louise Talon's face blanched. Hawkins narrowed his eyes at Navarro. "You don't say. . . ."

"Have you seen 'em?"

"No, we haven't seen them," Mrs. Talon said with amazement, the light leaving her eyes. "But we're looking for them, too."

"They took our girl, Billie, who worked at the stage station," Hawkins said. "Been trailin' 'em just over a week now. We 'bout rode our horses to death, ridin' in circles the last coupla days. Stopped here to rest 'em . . . and ourselves."

Navarro glanced around the camp. Three horses stood tied to a long picket line back in the tree shadows. Saddles and a wooden pack frame lay nearby. "You come all this way alone?"

"We had no time to form a tracking party," said Mrs. Talon, a trifle defensive. "As it was, we lost the trail several days ago, anyway."

"We're tougher than we look," muttered Hawkins as he blew ripples on his coffee, and sipped. "Might as well throw in together, though. We're all headin' the same direction. Me, I can shoot and trap and field dress a griz or buff in the time it takes most men to crap — uh, sorry, Mrs. Talon — but I can't navigate fer shit in these desert

278

mountains."

Tom glanced at the woman, sipped his coffee. "I reckon not," he said, throwing the dregs of the coffee out and extending the cup to Hawkins. "I appreciate the joe. There's several hours of good light left. I'll push on."

He pinched his hat to Mrs. Talon and Hawkins, who'd taken Tom's cup, then turned and, adjusting his cartridge belt on his hips, strolled back toward the creek.

"You don't believe in sharing the trail with a woman — is that it, Mr. Navarro?"

Tom turned to the woman, who stood by the fire, staring at him with a flush burning behind her suntanned cheeks. "Not in this country, ma'am. There's enough trouble without calling it in."

He turned again and waded into the stream. He hunkered down on his haunches, doffed his hat with his left hand, and cupped water to his face with his right. On the tea-colored water beside him, the woman's shadow slid out from the bank.

Water dripping down his sun-charred features, Navarro glanced over his shoulder. The woman stood behind him, fists on her hips, hard determination in her eyes. "I'll admit, coming down here where women stick out like sore thumbs is risky, and I'll also admit that having me along might attract trouble to you. But Mr. Hawkins and I have been having some difficulty following our map." She paused. "Billie is like a daughter to me. I'll do anything to get her back."

"You don't even know me, ma'am."

"If you'd had untoward intentions, I would have seen them back at my swimming hole."

"You had a gun."

"It wouldn't have stopped a badman."

"You ought to go home."

"I'm not going home without Billie. I took that girl in, and I've raised her like my own daughter."

Navarro sank back on his mental heels. He understood how the woman felt. He felt the same way about Karla. He glanced around the woman at Hawkins standing behind her, his cup of coffee in his hand.

"This is a headstrong woman," Tom remarked.

"She is that."

Navarro turned to the horses. Scowling thoughtfully, he replaced the bridle bits in the horses' mouths and was adjusting the pannier straps on the packhorse when he turned suddenly to Mrs. Talon and Hawkins awaiting his answer. "Wait a minute — you mentioned a map. What kind of map?"

Mrs. Talon said, "We met a couple pilgrims the other night, drifters heading north from Baconora. They drew us a map."

"A map to where?"

"Baconora," she said, as though speaking to a slow child.

"What's in Baconora?"

Walking slowly toward him, his coffee cup in his right hand, Hawkins said, "According to the pilgrims, that's where the slavers are takin' the girls. To a whorehouse down there for miners."

"Didn't you know?" asked Mrs. Talon.

"No. I've been trying to cut the bastards' sign." Tom was thoughtful, his heart clenching and unclenching. He'd had an idea why the girls had been taken, but hearing it spoken rang a bell in his head. His stomach churned, making him feel a little queasy.

"For *miners*?"

"There's an American- and British-owned gold mine down there," Hawkins said. "Apparently, the mine manager sends away for Mex girls to pleasure his American miners, and American girls to pleasure the Mexicans. Keeps all the peons, greasers and gringos alike, happily workin' for little but pennies and piss water."

Tom stared at the man so hard that Hawkins rolled his lips inward, blanching.

"I'm sorry," the woman said to Navarro. "I'd assumed you knew."

Tom looked at her sharply. "Let me see that map."

Hawkins stepped forward, reaching into a back trouser pocket and producing a folded sheet of lined tablet paper.

"Wait," Mrs. Talon said, holding up a hand to Hawkins. To Navarro, she said, "Will you help us find this place?"

"Do I have a choice?"

Hawkins extended the map, and Tom snapped it from his hand.

Two days later, in the late afternoon, with the air fresh from a passing shower, Tom lay atop a ridge with a pair of good German glasses held to his eyes. The town in the canyon below, strewn out along a narrow, winding stream, was an amalgam of crumbling old adobes and new, unpainted board structures the mining company had apparently slapped together for stores, saloons, dance halls, cafés, and bunkhouses.

Navarro figured the town had probably been an eighth its current size before gold was discovered on the slopes rising southeast of the town, and from which a wide road reinforced with logs and boulders snaked down through the sparse acacias and long-leafed pines from three broad mine portals yawning impressively from the cliff face.

A steady stream of heavy Murphy freight and Owensboro mountain wagons, loaded with ore, was drawn down those gradual switchbacks by four- and sometimes six-mule hitches. Leveling out at the base of the slope, the wagons and lumbering mules ran out along the stream on the other side of the town, heading apparently for the stamping mill Navarro could hear, the rock crushers sounding like relentless thunder blasts, somewhere among the craggy slopes over west.

A permanent smoke haze hung low in the valley dappled with cloud shadows. With the mines running around the clock, most of the stoves in town were no doubt stoked nonstop for hungry, thirsty miners between shifts. Below the stamping mill's monotonous pounding, a piano banged away in one of the several saloons.

"Those pilgrims give you any idea where the girls were being held?" Tom asked as he studied the layout of the town.

"I didn't think to ask," Louise said, belly down on her elbows to Tom's right.

Lowering the glasses, Navarro turned to

Hawkins on his left. The oldster shrugged. "How many whorehouses could there be out here?"

Tom held the glasses out to him. When Hawkins had glassed the town for a minute or so, he lowered the binoculars and growled, "I'll be damned. Regular little Gomorrah down there."

"Let me see," Louise said. Hawkins handed the glasses to Louise. When she'd given the town a scan, she turned to Navarro. "Well, what're we waiting for?"

"Nightfall."

"Why?"

"If this company town's bringin' in slave girls, it's no doubt run pretty tight. See all those gray uniforms down there? Those are *rurales.* Rural police. I'd bet the ranch they've all been bought and paid for by the company, and they keep a sharp eye out for strangers — especially gringos who might come down here to see what's become of their kids."

"Riding in there by day, we'd be about as conspicuous as a Lutheran sky pilot at a prairie Injun sun dance," Hawkins said.

Staring through the glasses again, Tom said, "That's one way of putting it."

Louise stared at Tom, puzzled. "I don't understand, after all the hard miles we've put behind us, how you can just sit here. Can't you imagine what must be happening to those girls . . . at this very minute?"

"Yep." Navarro lowered the glasses and canted a glance at the redhead. "But I can also imagine how much good we'd do them locked up in a *rurale* jail. And how much fun the *rurales* would have with you."

Louise held his gaze, slightly squinted one brown eye. "You're a pleasure to have around, Mr. Navarro."

"Yeah, well, I don't relish bein' here." He turned onto his back, lowered his head, and tipped his broad-brimmed Stetson over his eyes. "No, we'll wait for good dark before we go down there and start sniffin' around all public-like."

Louise looked at Hawkins, who threw his hands up and shrugged. "Time flies when you're havin' fun and crawls when you have a toothache."

Louise lowered her gaze to Navarro. His broad chest rose and fell evenly; his hands were clasped on his flat belly. She knew he was as anxious about his girl, Karla, as she was about her Billie, but he seemed to have just let go of everything.

She watched him, admiring in spite of herself the taciturn man who'd nearly run her ragged across these bald desert knobs.

Finally, taking his example, Louise lay back, as well, in the shadow of a large boulder. It took her a long time to quell the worries and wild imaginings before she finally fell into a doze. She had no idea how much time had passed before someone nudged her brusquely. Her eyes snapped open to an inky black sky speckled with stars.

"Let's go," Navarro said, looking down at her. He turned and headed down the slope toward the horses.

CHAPTER 22

Deciding they might attract more attention avoiding the main road than taking it, Navarro, Louise Talon, and Mordecai Hawkins rode back along the ridge, picked up the main wagon trace, and followed it into the valley and on into the town.

The streetlamps and torches had been lit, giving a surreal appearance to the two- and three-story wood-frame establishments still smelling of pine and wedged in amongst the ancient thatch-roofed adobe cantinas and *restaurantes,* on both sides of the cobblestone trace buried in horse and mule manure.

The boardwalks swelled with rollicking miners, the Americans apparently restricting themselves mainly to the newer, Dodge City–style saloons while the Mexicans were bunched up before the low-slung cantinas from which mariachi music flitted, competing with the ubiquitous pounding of the stamping mill.

As they rode amid the shunting shadows, Tom spotted the whores, freighters, drifters, and cardsharps — gringo as well as Mex — attracted to any mining berg, company-owned or otherwise. Several farm wagons were parked before the cantinas, and campesinos in the traditional coarse cotton slacks, oversized blouses, and ragged-brimmed sombreros milled with the Mexican miners in duck trousers and hob-nailed boots. The mixed crowd was a good sign that he and Hawkins might not stand out as much as he'd feared.

Louise, however, could pose a problem.

To solve it, Navarro looked around for a hotel. Turning left around the regal old Palacio Federal abutting a new mercantile store, he led his two companions and their packhorses down a dark side street and reined up before a two-store adobe bearing a sign reading HOTEL GRANDE DEL ORIENTE. The dirt-streaked hotel had a second-story balcony with a scrolled wrought-iron railing. The building was fronted with columns supporting an arched ceiling over a tile-floored front ramada, where a rain barrel sat against the wall and shipping crates were stacked.

"What are we doing here?" Louise asked.

"We're getting you off the street," Navarro said, slipping down from his saddle and approaching the hitch rack.

"I didn't come here to sleep." Louise kept her vehement voice low. "I came here to find Billie."

"You're not gonna find anything in this town but trouble. I'm gonna hole you up in a room. Then Mordecai and I are gonna peruse the saloons."

"While I'm doing what?"

"Playing fiddlesticks, for all I care!" Navarro looked around, wincing, hoping no one had heard his explosion. This strong-willed woman reminded him of another — whose pigheadedness got herself and him into this mess in the first place. And two good men dead.

"I can't just lounge around a room while Billie is —" Louise cut herself off, shaking her head. "I'll go *crazy*!"

"Well, do it quiet-like." Navarro reached up, brusquely pulled her down from her saddle, and mounted the porch.

Behind him Mordecai said quietly, "He's right, Mrs. Talon. You —"

"Oh, I know!"

Inside, an elegant old Mexican with close-cropped gray hair stood at the front desk, reading an *Illustrated Police Gazette* laid open beside a water glass half-filled with *habanero,* a Cuban-style rum that was probably less toxic than the local *aguardiente.*

"Buenas tardes," the old man greeted. *"Qué quiere?"*

"A couple of rooms," Tom said. "One for my foreman there" — he canted his head to indicate Hawkins before planting a hand on Louise's slim shoulder — "and one for myself and my lovely wife. We're down from Arizona on a horse-buyin' expedition. It'll be nice to finally sleep in a bed, won't it, honey?"

Louise didn't miss a beat. "It sure will, my love." To the old Mexican she said, "Could we get one of those rooms up front with a balcony? I get a little tight in the chest when I can't see what's happening on the street."

When they'd secured the rooms and were heading up the stairs lit by too few smoky candles, Louise turned to regard Navarro coming up behind her. "You're taking quite a bit for granted, don't you think?"

"I've seen how you look at me."

Hawkins snorted.

Louise asked Tom, "Why is it that you get to play my husband, and not Mr. Hawkins?"

"For the simple reason that you and I are closer to the same age. We can switch when we get to the rooms, though, if it'll make you feel better."

Louise stopped before her and Tom's door and stabbed the key in the lock. "No, we might end up with a snoopy chambermaid."

When Navarro and Hawkins had hauled their gear to their rooms, both men took a whore's bath in Hawkins' room, cutting through the thick layers of dust on their faces, then headed back downstairs. They stopped at the front desk, where the old Mexican was pouring himself a fresh drink from a crock jug, his brown eyes looking bleary.

When Tom had inquired about a good livery barn, he poked his hat back on his head, feigned a bashful expression, and rested his arms on the native-wood desk. "Senor, one more question, if you don't mind." He looked around the lobby as if to make sure no one was eavesdropping, then jerked a thumb at Hawkins flanking his right. "My foreman here has a lusty streak. He's wondering where he might find some women of the sporting variety."

"Ah, *putas*."

"Yes, *putas*."

"You are in luck, senor," the old Mex told Hawkins thickly. "Baconora is — how do you say? — rife with *putas*." He threw his head back and laughed, showing a gold front tooth. "You need not walk too far. They will find *you.*"

Tom again leaned forward to speak confidentially with the old Mexican. "Now would there be *Norteamericano putas* here, as well as *Mejican?* We've been away from home a long time, and my foreman's a little homesick. He has nothing against the lovely *Mejican putas,* for sure, but tonight he would like to lie with a *Norteamericano.*"

"Ah, *Norteamericano,*" the old Mexican said, lifting his glass of clear liquid and stroking his imaginary long hair. "*Sí.* Our Lady of Sorrows."

Frowning, Navarro glanced at Hawkins, then turned again to the old Mex. "Pardon?"

"Try Our Lady of Sorrows. The *catédral.*" He crossed himself soberly, shaking his head, then lifted his jug. "A drink for the road, senors? It has been a quiet evening on this side of town, and I have nearly finished my *periodico.*"

Navarro wanted that drink about as badly as he wanted his fingernails torn off in the slow Apache style, and he could tell that Hawkins felt the same. They needed to get after the girls. But both men, not wanting to look too eager, sat down in overstuffed chairs by the chaparral fire on the other side of the lobby, and had their drink. The Mexican railed in his slow Spanish-spattered English about how the town had changed for the worse since the gold mine came to town, with a dandified Englishman named Blane Ettinger at the helm.

Navarro wanted to know more about this Ettinger but the man clammed up when Tom started to probe, a fearful light entering his rheumy eyes. When he and Mordecai had finished their drinks, they said that, like them, the night wasn't getting any younger. They shook the old Mexican's hand and strode out the heavy double doors into the torch-lit side street.

"What in the hell are we looking for?" Hawkins asked as they turned before the Palacio Federal and entered the boisterous main drag.

"Some place they call the cathedral, I reckon. More of this Ettinger's influence, no doubt. Leave it to a Protestant-raised Brit to open a saloon in Mexico called Our Lady of Sorrows."

Keeping to the south side of the street, they threaded their way through clumps of loud, drunk miners of both American and Mexican persuasion, heading eastward, peering into every saloon and cantina they passed. The music had gotten more raucous since they'd entered the town, as if the mariachis were openly competing with the American piano bangers and fiddle players one or two doors down or directly across the street.

All seemed to be competing with the occasional bursts of celebratory gunfire and the ubiquitous thunder of the stamping mill.

Navarro and Hawkins were waylaid twice by fistfights, which were quickly broken up by big men armed with double-barreled shotguns and wearing the badges of mine company constables on their jacket lapels.

When they were returning westward along the other side of the street, Navarro stopped suddenly when someone shouted above the crowd's din, "Edgar, you old dog! I woulda bet my right oyster you couldn't fill a straight from that hand! Ha!"

Navarro grabbed Hawkins's arm, canting his head to indicate the saloon they were standing in front of. Hawkins nodded and followed Navarro through the crowd bunched along the boardwalk, and through the batwings. They stood among the sitting and standing miners, Navarro sweeping the crowd with his gaze.

"The more liquor you force down his throat," the same voice rose again, "the *bet-*

ter he *gets.* I just don't *understand* it!"

Navarro settled his gaze on the yeller — a slender unshaven lad sitting at a table with seven others. Playing cards, shot glasses, and beer mugs were strewn before them. To the young man's right, and scooping up a pot of greenbacks and silver coins, with a round-faced Mexican girl perched on his knee, sat a man with a battered derby pulled down over blond curly hair. He had dark-ringed, crazy-looking eyes, and two gold rings looped through his ears.

"Son of a bitch."

"What's that, Tom?"

Navarro turned. Hawkins was looking at him curiously. Tom hadn't realized he'd spoken aloud. Turning, he bulled through the batwings and pushed through the crowd. When they were alone he said to Hawkins, who was shuffling along behind him, half running to keep up, "Did you notice the pilgrim with the two gold earrings?"

"How could I help it?"

"That's Bontemps."

"You don't say!" Hawkins wheeled, one hand going for the .36 Navy Colt conversion on his hip. "Well, I reckon we can find out right quick where he's stashed them girls!"

Tom grabbed the man's arm. "Don't be a

fool. You seen all the men surrounding him?
I'd bet my front teeth they're all part of his
bunch. One I recognized as Sam 'The Dog'
Calvino, a Confederate guerrilla like Bontemps, who rode with Sibley's West Texas
Raiders. To a man, they're shooters with a
capital 'S'."

"What do you propose we do?"

Navarro was walking forward along the
boardwalk, Hawkins again half running to
keep up. When an isolated drunk approached, staggering, Tom tapped the man's
shoulder and asked where a place called the
Cathedral or Our Lady of Sorrows might
be.

"Well, shit, amigo," said the sour-smelling
Irishman, "where it's always been. Right
there at the other end o' the square. Say,
you couldn't help a mick out with a drink,
could ye? Snodgrass and Thorndike just
cleaned me out over at said *house of wor-
ship* — though it ain't like any *churches* we
have back home in sweet County Cork!"
The man winked and held out a big pale
paw, palm up.

When Tom had given the man some silver,
he and Hawkins stood staring across the
square. Fifty yards up the street, beyond a
large dry fountain, was a giant adobe cathedral behind a low wall. It was a cathedral

296

like any other the Jesuits and Franciscans had long ago erected in every little town within a year's ride of Mexico City, north and south of the Rio Grande.

Hawkins said, "He can't mean the *real* Lady of Sorrows, can he?"

Tom stared at the big structure, with its wooden cross stabbing starward from the square bell tower high above the big double doors.

"Why can't he?"

As Navarro and Hawkins approached the building, they saw the saddled horses standing before the three hitchracks fronting the seven-foot-high wall.

"Whoa, boys," said one of the two guards smoking before the open wrought-iron gate. "No guns inside. House rules. You wanna go in, you leave the hardware in the box here. Pick 'em up on your way out."

When Tom and Mordecai had set their pistol belts in the apple crate, atop a dozen others, the two guards, armed with shotguns and bung starters and with cartridge belts crossed on their chests, frisked them thoroughly before letting them head across the tiled courtyard to the four stone steps rising to the pair of open front doors. Fluttering torches flanked both doors, as though marking the entrance to purgatory.

If he hadn't been looking so hard for Karla, Navarro would have chuckled when he saw what the church had become. As it was, he swung his gaze left and right across the great hall before him, at the swarthy smoky-eyed Mexican miners sitting on the couches and fancy chairs and at tables with light-haired, light-eyed girls on their laps, their hands on the girls. He felt a big gray cat swish its tail down deep in his belly. That cat got up, stretched, and swished its tail again when Tom spotted Karla.

CHAPTER 23

Tom hadn't spotted Karla on his first glance around the room, because she was dressed in a low-cut, impossibly short yellow satin dress, with black net stockings and purple high-heeled shoes. She wore three purple feathers in her upswept hair and a black choker around her neck.

She sat with three Mexicans on a couch beneath a staircase angling down from the second story. One of the Mexicans had his hand in her dress. Karla gazed off into space, glassy-eyed, as though drugged, quirking a vacant smile when the Mexican whispered in her ear.

The other two Mexicans sat with their high-crowned hats in their laps, feet on the floor, grinning stupidly as they watched the other man's hands rummaging around in Karla's dress.

Karla's indolent gaze slid toward Navarro. He turned away abruptly, hoping she wouldn't recognize him and call out. His back to the girl, he said softly to Hawkins, managing a smile, as though he were quite taken with the place and thoroughly enjoying himself, "Let's sit."

Most of the tables in the place were occupied, but Tom and Hawkins found a small one against the left wall, before a stained-glass window depicting Adam and Eve in the Garden of Eden. The men sat down across from each other. It wasn't long before a pretty Mexican in a dress similar to Karla's wandered up and took their orders.

This girl's eyes were not glazed. She appeared to be one of the few willing girls in the room. Most of the half dozen others, sitting on knees or laps or surrounded by admiring miners or *rurales* in their stitched whipcord slacks and boots, were stoned on something stronger than alcohol.

"That's your girl over there, ain't it?" Hawkins asked.

"Any sign of Billie?"

"At the table by the bar. The little hazel-eyed girl sitting on that dandy's knee."

Tom swung a glance to the girl with the elfin face sitting on the knee of a fat-faced, blond-mustachioed gent in a panama suit and a planter's hat. He was playing five-card stud with four other men, lesser lights allowed well-oiled Colts and Remingtons on their hips.

The four wore the white shirts, whipcord trousers, silver-tooled belts, and hats of the border buscadero. Probably body guards. The man in the silk suit was rambling on in an exaggerated British accent while taking frequent sips of sangria from a cut-glass decanter and puffing on what appeared from this distance to be a genuine Cuban cigar.

Navarro felt that lightness in the fingers he felt on the rare occasion he wanted to shoot someone. He wanted to shoot this bastard in both arms, both legs, and his belly. . . . Let him die slow. . . .

"Tom, you're staring," Hawkins said, smiling across the table at him. "Have some beer." He raised his mug and sipped, keeping his eyes on Navarro.

"Ettinger?" Tom said.

"I would imagine. I'm glad they took our guns. If I had mine, I'd kill that son of a bitch and probably get Billie and us killed in the process."

Tom flicked another glance at Ettinger, then quickly raked his eyes across the room. Several men had left, several more had entered, and a beer keg–sized Mex in a red straw sombero had started pounding away on a piano near the confession booth, which had a padlock on its door.

Hawkins took a long pull off his beer, licked the foam from his mustache. He shook his head as he set the beer back down in the ring the glass had left on the table. "This doesn't look good."

When Navarro didn't say anything, Mordecai said, "Tom, I don't like that look in your eyes. Last time I seen that look in a friend's eyes, I woke up in a basement jail in Deadwood. . . ."

Navarro tempered the steely determined glint in his gray eyes with a festive quirk of his lips, showing the pearly tips of his teeth. He'd turned in his chair to face the room, his right boot resting on his left knee. Just a drifting horse seller or buyer enjoying the way the church had been redecorated and maybe thinking of counting out some change for a whore.

He had to raise his voice to be heard above the piano. "I thought when we first walked in here without our hardware that this was gonna have to be a scouting mission only."

"And now . . . ?"

"Now I'm thinkin' tonight's as good as any to make our move. Both girls are here in the room with us. It ain't gonna be any easier to get in or out, and the more time we have to think about it, the more time we have to knot it up."

Sweat ran in rivulets down Hawkins' face. "Shit, we don't even have our guns."

"Those men over there have hoglegs," Navarro said, sliding his eyes to the border bucks at Ettinger's table.

"You're talkin' suicide now, my friend."

"Their tonsils are pretty well oiled."

"What about the guards outside?"

"They're up to you, after you've fetched Louise and the horses."

When Tom laid out his plan, which wasn't really much of a plan, Hawkins finished his beer and looked over the table at him. "You think we can pull it off?"

"I came down here for that girl over there. I ain't leavin' without her."

"I'm thinkin' the smarter choice might be to head home and report this wasps' nest to the territorial governor and, hell, to good ole Rutherford B. Hayes himself. The feds won't have any choice but to take action against Ettinger's company when they hear what he's pullin' down here."

"Yeah, they'll close down the mine and free the girls, but how long do you think it'll be before we see 'em again? And is there any guarantee they'll still be alive?"

"You'll grab both girls?"

Navarro nodded.

"What about the others?"

"We'll have to settle for freeing *our* girls, and let the so-called authorities free the rest."

"If we get the girls outta here, Ettinger's men are gonna be after us like possums after persimmons."

"Hope the horses are well-rested."

Hawkins regarded Tom soberly, lifted the mug again to his mouth. Realizing he'd already finished the beer, he set the mug back on the table, stood, and stretched, as though he'd had enough fun for one evening and it was time to locate a mattress sack.

"Good night, amigo."

Tom watched the bandy-legged old hide hunter saunter through the handful of men dancing with a couple of drugged-looking Mexican girls and the one white girl who seemed to be enjoying her job. Hawkins strode through the double doors and disappeared into the night.

With occasional glances at Karla, who had now been forced to sit on the lap of one of the other miners, Tom finished his beer, ground his teeth, and rubbed his gun hand on his thigh.

He had another twenty minutes before Hawkins and Mrs. Talon would show with the horses. He ordered another beer, and when one of the bright-eyed Mexican whores came around, smiling coquettishly, he pulled the girl onto his knee. He made a show of being interested, running his hands down her bare thighs and nuzzling her neck, keeping one eye on the room.

The girl's attention was drawn to the front door, her expression turning suddenly sour. Following her gaze, Navarro saw Edgar Bontemps and a tall Mexican enter the "church." Bontemps wore his dusty trail garb, ratty wool poncho, and torn moccasins, with a brace of .45s on his hips.

The tall Mexican wore the braid-encrusted sombrero and stitched boots of a *rurale* officer, probably a captain or a major, judging by the quality of his clothes. His jet-black mustache was carefully waxed and upswept to frame his pitted nostrils. The two big Dragoons on his pistol belt were pearl-butted and custom-engraved; the sawed-off shotgun hanging down his back was silver-plated, the stock inlaid with colored glass. Over a white silk shirt he wore a short charro-style jacket of gray-green brocade.

He and Bontemps shouldered through the crowd to Ettinger's table. Ettinger stood, smiling broadly and shaking the *rurale*'s hand, as if he couldn't be happier to see the man.

As Ettinger and the *rurale* conversed standing up, Bontemps tapped the shoulder of one of the buscaderos, who reluctantly set his cards down, stood, and strolled up to the bar. Grinning, the slaver adjusted his pistols, doffed his bowler, and sat down, taking over the bodyguard's hand.

A minute later, Ettinger and the *rurale* walked away from the gambling table. Tom's heart started beating irregularly when the two men stopped at the couch where Karla sat with the three Mexican miners. Ettinger lifted her chin, giving the *rurale* a look at her face. The *rurale* nodded and grinned.

Smiling like a proud horse trader, Ettinger pulled Karla off the miner's lap. The *rurale* held his arm out formally. Karla looped her own arm through his, and the man led her through the crowd toward the stairs at the room's rear.

Behind them, Bontemps grinned and, cupping a hand to his mouth, told the man to enjoy himself and that he'd have a bottle of his best mescal sent to his room.

Navarro watched the *rurale* and Karla disappear up the staircase. His ire must have been written on his face, because the Mexican dove had stopped squirming. Regarding him cautiously, she stood, muttering under her breath, then sidled off to be swept away by a knob-nosed, bull-necked miner in a cloth cap and denim jacket.

Standing, Navarro manufactured a neutral expression, and strode toward the right end of the bar at the front of the church. Tending the altar bar was a fat, middle-aged brunette in a silly pink dress with white ruffles, and a tall, sallow-faced American gent with pomaded hair and a stained green shirt buttoned to his throat. As the woman drew beers, sloshed liquor into shot glasses, and swept change from the bar with her pudgy white hands, she kept up a running harangue against the sallow-faced gent's inability to move faster "than an April calf in a mud creek."

Angrily, she turned to Navarro and shrieked, "Name your poison — I ain't got all night!"

When Navarro's tequila shot was plunked down before him on the plank bar winging out from the altar, he watched the woman bustle away to fill another order. He tossed back the shot, slid his eyes right and left. Sure no one was watching him, he took three steps straight back and crouched at the foot of the stairs. Turning and staying below the wainscoted railing shielding him from the rest of the room, gritting his teeth as he hoped against hope no one had seen his crazy move, he crawled on hands and knees to the top.

As he gained the shag runner in the second-floor hall, he took a deep breath and stood. Hearing the near-deafening roar from below — the piano player was banging out a rousing Mexican festival tune while others clapped and stomped to the beat — he moved quickly along the hall lit with a wavering umber glow.

Several doors were open, revealing empty, tidy rooms. Through several others he heard heated murmurs and squeaking bedsprings, the soft thuds of a headboard hitting the wall.

Navarro had no idea which room Karla and the *rurale* were in. He began sweating in earnest, his chest squeezing, when he heard the deep rumble of Spanish-uttered curses. Karla groaned a protest.

Navarro reached for the doorknob. Locked. Taking two steps back, he whipped his right boot back, then forward, connecting soundly with the door. It snapped wide, slammed against the wall. On the bed before him, the naked *rurale* lay sprawled atop Karla, who was still dressed, her gown pulled down around her waist. The *rurale* was on his knees, tying Karla's wrists to the bedframe with his pistol belt.

The man had just whipped his head toward Navarro when, bolting forward, Tom punched him soundly across the jaw. Several bones in the man's face broke with a dull crack. With a clipped scream, he flew off the other side of the bed.

Tom grabbed one of the big Dragoons from the man's pistol belt, leapt upon the bed, and plucked a pillow from beside Karla. He stepped off the bed, knelt over the groaning *rurale,* and slapped the pillow over the man's face. He cocked the Dragoon, jammed the barrel into the pillow, and fired one belching round. Black smoke wafted, and feathers flew.

The *rurale*'s arms fell to the floor, and his body relaxed.

Leaving the smoking pillow over the man's head, Navarro leapt onto the bed, and untangled the pistol belt from the headboard, freeing Karla's wrists.

Pulling her dress up, she stared groggily at him, tears veiling her eyes. "Tommy?"

"I'm gettin' you outta here, kid." Navarro shook her harshly. "Can you follow me, run when I tell you?"

She blinked and nodded, tears flowing over her eyes and down her pale cheeks.

Navarro grabbed the *rurale*'s double-barreled shotgun off the dresser, broke it open to make sure it was loaded, snapped it closed, and looped the lanyard over his neck and right shoulder.

He grabbed the second Dragoon from the pistol belt, shoved both behind his waistband, and pulled Karla off the bed.

"Let's go!"

CHAPTER 24

Holding the double-barreled barn-blaster barrel out before him, and Karla's right hand in his left, Navarro stole a glance up and down the hall.

A door had opened across the hall. A bare-chested man with a thin blond mustache peered through the crack, drunk eyes bewildered.

Navarro shot him a poignant look and raised the shotgun. The man stepped quickly back and slammed the door.

All the other doors were closed. The din rose up the stairs, as raucous as before. Apparently, only the man across the hall had heard the pistol shot, or paid it any heed.

Moving sideways down the hall, Navarro glanced over his shoulder at Karla stumbling along behind him on bare feet. "We're gonna walk down the stairs nice and slow," Tom told her. "You keep just back from my right shoulder. When I say go, you light out for the front door and hightail it across the street. There'll be a woman and an old man waiting for you with horses."

Eyes wide, Karla bobbed her head.

Navarro led her down the stairs, moving at a normal pace, not too slow, not too fast. His back was stiff, nerves taut. He stared straight ahead, sliding his eyes left to peer into the main hall below, all but invisible beneath a heavy layer of tobacco smoke.

He felt the vibrations of the piano in the steps beneath his boots.

Men howled, cheered, cheerfully berated one another.

The fat woman and the dour man scurried around behind the bar, drawing sudsy beers or tipping bottles over shot glasses. Before the bar and about halfway across the room, Ettinger and Bontemps played cards with the border bucks.

Holding the shotgun down low at his right side, his finger curled through the trigger guard, Navarro pulled Karla to the bottom of the stairs, then slowly turned, and walked along the bar. Ettinger and the others at their table were intent on their cards or each other.

When he and Karla had walked ten feet, Navarro turned again and strode past the piano player and through the crowd toward the front door. He glanced around the room, neck hairs tingling. When it came, it would come from Ettinger's table on his right flank.

He squeezed Karla's hand and stared at the doorway a hundred feet beyond. If he could get Karla halfway there safely, he'd go back inside for Billie.

Sudden movement on his left. Navarro turned, raising the shotgun. The miner upon whose lap Karla had been sitting before Ettinger had turned her over to the *rurale* faced him, his Indian-dark face burnished red with exasperation.

"Qué es esto?"

Tom glanced at Karla. "Run."

Karla bolted past the incensed miner, hair flying as she dashed for the door. Tom turned around, bent his legs to Ettinger's table. Billie was sitting on Bontemps' knee. He grabbed her arm, jerked her off the slaver's knee, and heaved the girl out ahead of him, rasping in her ear, "Run to the door!"

Billie whipped her stricken gaze at him.

Backing away from the table, Navarro trained the shotgun on Bontemps, who'd bolted out of his chair and froze, crouching, with both hands on his .45s. The busca-deros stared at Navarro blandly, cigarettes or cigars in their teeth, cards in their hands.

Ettinger slid his chair back and heaved to his feet. "Just who in the hell do you think you are, you son of a bitch?"

"Why, it's 'Taos Tommy' Navarro," Bontemps said, glee dancing in his eyes. "I thought you was dead!"

The room had fallen nearly silent beneath muttered exclamations. Still backing away from the table, holding his shotgun on Bontemps, Navarro glanced behind him to see Billie stumbling toward Karla, who was waiting at the back of the room.

Navarro swung his gaze forward. Ettinger triggered a pocket pistol. The bullet nipped Navarro's left leg. Someone behind him screamed, and a thump rose as a miner hit the floor.

Bontemps slapped leather with both hands.

Navarro swung the shotgun to Ettinger and tripped the right trigger. The shotgun boomed and jumped. In the periphery of his right eye, Navarro saw the screaming mine manager bounce off the bar clutching his gaping middle.

Tom swung the barn-blaster back toward Bontemps, and dropped the left hammer. The slaver dove to his right, and the head of the buscadero behind him erupted in a fine red spray.

As the other buscaderos leapt to their feet, filling their hands, Tom chucked the empty shotgun toward Bontemps, who was crawling around behind a table, and pulled both Dragoons from his waistband. One of the bodyguards had beat him to the mark. The bullet whipped past his right ear and shattered a stained-glass window behind him. A girl shrieked.

Dodging two more pistol shots, Navarro crouched and cut loose with both Dragoons, shattering glass behind the bar and punching lead through two buscaderos. A pistol roared on his left. He quarter-turned and fired three quick rounds at Bontemps, punching holes in the table the slaver crouched behind and, as the man flinched, bloodied his right eye.

"Ahhhh!" the slaver screamed, dropping both pistols and clutching his wounded eye as he dropped to the floor.

Navarro wheeled and ran toward the door, leaping the men and the girls who'd dropped to the floorboards, arms crossed on their heads. He was ten feet from the door when a gun barked behind him. The slug burned a path along Tom's right elbow. Wheeling, Navarro fired his last three rounds.

The tall bartender slammed back against the broken mirror and dropped with a wheeze. At the same time, the fat woman rose up from behind the bar and rested a long-barreled shotgun along the bar top, squinting down the barrel.

The gun exploded as Navarro leapt through the front door and ran toward the open wrought-iron gate, where the two main guards lay sprawled in glistening blood.

Navarro cast a look into the street beyond the gate. Twenty yards right of the fountain, four horses stood staring toward him, twitching their ears and swishing their tails.

Louise Talon and Billie sat one. Hawkins was helping Karla onto Navarro's pack-horse.

Waving an arm, Navarro shouted, "Go!" He grabbed his and Hawkins' gun belts from the apple crate, slung each over a shoulder, and ran limping across the yard toward the bay Hawkins was holding for him.

"Tommy!" Karla cried, whipping a look behind as she and the other two women galloped east.

A shot popped to Navarro's left, the slug pinking the fountain with an angry twang. Tom turned to see several men sporting mine company badges running toward him.

"Hold it!" one shouted, leveling a shotgun.

Navarro grabbed the reins from Hawkins' hand, tossed the old hide hunter his cartridge belt, and leapt into his saddle. As Tom and Mordecai spurred their mounts into lunging gallops, the shotgun exploded. The shooter was too far away for the buckshot to do anything but sting Navarro's back and cause his horse to shake its head and whinny.

Pistols barked, the slugs tearing dust clods at the horses' hooves. In seconds, the mountain man and the Bar-V segundo were splitting the wind amid the shacks at the ragged eastern edge of town, bringing the women into view ahead.

"Jesus H. Christ!" Hawkins yelled, glancing at Tom over his right shoulder. "I never figured that old dog could hunt!"

"He can't," Navarro yelled, urging the bay even faster as the street became a road. "He just got lucky!"

A hundred yards before the river, which was gleaming silver in its wide, shallow bank, Navarro rode up abreast of Karla. He reached over, grabbed the reins from the girl's hands, then gigged the bay on ahead of her and on past Louise and Billie, swinging right at the river and loping upstream, into the broad, dark night.

At a hide-parting clip, Tom led the group along the stream for nearly a mile, then followed a cart trail up the snaggle-toothed ridge rising northward. Near the ridge's lip, he turned his horse off the trail, stopped, and reined back toward the valley. The women were approaching, weary horses blowing and lunging floppy-footed into the grade.

"Keep pushin'!" Navarro called to Louise. "Take the girls on over the ridge."

Slumped forward in her saddle, Karla followed Louise and Billie up the ridge. Hawkins halted his horse on the trail before Tom, rested both hands on his saddle horn.

"Those badge-toters must've grabbed some horses off the street," Hawkins said, breathless.

Navarro stared out over the valley, listening. The moon was rising over the far ridge like a big dented quarter. Above the usual night sounds rose the thumps of pounding hooves and men's voices raised in anger. Back down the trail, shadows moved along the stream.

"My eyes ain't what they used to be, but they look to be four."

"Five," Navarro said. "Keep the women moving."

"What're you gonna do?"

"We can't keep this pace up forever. I'm going to get these five off our trail. Discourage anyone else from following suit."

Hawkins pulled his rifle from his saddle boot. "You're gonna need help."

Tom shook his head and shucked his own Winchester. "Keep moving. I'll catch up to you in a few minutes."

Hawkins chuffed and, gigging his horse on up the ridge, grunted over his shoulder, "That ole dog's luck ain't gonna hold forever."

Hearing Hawkins's hoof falls dwindle down the other side of the ridge, Navarro turned his horse from the valley, followed the trail for another thirty yards, then turned into the rocks along the crest. Dismounting, he tied his horse to a shrub, then made his way back through the rocks. He levered a shell, lowered the hammer to half cock, and hunkered behind a boulder on the right side of the trail.

He removed his hat and cast a glance into the valley, shimmering silver under the rising moon, the opposite ridge climbing darkly on the other side of the stream. A hundred yards down the shaggy cart path, shadows danced in the moonlight. The running hoofbeats and leathery tack squeaks grew louder.

As the riders approached riding two by two, Navarro made out several badges pinned to shirts or jackets. Two of the five wore high-peaked sombreros. Probably *rurales* out to avenge their leader's death in Ettinger's Lady of Sorrows.

Navarro waited till the men were ten yards down the grade, their horses slowing as they approached the crest. Navarro stood, snapped the Winchester to his shoulder, and fired four quick rounds into the group.

As the men fell from their saddles and horses screamed, rearing, Tom ran into the trail, drew a bead on a badge glittering in the moonlight, and fired, the ping resounding as his bullet plunked through the tin and into a heart.

The man grunted and tumbled off his buck-kicking horse's rump and lay groaning in the sage right of the trail, his three fallen comrades spread out around him.

Navarro had taken the group by complete surprise. Only one man managed to snap off a shot, the slug spanging off the rocks around Navarro as the shooter tried to get his pitching mount under control.

Tom lowered himself to a knee, drew a bead on the man, and dropped the hammer. The bullet punched through his left shoulder. The *rurale* screamed and twisted around as his horse leapt high, its front hooves flailing skyward.

Pitching off the left side of his horse, he hit the ground with a dull thud. His horse ran screaming straight up and over the crest and down the other side.

Two other wounded men groaned and cursed along the trail. The thuds of the fleeing horses dwindled in the quiet night.

The *rurale* had dropped behind a rock. Crouching, Tom waited. The man's silhouetted head appeared, hatless. His gun glittered. Tom fired, his round barking off the rock a few inches from the *rurale*'s head.

The man cursed in Spanish, bolted to his feet, turned, and ran east along the ridge's rocky spine. Tom triggered a shot and followed, leaping rocks. The man snapped off two shots as he ran.

Running toward him, Tom returned fire, jacking and levering his saddle gun. His third shot evoked a grunt, but the man kept running, his shadow staggering. The *rurale* triggered off another wayward shot, and Tom returned it.

The man groaned. His shadow fell.

Tom approached the fallen man at a walk, holding the Winchester out at his waist.

The *rurale* was down on his left side, clutching his right thigh with his right hand.

321

He held his old Remington in his left, but he didn't try to lift it. He raised his head to Tom, his eyes snapping wide.

"Please have mercy!" he cried in Spanish.

"I always heard there wasn't any mercy in Mexico."

Navarro triggered the Winchester from his hip, drilling a round through the *rurale*'s heart, then turned and walked back to the trail. He put the other two wounded men out of their misery, then stood in the middle of the trail, peering into the valley bisected by the silver stream. He watched and listened.

No hoofbeats or moving shadows. Only crickets and the breeze ruffling the sage and Mormon tea.

Leaving the dead men where they'd fallen, Navarro mounted his bay and gigged it over the ridge.

CHAPTER 25

Navarro's group traveled for two more hours, heading steadily northward, navigating by moonlight. When Karla and Billie were nearly falling from their mounts with exhaustion, Navarro found a hollow below a rocky pass. He and Hawkins picketed the horses near a grass-lined spring, while Louise set up camp and rolled out blankets near a small fire for the girls.

When the horses had been fed, watered, and rubbed down with dry grass, Navarro walked into the small circle of firelight reflecting off the jumbled boulders behind it. Karla and Billie lay curled beneath their blankets while Louise filled a speckled blue pot from a hide-covered canteen.

"They all right?" he asked the woman.

"As far as I can tell, there are no lasting physical injuries. It looks like they've both been drugged."

"Opium, no doubt."

"Tommy?"

Navarro turned to Karla. She lay regarding him from beneath her blanket, firelight flickering in her drawn hazel eyes. He knelt beside her and she rose up on her hip, threw her arms around his neck, and sobbed, "I'm so sorry!"

"Shhh," Tom said, smoothing her hair down the back of her head. "You rest now. We got some hard ridin' ahead of us."

She sobbed again, then lay her head back down, and her eyes closed. A minute later, her shoulders rose and fell slowly and her breaths grew deep and regular. The blanket had slipped up her leg, revealing a smooth curve of tender thigh and a bare foot. Tom thoughtfully pulled the blanket down over the bared skin, drew it up snug to her neck.

When Louise and Hawkins had turned in, Navarro climbed a rise on the other side of the spring to keep the first watch. The night was quiet, and for that, he felt great relief. He was sitting with his back to a boulder, fighting sleep, when something rustled on the slope behind him, toward the camp. He turned his head quickly to see a shadow moving toward him.

"It's me," Louise said, weeds crunching beneath her shoes. She knelt down beside him, extending the steaming tin cup in her left hand. She held another in her right. "I thought you might need this."

"Just what the doctor ordered." Navarro took the coffee and sipped. "I figured you'd be asleep."

"So did I," Louise said, sitting down beside him and resting her back against the rock. "But when I lay down, I felt like I was still riding. I can take the first watch, if you'd like."

"Me and Mordecai can manage."

She sipped her coffee and turned to him with a wistful smile. "Don't trust a woman?"

"You got the girls to tend."

Louise rested her head back against the rock and stared out at the desert rolling away below the pass, beneath a sheen of milky light shed by a high, shrunken moon. After a while she said, "She's beautiful."

Navarro looked at her.

"Your Karla's a beautiful girl."

Navarro shrugged and scratched his neck. "She's had her share of suitors. It was a Mexican boy who caused to her run off like she did."

"If I'm not being too shamelessly forward, may I ask what your relationship is?"

"I reckon that's a might forward," Navarro allowed with a grunt, blowing on his coffee. "She's like a daughter to me. The daughter

I never had, never *will* have. Nothing more, nothing less."

Louise set her cup down beside her. "Never *will* have? How can you be so certain?"

"I'm certain."

"Even if the right woman came along?"

"The right woman won't *come* along. I'm an ornery old cuss with a bad reputation. I'm going back to my cabin in the desert, and I'm going to stay there."

"If I've learned one thing in my thirty-six years, Mr. Navarro, it's that one should never feel so certain about anything in this life."

Navarro grunted. "What about yourself?"

She turned away, but he thought he saw a flush rise in her cheeks. "I've closed no doors. I reckon, if the right man came along. . . ."

Tom looked at her, only inches away in the misty darkness. She was indeed a woman to twist a man's heart. Looked good, with those brown eyes and that deep red hair. Smelled good, too, even after a long day's ride. He liked the way he felt when she was near.

Why in the hell did he have to be so set in his solitary ways?

She'd turned to him again. They locked

glances. His heart thumped, and he placed his hand under her chin, gently lifted her face, and closed his lips over hers. She pressed closer, placed her right hand on his arm, squeezed gently.

They drew away from each other.

"Maybe," Navarro said, finding his voice, "if I'm down Benson way sometime, I'll stop in for a visit."

Louise picked up her coffee cup and stood, brushing grass and sand from her skirt. "I best get back to the girls, see if they need anything. Good night, Tom." She moved away, stopped, and turned back to him. "You stop by anytime." Her soft footfalls rose as she descended the knoll to the camp.

The next morning, Navarro was asleep against his saddle, hat tipped over his eyes, when a hand nudged his shoulder. He opened his eyes and raised the rifle he'd slept with in his hands.

"It's me, Tom," Mordecai Hawkins said softly, hunkered down by Tom's left shoulder. The sun was full up, and birds were winging overhead. Louise, Karla, and Billie were still curled asleep beneath their blankets, on the other side of the fire, over which a coffeepot chugged.

Keeping his voice low, Hawkins said,

"This might not be nothin', but there's a covered wagon comin' up the pass, 'bout a mile away."

Immediately awake, Tom straightened his hat, stood, grabbed the field glasses from beside his saddle, and moved quickly but quietly across the camp. On a rocky ledge overlooking the trail, he trained the glasses down the pass, where the trail snaked through the creosote, cholla, and the occasional cottonwoods reaching up from low depressions.

The sun was just above the eastern horizon, gilding the white canvas tarpaulin bowed over the oncoming wagon's box. Compressing slightly as it started up the incline toward the pass, the Conestoga's bulky shadow ran along the sage tufts on the west side of the two-track trail. The driver snapped the whip over the backs of the two mules in the traces, the animals leaning into their collars as the terrain rose beneath their hooves, the driver shouting shrill epithets. Even from this distance, the voice sounded familiar.

Tom leveled the glasses on the driver's face, adjusted the focus. Frowning, he said, "What the hell . . . ?"

Beside him, Hawkins said, "Recognize that fella?"

Navarro handed the glasses to Hawkins. Squatting, the old hide hunter doffed his floppy-brimmed hat, brought the glasses to his deeply spoked eyes, and chuckled a surprised curse. "Well, hell's bells, that ain't no fella!"

Navarro took the glasses from Hawkins, said, "Let's get out of sight," and dropped down off the rock, slipping between two boulders on the east side of the trail. When he could hear the mules blowing wearily and the squawk of their leather collars, Tom stepped into the trail and held his rifle in one hand, barrel down at his side.

The Conestoga was about twenty yards away, just down from the saddle. The driver was peering off to her left. Spying Navarro in the periphery of her vision, she snapped her cow-eyed gaze forward, gasped, and leaned back on the ribbons, shouting, "Whooooo-ah! Whooooo!"

When she had stopped the team, she stared over their sagging heads, drilling Navarro with a belligerent stare. He stared back at her — the female apron from Our Lady of Sorrows. Her round, fat face was flush-splotched; her heavy bosom rose and fell sharply as she breathed. Her cream-and-brown dress, cut low to reveal a good half of her milky bosom, was caked with seeds and trail dust. Her dark brown hair had partially escaped its bun, with several wisps pasted to her sweat-glistening cheeks.

"I don't have any money, if that's what you're after!" she yelled, her pig eyes narrowing. "Now get the hell out of my way or I'll run ye down!"

"I don't think so," Navarro said.

She stared at him. "Where have I seen you before?"

Navarro said nothing.

The woman's eyes brightened suddenly, and her chin snapped up. "You!" she rasped. With her right hand, she reached under the driver's box, then pulled out an old Spencer carbine. She was raising the rifle and thumbing back the hammer, when Hawkins slipped out of the rocks beside the wagon, reached up, and wrestled the long gun from the woman's pudgy hands.

"What do you have in the box?" Navarro asked the woman. She was screaming so loudly at both of them, making up epithets as she went, that she couldn't hear the question.

Finally, Navarro walked around behind the wagon, loosened the puckered canvas over the tailgate. He peered inside. Several blankets had been strewn across the floorboards. Six girls in skimpy, soiled, sweat-stained dresses sat along the sideboards, their wrists and ankles tied with rawhide. One had a single pink feather dangling in her tangled hair.

The wagon smelled of hot canvas, sweat, and urine. A tin pan sat in one corner of the wagon box, a few glistening drops sharing the pan's bottom with a single dead fly.

"Christ!" Navarro growled, stepping back and fumbling with the tailgate latch.

"You leave those girls right where they are, mister!" Sister Mary Francis screamed as she came running with surprising speed around the wagon's east side.

Hawkins tried to stop her, but she balled her right fist so tight it turned crimson. She brought it up from her knees, connecting soundly with Mordecai's right jaw. Hawkins fell with a groan.

Losing her balance, she nearly fell, too, but managed to stay standing and whirl toward Tom, balling the same fist she'd used on the old hide hunter.

Having none of it, Navarro cocked his saddle gun one-handed and aimed it from his right thigh at the woman's bulging belly.

Seeing the rifle, she stopped. "They're mine, goddamn you. I'm sellin' 'em all in Nogales." A thought flitted across her eyes. "Less'n you boys want to buy 'em with gold or cash money . . ."

Navarro replied by tattooing her forehead with his Winchester's butt plate. Eyes crossing, she staggered straight back and fell like a sack of potatoes.

They spent the next two nights camped in a long green horseshoe of the Rio Bavispe. The freed girls ate the venison and rabbits Navarro shot, and slept off the effects of the opium.

Karla and Louise helped the girls scrub the paint from their faces, and as Navarro and Hawkins smoked and drank coffee from a nearby bluff, keeping watch, they splashed around in the water, laughing, skipping stones, and talking about how good it would be to see their families again.

Both nights, Mordecai Hawkins lulled the girls to sleep with gentle notes from his rusty harmonica. Young Marlene, who rarely strayed more than four feet from Karla, slept curled against the older girl's side.

Tom bound Sister Mary Francis, whom he intended to turn over to Phil Bryson at Fort Huachuca, and when the fat woman couldn't keep her mouth shut, he gagged her. She may have been a nun at one time, but it probably hadn't been much of a chore for Ettinger to recruit the pudgy slattern to run his brothel.

The group pulled out the third morning, Louise driving the wagon, all the girls except Karla riding inside, Sister Mary Francis tied to one of the packhorses. They were riding single file through a narrow canyon, Navarro in the lead, Hawkins riding drag.

Karla followed Tom on her high-stepping Arab. She kept a blanket draped over her bare shoulders; the sun had come out again after a strong wind and a brief, passing shower.

Halfway through the canyon, Tom's bay lifted its head sharply and whinnied.

A rider stood atop a sandy knoll about thirty yards ahead and right of the rocky wash, partially concealed by a wind-gnarled pine. " 'Taos Tommy' Navarro!"

The man was a long-faced, ghoulish-looking hombre in a battered, feather-trimmed derby, with gold rings in his ears. Over his right eye he wore a white bandage wrapped crosswise around his head, beneath the hat. The bandage was stained dark red. The blood had dripped out from under the bandage to run in a grisly rivulet down his cheek.

Navarro halted his horse abruptly, one hand on his pistol butt.

"Leave that hogleg where it is," Bontemps warned, lifting his rifle to his shoulder and aiming at Karla. "I may be a poor, one-eyed sumbitch, but I can still kill that girl from here."

Silently cursing himself for not spotting the man earlier, Navarro slid his hand from the .44's butt to his holster. "The girls are goin' home where they belong."

"I don't care about the girls. I want you. You're gonna pay for my eye, you old bastard."

Navarro stared at the man, feeling as tired as he'd ever felt. He wasn't sure he had the strength to lift his gun from his holster again. But he had to get the others out of here. "You'll let the others go?"

"I don't give a tinker's damn about the others."

Navarro turned in his saddle. "Ride on," he told Louise, who was sitting the wagon's driver's seat.

"Tommy . . ." Karla said.

"Go," Navarro said, more urgently this time, looking around the women at Hawkins.

One hand on his pistol butt, jerking Sister Mary Francis' mount along behind him, the old hide hunter gigged his horse up abreast of Karla. He reached over and grabbed the

Arabian's bridle. "Come on, honey."

"Tommy, he's fast," Karla said as Hawkins pulled her mount around Navarro's bay. "I've seen him shoot."

"Take them on out of the canyon," Navarro told Hawkins. "I'll be along shortly."

Giving Tom a worried glance, Louise urged the mules on past him, Billie and the other girls staring fearfully out the wagon's rear pucker at the man on the knoll beneath the gnarled pine.

When the women and Hawkins had ridden out of sight, Bontemps slid his rifle into the boot beneath his right thigh. He popped the cork on the bottle resting on the pommel of his saddle, and took a long drink, his Adam's apple bobbing like a plum in a rain barrel.

The slaver lifted his chin and poured the whiskey over the bandage. Sighing and shaking his head, he corked the bottle and gigged his speckle-gray down the knoll, riding stiffly, the bottle in one hand, reins in the other. The brace of .45s on his hips flashed in the afternoon sun.

Bontemps reined his horse to a halt only a few feet in front of Tom's bay. He raised the bottle. "Drink?"

Tom shook his head.

"It's right soothing on my eye, which

hurts like hell, as you might imagine."

Tom stared at the man, unblinking. Bontemps had positioned the sun behind his left shoulder. It bounced like javelins off the rocks. The man might have had only one eye, but Tom knew Bontemps was fast. He'd heard the stories, like the stories others had told about Navarro himself.

He didn't especially want to die by the gun of a human hookworm like Bontemps. But suddenly he wondered if his time had come. He felt limp as a worn-out fiddle string, his reactions slow as a cat walking through mud. Maybe he'd burned himself out. Even if he was faster than this bastard, did he still have his edge?

It didn't really matter. He'd sprung Karla and the other girls. How many good years did he have left, anyway?

"Here I am," Bontemps said, contempt pinching his voice shrill, "facing the infamous 'Taos Tommy' Navarro! I'm just sorry you're so old and dried up."

"You can call me Tom," Navarro said, surprised by the steel he heard in his own voice. He suddenly had the very real urge to pay a visit to that stage station in Benson someday. "Since you're fixin' to die."

The men stared at each other, the grin slowly fading from Bontemps' eyes, his cracked lips straightening.

The slaver flexed his right thumb. His hand streaked to the pistol on his right hip.

Tom's .44 came up automatically, stabbing smoke and fire. As the bullet tore through the slaver's chest, Bontemps crouched over his saddle horn and triggered his own revolver.

Navarro's bay crow-hopped, quarter-turning, carrying Tom from the path of the slaver's slug. Bontemps' own horse bucked, and the dying slaver fell down its side, catching his right foot in the stirrup.

The speckle gray bolted down the canyon, Bontemps bouncing along the trail beside it, arms flung out above his head.

Navarro sleeved sweat from his brow and watched until the horse and slaver disappeared around a thumb in the canyon wall. He holstered his pistol and squinted up at the sun, arcing slowly toward the bald crags in the west.

Several hours of good light left. With luck and hard riding, they'd make the border day after tomorrow.

Navarro straightened his hat and kneed the bay into a canter, heading down canyon toward the Arabian and its tawny-haired rider galloping toward him.